HOME BY NIGHTFALL

Center Point
Large Print

Also by Charles Finch and available from
Center Point Large Print

The Last Enchantments

The Charles Lenox Series
   The Laws of Murder
   An Old Betrayal

**This Large Print Book carries the
Seal of Approval of N.A.V.H.**

HOME BY NIGHTFALL

Charles Finch

CENTER POINT LARGE PRINT
THORNDIKE, MAINE

The text of this Large Print edition is unabridged.
In other aspects, this book may vary
from the original edition.
Printed in the United States of America
on permanent paper.
Set in 16-point Times New Roman type.

ISBN: 978-1-62899-974-7

Library of Congress Cataloging-in-Publication Data

Names: Finch, Charles (Charles B.) author.
Title: Home by nightfall : a Charles Lenox mystery / Charles Finch.
Description: Center Point Large Print edition. | Thorndike, Maine :
Center Point Large Print, 2016. | ©2015
Identifiers: LCCN 2016008252 | ISBN 9781628999747
    (hardcover : alk. paper)
Subjects: LCSH: Lenox, Charles (Fictitious character)—Fiction. |
Private investigators—England—London—Fiction. | Large type books. |
GSAFD: Mystery fiction. | Historical fiction.
Classification: LCC PS3606.I526 H66 2016 | DDC 813/.6—dc23
LC record available at http://lccn.loc.gov/2016008252

ACKNOWLEDGMENTS

What do you say when a line in the acknowledgments isn't enough? I owe so much more than a simple thanks to my editor, Charlie Spicer, and my agent, Elisabeth Weed—two people who love and understand books, who work beautifully in concert, and who have supported me and this novel in innumerable crucial ways. Consider this a placeholder until I can buy each of them a private island.

Charlie's colleagues at St. Martin's have been typically sterling in their efforts on behalf of *Home by Nightfall*, inventive and perceptive: my deepest thanks to Sally Richardson, Andy Martin, Hector DeJean, Sarah Melnyk, April Osborn, Paul Hochman, and Melissa Hastings. The same goes for all of Elisabeth's colleagues at The Book Group, particularly Dana Murphy.

Friendship has never seemed more important to me, and I've been grateful for that of so many different people in the last year, including Rachel Brodhead, Matt McCarthy, John Phillips, and Ben Reiter; Hendrik and Alya Woods; Alexander Uihlein; June Kim and Daniel Hwang; my newest pals, Amelia, Madeleine, Henry, Nathan, and Jane; and so many others, who were probably thanked in the last book or will be in the next.

To Mom, Dad, Rosie, Julia, Henry, Isabelle, and Jamie, my unending affection and my ongoing feeling of wonder that I am lucky enough to be related to you.

Emily, Annabel, Lucy, thank you for being the sweetness of my life, in times that might otherwise have been hard. With you beside me even tempests are kind, and salt waves fresh in love.

• • •

This book is dedicated to
Dennis Popp and Linda Bock,
with love, gratitude, and affection.

CHAPTER ONE

It was a blustery London morning in the autumn of 1876, wind and rain heavy in the trees lining Chancery Lane, and here, damn it all, stood before Charles Lenox something that nobody should have to tolerate before breakfast: a beaming Frenchman.

"What is it, Pointilleux?" he asked.

"I have solve the case."

"Oh?"

"I believe he has never enter the room at all."

Lenox sighed. "Are those the papers you're holding? Could I see them?"

"Do you not observe the elegance of it, though! He has *never enter the room at all.*"

Pointilleux handed over the neat pile of newspapers, face expectant, and Lenox, tired and moody, felt an unbecoming glee at being allowed to dash his enthusiasm. "Three people saw him go into his dressing room. And the glass of wine that he always had waiting for him after a concert was drunk up, all but a few drops."

Pointilleux's face fell. He was a tall, straight-backed, handsome young person of nineteen, very earnest, with large dark eyes and jet black hair. A late-summer attempt to grow side-whiskers had ended in ignominious defeat; his face was clean-shaven again.

"You are certain?"

"Yes. I had it from the detective inspector himself."

"This information does not present itself in the newspapers."

"They're holding back as much as they can to distinguish false tips from real ones. So you'd better keep mum."

"Mum." Pointilleux looked dissatisfied. "I was very sure."

"Better luck next time," said Lenox, tiredly. He was past forty-five now, and it took more of the day for him to overcome a late night. "And now you'd better get to your desk—I have a great deal to do, and not much time before my first appointment is due."

This was true. His professional life had rarely been better, more gratifying, more full of excitement; nor had it often been more exhausting, more burdened with care, more tedious.

Newby, his appointment, was a country fellow, a prosperous brewer of apple cider in Somerset. He arrived precisely at eight o'clock—but looking much battered, red in the face, with mud spattered three-quarters of the way up his trousers.

"You found your way easily enough?" asked Lenox.

Newby gave him a look of outrage. "I call it a

8

pretty kettle of fish," he said, settling his great bulk into the chair across Lenox's desk, "when a fellow in the prime of his life cannot walk down the streets of England's greatest city without getting trod on by a horse, or knocked about by a woman selling oysters, or pushed over by an omnibus!"

Lenox frowned. "Oh dear."

"I am accustomed to a pretty hearty traffic in Bristol on market day, too, sir!" he said. "Pretty hearty traffic!"

"That's very bad," said Lenox.

"These young women selling oysters ought to be in jail."

"I can have a word with someone."

"Would you? I think someone should, honestly."

It was the usual story—London was a hellish place to walk if you weren't accustomed to it. There was a famous story about Charlotte and Anne Brontë coming from the country to visit their publisher; they'd stayed at a hotel not two hundred yards from his offices, but their morning walk to reach it had taken them more than an hour, including long periods for which they stood completely still, in something near blind despair, as foot traffic moved around them.

Lenox, used to it all, the children ducking under the heads of horses, the city men whose strides gulped great stretches of pavement, hadn't had such troubles in many years, but he was happy to spend five further minutes listening to Newby bemoan the impossibility of walking down Holborn Street in broad daylight without being knocked over like a spring flower every thirty seconds, what did they have an empire for at all, and in older days people hadn't been quite so busy and *they* had managed very well if you asked him, thank you, and really things had come to a fine pass—and all that kind of thing, the statement of which gradually lulled Newby into a better mood than Lenox had ever seen him in before. It occurred to Lenox that if he instituted the practice of spending the first ten minutes of every meeting listening to their thoughts on the state of the modern world, his clientele would be the most contented in London.

At last, Newby came to his business. "I'm convinced that our distributor in Bath, Jonathan Fotheringham, is skimming money from us."

"Can you change distributors?"

"He's our best and only option there, unfortunately."

Lenox frowned. "What makes you think he's stealing?"

Newby was provincial, but he was no fool. From his valise he pulled a sheaf of papers, which showed that in each of the last five quarters there had been an incremental decline in the revenue of Fotheringham's district, while everywhere else there had been a rise in revenue. Lenox asked a variety of questions—Was it possible there was a new competitor? How long had Fotheringham been a reliable partner?—before at last nodding, thoughtfully, and promising to send Atkinson to Bath.

"Is he good?"

"Our top man," said Lenox, nodding. "He was at Scotland Yard until last year. First person we hired."

"What about you, or Strickland, or Dallington? The fellows on the nameplate?"

"They're both on cases, and I'm working primarily in a supervisory capacity nowadays. Believe me, Atkinson is excellent. If I didn't take this seriously, I would send our new chap, Davidson. He's promising, but greener than one of your apples."

Newby seemed satisfied by the answer. He accepted a fortifying glass of sherry, then rose and braced himself to wade back into the midden of London, with a grave final word before he left about the city's general decline, and what it portended for them all.

These were Lenox's days now. About ten months before, at the start of the year, he and three other people had started the first detective agency in England. After a difficult beginning, particularly for Lenox, who had spent the better part of the previous decade sitting in Parliament, falling hopelessly out of practice as a criminal investigator, they had made a success of it.

Well—something of a success. One of the partners, the Frenchman LeMaire, had left the firm during its initial wobbles, certain that it would never make a profit, and founded a competing agency of his own. Fortunately, just when LeMaire's pessimism seemed as if it might have been quite clear-eyed, the three remaining partners had found their feet. In part this was because the other two were superb: Lord John Dallington, an aristocrat of nearly thirty, and Polly Buchanan, an enterprising young widow who worked as "Miss Strickland" and was a specialist in all the small mysteries the middle class produced, stolen silver, vanished fiancées, that sort of thing.

An even greater percentage of their success came from Lenox, who had theretofore been far and away the least productive of them all. The difficulty had been some resistance in him, at first, to treating it as a *business*—a gentleman by birth, with a private fortune, in his previous life he had been an amateur detective, working from his town house in the West End, taking cases as it pleased him.

When he had finally realized—after those crushing first months, after LeMaire's depar-ture—that he was actually in trade now, his attitude had changed. With systematic determina-tion, he had set out with a new idea: that he would win clients from the City, the business world.

Using all of his many contacts from Parliament and the social sphere in which he and his wife, Lady Jane, moved, he had amassed some two dozen regulars just like Newby, who kept Lenox, Strickland, and Dallington on retainer. They were the agency's prizes, their names and files kept in a small gray safe, secure from the snooping eyes of anyone who might be willing to offer them to LeMaire. The firm regularly checked in on each of these clients, and also remained on call should anything unusual occur—a work stoppage, the theft of materials or money, bookkeeping discrepancies. Lenox and his colleagues prided themselves on handling such issues much more quickly and adeptly than Scotland Yard could. That speed and discretion was where they made their fees worthwhile.

The triumph of this strategy—the agency had had to hire four additional detectives now, and several more clerks—had come at some cost to Lenox. It was the beginning of October now, and he hadn't personally handled a case since July. Instead he spent a great deal of his time managing men like Newby and delegating their problems to the firm's active detectives, Atkinson, Weld, Mayhew, and now Davidson. Polly had her small but lucrative cases to handle—"Miss Strickland" continued to advertise in the papers—and Dallington his own idiosyncratic custom, much of it criminal, which came in part from the close work with the Yard that Lenox had handed down to him upon taking up his political career.

And in fact, that was precisely the kind of work that he had returned to this field to do. He loved above all the pursuit, the infinitesimally small details upon which a murder investigation might turn, the dirt in a shirt cuff, the abrasion on a windowsill, the missing ten pounds. Well; he would return to it, in time. At the very least, dealing with Newby was vastly, incomparably better than the dismal state of affairs he had experienced from January through the spring, when he had had no clients, had contributed nothing, had been a positive millstone around his partners' necks.

Shouldn't he be appreciative for that?

Yes, he thought, with resolve—and for the rest of the morning he handled the business with great good cheer, just as he had past midnight the evening before, putting his signature to papers, assigning work to the clerks and detectives, making time for a rapid and humorous cup of tea with Dallington, and glancing in his free moments at the account book, which was pleasingly cross-hatched and filled in and prosperous-looking.

By noon, therefore, he was in an excellent mood. "Pointilleux!" he called out.

The young Frenchman appeared, one hand on the doorway, head popping around it. "Yes?"

"Are you still investigating that break-in in Bayswater? The butcher's shop?"

Pointilleux nodded and stepped into the office. He was actually LeMaire's nephew—had stayed behind after his uncle left, a serious, pleasant presence, very young, and beloved by them all, only in part because he'd kept faith in their project. Though he was barely nineteen, they assigned him some of their smaller cases, as part of an agreement they had made to train him. "I am come to suspect the wife very strongly. She has conduct an affair of the heart with the constable."

"Then take the afternoon off," said Lenox.

Pointilleux's face opened into a beam. "Ah!" he said. "Excellent! I will!"

Lenox, pleased at having atoned for his previous irritability, bade the young man good-bye and then turned his eyes to his own appointment book. What was next? He knew there was a meeting with Carter later that afternoon, an important client who owned a cloth wholesaler in Lambeth. But was his lunch hour spoken for?

And then Lenox's own face fell, his heart with it. All the vim he felt from having achieved so much on a Monday morning vanished.

He was engaged to have lunch with his brother, Edmund, he remembered now; in fact, he had to leave soon, if he was going to get to the restaurant on time. With a sigh, he rose and fetched his hat from its stand, dreading how difficult it had become to see one of the three people in all the world that he cared about the most.

CHAPTER TWO

He stepped out into Chancery Lane and looked left and right for a cab. In that instant, at least, he could see London through Newby's eyes—chaos. Toward the Holborn end of the street there were two carriages hopelessly wedged together, as they stood abreast almost exactly as wide as the lane, and closer to Lenox was a great congregation around the local coffee stand. The young clerks of the businesses along this avenue liked to gather here; there was a great bright copper boiler over a brass-handled smudge pot, and its hawker in his green smock was calling out "Cup and two thins, only a penny, mind!" to all who passed. Two of Lenox's own clerks were standing nearby, eating their two thins—pieces of bread and butter, thickish ones in fact—with between them a piece of cold beef, another ha'penny.

Lenox turned up toward Holborn. What he knew and Newby didn't, of course, was the secret regularity that existed within this commotion. Though it looked like there was a mad press at the coffee stand, every person knew his place in line, and even now one of the carriages at the top of the road was sliding forward, the other one just backward. Both would be on their way within a minute or two.

Even the swarming walkers on the pavement—the only secret there was to keep to the right and walk at a steady pace. There were men of the city who traveled four or five miles to work by foot every morning and read their newspapers the whole way without lifting their eyes, because they were so confident of their paces.

As he reached the corner, he came to a man selling newspapers, with large placards on his cart announcing the most recent news about the disappearance of Muller, the great German pianist.

The fellow tipped his cap. "Mr. Lenox, sir," he said.

"Anything new in there, Parsons?"

"Not a mote o' news, sir, no. 'Tis the midday edition, however."

"Ah, well, give me one for the ride, then."

"Much obliged, sir," said Parsons, taking his coin.

Lenox found a hansom cab and settled into it for the westward journey, scanning the headlines.

They were all about Muller. It was this mystery that Pointilleux believed he had solved that morning—an error by which he had perhaps become a true Londoner for the first time, for seemingly every soul in the metropolis believed that they and they alone knew the answer to the puzzle that had so trialed and tribulated Scotland

Yard this past week. Across every class that autumn, in the butchers' stalls at Smithfield market, on the crowded buses full of clerks and respectable widows, in the glittering drawing rooms of Hanover Square, Muller was the only subject of speculation.

The facts were these: that on the fourth of October he had played a concert, his fifth of nine that were planned (though the promoters had already been urging him to add several more performances, based on the enthusiastic reception he had received in the city); that at the end of the final piece, the overwhelmingly popular *Fantasia on "The Last Rose of Summer"* by Mendelssohn, he had stood up, bowed once in his customary fashion, and left by stage right; that he had said to an employee of the Cadogan Theater, "I feel very tired—hold my visitors for half an hour," before going to his dressing room; that, after a tentative tap on the door thirty-five minutes later, the theater owner and Muller's own manager had opened the door and found the room empty, without any sign of violent struggle, or indeed anything out of place at all; and that nobody had set eyes on him since.

And yet it was impossible! That was what made the case so interesting, of course—the impossibility of it. For between Muller's private room and any conceivable exit of the building there were dozens of staff, managers, well-wishers, cleaners. On an average night, the *Post-Courier* had calculated, in an ingenious bit of journalism, Muller had seen thirty-six people between leaving his dressing room after a performance and stepping into his carriage.

Aside from the dread possibilities of what might have befallen the pianist, his disappearance was known to be an embarrassment to the Queen and her retinue. She was part German herself, of course, Prince Albert had been entirely German, and many of their retainers were, as well. All of them had watched Muller perform on his opening night; now the Queen's cousins across the channel were extremely aggrieved at the disappearance of one of their finest artistic exports.

Lenox had seen him play and had to admit the fellow was magical—a short, slim, swarthy, balding, unprepossessing person, and yet when he sat before a piano, suddenly transformed into the most sensitive and subtle conduit of artistic beauty. His pauses, his rhythms, gave new meaning to music that a whole audience had heard dozens of times, and thought they knew.

Where could he be?

The room showed no sign of violence; nothing was discomposed or shifted, except that Muller's black silk evening jacket was thrown across an armchair, and that glass of wine had been emptied, as Lenox knew from a private conversation with Inspector Nicholson. In the same conversation,

Dallington and Lenox had offered the assistance of their agency, free of charge, and been immediately rebuffed. The Yard was extremely sensitive, at the moment, to any implication that they might be failing in their duties, Nicholson said. It wouldn't do.

"But of course you *are* failing in your duties," Dallington had replied. "A pig with a magnifying glass would be as much use as the lot down at the theater."

Nicholson frowned. "A pig couldn't even hold a magnifying glass."

"I won't have you besmirch pigs in my hearing," said Dallington moodily. He desperately wanted a chance to find Muller; indeed, Lenox suspected that he had been absent from the offices so much that week because he was conducting his own investigation. "Some of the finest chaps I ever met were pigs."

"Well, as you know, I'm not on the case myself, though I would very much like to be. Anyone who finds Muller, particularly alive, is guaranteed promotion."

"I still think you ought to come work for us," Lenox had said.

They'd been sitting in the Two Princes, a dim pub with a bright little coal fire and very good ale. Nicholson, packing his pipe, had shaken his head. "I love the Yard. I'll never leave, if they'll keep me." Both Dallington and Lenox must have looked doubtful, because he had felt compelled to add, "It's my Oxford, you see."

Lenox nodded. He liked Nicholson. The three had grown close earlier that year, working together on a case. "So then," said Lenox, "can't you ask to be put on the case?"

"I have. McKee is protecting his turf very carefully."

"We kept a pig when I was a boy," said Dallington, taking a sip of his dark beer. "His name was George Washington."

"What an utterly fascinating story," said Lenox.

"He could eat thirty potatoes in a sitting if he got a head of steam up."

"*Thirty* potatoes? Really, I mean to say, you ought to tell people about this at parties."

Dallington had looked at him suspiciously and then broken into a laugh, which Nicholson joined. Nicholson shook his head as it died down, tapping his pipe on the table to pack it more tightly. "Ah, that glass of wine," he said. "The two stewards swear up and down that they filled it after the intermission, when Muller was already back out playing. But then where could he be?"

Lenox pondered the question as the cab moved across Grosvenor Square, in the direction of his brother's house. Parsons had told the truth—there was nothing new in the midday paper, though there was a great deal of specious theorizing. When he stepped down from his cab he had learned no fresh information. Alas. Well, here he was: his brother. He took a deep breath, bracing himself.

Sir Edmund Lenox was two years older than Charles, and they had passed their childhoods as close as two brothers could be, first at their family home, Lenox House, in Sussex, then together at Harrow School, in London, and finally two years apart at Oxford. Their paths had diverged slightly after that. Edmund favored the country, Charles the city, and when their father died, and Edmund inherited both the baronetcy and the house, he had married and settled there. Then, however, around his thirtieth birthday, he had won the parliamentary seat of Markethouse, the village nearby, and since then he had divided his time more or less equally between London and the country. That had pleased his younger brother; for the past fifteen years, he'd been able to see a great deal of Edmund, between the time he was up for Parliament and the two weeks that they all spent at Lenox House over Christmas, by custom.

Edmund's house in the city was the same one Lenox's family had lived in during the season since the early part of the century, a bright, airy, wide-windowed, white-walled town house on a Mayfair side street.

Now, however, it was darkened—a black cloth wrapped around the door knocker, an unlit candle in the front window, black crepe lining the flower boxes, which ought at least to have had mums in them, at this time of year.

Lenox, a lump in his throat, reached up to the cab's seat and paid the driver, who accepted the money with a finger to his hat and then whipped his two horses onward to their next fare.

The younger brother stood on the pavement for a moment, looking up. His brother's dear, beloved wife, Molly, was dead, aged only forty, and though Edmund had kept his demeanor even, in the five weeks since it had happened, anyone who knew him even slightly saw how impenetrable, how implacable his grief was. He had become a ghost of himself, and Lenox had realized to his horror that it wasn't impossible to imagine that Edmund might follow, soon, behind his wife.

CHAPTER THREE

T hey walked together to White's. This was
Edmund's favorite club, where they got a
quiet table near the window. Was the waiter
unusually solicitous, or was it merely good
service? Lenox saw his brother calculating the
chances on either side of the question while they
ordered their luncheon.

"Well then," said Edmund. "Muller. You must
have some idea?"

"None at all!" said Lenox cheerfully.

There was a very faint flicker of interest in
Edmund's face. "No?" he said. "Not even a
conjecture?"

"Do you have one? I should be very happy to
take it and pass it off as my own, in particular
should it prove correct."

"I? No, I have not followed it very closely,"
murmured Edmund.

Lenox would have greatly preferred it if his
brother had been experiencing a more dramatic
and tragic grief—if he drank too much wine, or
refused all food, or stormed about the turf near
Lenox House at midnight. Instead, he was
passably social, drinking a little wine, eating a
few bites of food. He was simply not altogether
there. In the soft, luminous whiteness of

midmorning, sunlight falling in slants through the windows, it looked as if he were already half departed from the world.

How quickly it had happened! Molly had been a plump, pretty woman, with red cheeks and dark hair, of excellent but not especially illustrious stock. Edmund had met her at a Sussex dance. Then and later she had been countryish, quick to laugh, happy to chatter, even a bit silly at times—very different from Lenox's own sharp, cosmopolitan wife, Lady Jane Grey, though the two had grown close across the years, being married as they were to a pair of brothers. She had been the type of person who enlivened a room, Molly, and since Edmund himself was rather quiet, a reflective soul, they had been a wonderful match. And she had been a woman of parts, too, fine at the pianoforte, and a really quite superb draftsman, who had left behind her hundreds of small, endearing, utterly accurate drawings of the people and places she had loved.

Her death had been fast—shockingly fast. A mild headache on a Tuesday; a fever on the Wednesday; better on the Thursday and planning out her social calendar; very weak indeed on the Friday but optimistic she would see the illness out before the weekend; then, on Saturday morning, badly feverish, and by the afternoon, unconscious, the best doctors from three counties called to her bedside. On Sunday, dead.

One of Lenox's closest friends in the world was a physician named Thomas McConnell, a Scotsman who had often helped him in his criminal investigations.

"What killed her?" Lenox had asked after the funeral. "It would be nice to know."

They had been walking down the lovely avenue, lined on either side with lime trees, which led toward Lenox House. McConnell, a rangy fellow, given perhaps too much to drink at moments in his life but a surpassingly excellent doctor, had shaken his head sadly. "I cannot say, exactly. A fever."

"But you have spoken to Lincoln, Hoare?"

It had been a lovely day, one of those true summer days of September in Sussex, still, bright, mild, a few clouds in the brilliant blue sky. "There are moments when I congratulate myself on belonging to an age of sophistication, Charles— none of the slime-draughts and silver bark and bloodletting of last century, all remedies that killed more than they saved. We know infinitely more than our grandfathers did. And yet something like this—delirium . . . a fever . . . chills? We are no closer to understanding precisely what killed her than the Romans would have been. Go back farther, if you like—the ancient Egpytians."

"Poor Molly," Lenox had said.

"Poor Edmund," McConnell had replied, shaking

his head. "The dead are at least beyond whatever harm this world can do them."

McConnell worked at Great Ormond Street Hospital, which served severely ill children, regardless of whether they could pay—a charity that was one of the great credits to the empire, or so Lenox thought. McConnell had seen children die. "Yes," Lenox had said. "I'm sure you're right."

As he and his brother ate lunch now, talking with simulated engagement about political matters, Lenox tried to think of what he could do to help. The five weeks since that day with McConnell might have been five seconds for his brother. Edmund's face, his mood, were no different, his shock still total.

What made it so difficult was his brother's essential sweetness. London and his career as a detective had together sharpened Lenox into hawkishness, observance, and cynicism, not all the way perhaps, but far enough that there was little enough that could catch him off guard. Edmund, however, had never been altered, not from boyhood. Even as he maneuvered in Parliament—for he had reached a high position there—it was not through cunning but through his good nature, the ease with which people loved him, that he attained each success. He was intelligent, to be sure, but he had held on through the long years to his country openness.

Part of the credit for that was in all likelihood due to Molly, Lenox realized now.

"I'm down to the house in two days' time," Edmund said, as the waiter took away their plates.

Lenox frowned. "On Wednesday?"

"Yes. There's a lot to look after—I've been away too long. They'll want to know about the horses, and I hear that some of the tenants have complaints."

"Mather can deal with all of that," said Lenox.

This was the fellow who managed the estate, a young, energetic person, nephew of the old steward, who had retired to the village. "On the contrary, he needs a great deal of assistance," said Edmund.

Fortunately their coffee came then—for Lenox was extremely concerned, and he managed to conceal it only by busying himself with milk and sugar. He and Jane had invited Edmund to stay with them after the funeral, but he had declined absolutely. At least, though, he had been in London, and one way or another they had managed to see him most days since then. He would be terribly isolated in the country. He had friends there, but none closer than a twenty-minute gallop. And it was where Molly had died.

"Are you sure that it will be tolerable—mentally, that is?" said Lenox, with great care in his voice.

Edmund actually laughed. "Ha! No, no, I am not," he said.

"Skip it, then."

He waved a dismissive hand. "No, I must go. It was urgent two weeks ago. Now it is past urgent."

"You will be very gloomy down there, Ed."

"I don't doubt it."

This was typical enough. Edmund wasn't resistant to talking about his state of mind, particularly with Charles and Jane, and he did not pretend to be happy. It didn't seem to help him, though. If Charles asked him, he answered truthfully and politely, but every word of his reply was filled with a monumental sense of the pointlessness of such conversation, how little it had the power to change anything. The subject would move toward politics then, or Sophia, Lenox's daughter—and there at least Edmund could give his honest attention, with the part of his self that still remained down here among the living.

Lenox had a thought. "What if we came for a visit?"

Edmund frowned. "To Lenox House? I hope you'll still be there at Christmas."

"No, now. Wednesday."

"I couldn't possibly ask you to do that. The agency alone takes up so much time."

"Are you being witty? It would be a positive

relief to get away from the city. Dallington can manage the queue for a week or two."

"What if they ask you to help find Muller?"

"They won't, the devils."

Edmund considered this. Then he shook his head. "No," he said. "It's better that I spend these ten days there myself. It will be very dull, you know—all business, every day."

There was a brief pause, and then Lenox decided that he would simply be honest. In a low voice, he said, "I think there is nothing I can do to help you now, Edmund, but if it would make you even slightly less alone to have company at Lenox House, I would like to come with you. I know Jane and Sophia would, too. Please allow us. At least then I will feel better, whether or not you do."

Edmund looked at him levelly. "Very well," he said. "As you please."

"Ah, thank you," said Lenox. He leaned back in his chair and hailed the waiter. "Will you have a biscuit with your coffee?" he said to Edmund.

"No, thank you."

"Well, I call that foolish, because I know something you don't know—which is that they have the biscuits with raspberry jam in them. We passed a plate on our way in."

"In fact, I did know that," said Edmund. "They have them at every meal."

"That's the best case I've heard yet for London

30

being the center of civilization," said Charles, and then said, to the waiter, "We'll take as many biscuits as you can fit on a plate."

"Very good, sir," said the waiter.

Edmund, stirring his coffee, thought for a moment and then said, with a glimmer of interest, "Really, though, nothing about Muller? Nothing at all?"

Lenox smiled. "I think until we get more information we'll just have to assume the butler did it."

CHAPTER FOUR

To leave London meant to miss out on a great deal of work, and that afternoon Lenox tried to clear as much from his calendar as he could. It wasn't easy. He would ask Polly to take the meetings he couldn't shift—she was far better at dealing with clients than the mercurial Dallington—and his only ongoing investigation, one that he was making privately into the criminal behavior of a fellow named William Anson, was a long, slow one, without any immediate necessity for action.

It wasn't until seven that all three of the partners were in the office, and Lenox, putting his head around Polly's door, asked if they might have a quick word. She said she would be with him in a moment. Dallington was playing checkers against himself at his desk when Lenox came in and asked the same question. "Yes," he said, standing up. "Is everything all right?"

"Oh, fine," said Lenox.

They met in Polly's office; each partner had a small private room off the large central area, which was full of slanted clerks' desks. LeMaire had had one, too, but since he had vacated it three of their new detectives had gone shares in it, tight-quartered but comfortable. There was also a large meeting room toward the front of the suite, overlooking Chancery Lane, but this was an informal gathering.

Lenox told them that he had to leave for ten days.

"Ten days!" said Polly.

"Yes, unfortunately. I've pushed as many meetings as possible to tomorrow or the other side, but I was hoping you might take those I can't."

She furrowed her brow. "I suppose. I'm stretched already."

"How so?"

She sighed. "Too many cases. I would have bitten off your hand if you offered me that problem in the spring, but here we are."

She was a pretty, vivacious young woman, of good birth, though somewhat slighted socially. This was for two reasons: first, because she was inclined to speak her mind, cuttingly from time to time, and second, and perhaps more to the point, because she had been widowed young, making her an unpredictable quantity and earning her widespread blame for her attractions. "John, are you busy?" asked Lenox.

He didn't look it, the duke's son, handsomely turned out as ever, but he nodded. "Terribly," he said. "I was out at dawn this morning, and I'm seeing a fellow about a dog in half an hour."

"It's not an ideal moment for one of us to leave," said Polly.

"You were playing checkers against yourself five minutes ago," Lenox pointed out to Dallington.

He frowned. "I sometimes do that when I need to think."

"Fair enough. I suppose I can try to cut the trip short—particularly if you wire to tell me that things are becoming unmanageable here. But I would prefer to go."

"Ten days, though!" said Polly. "Where are you going?"

"To stay with my brother."

Both of their faces changed simultaneously.

"Oh, I see," said Polly.

"Take all the time you want, of course," said Dallington.

"I won't take any more vacation this year, you have my word on that."

"Charles," said Dallington firmly, "you must go stay with your brother as long as you like. We can manage very easily. I was telling Polly only this morning that you were next to useless."

She laughed, and though Dallington's face remained impassive, appropriately considerate of Lenox's feelings, a pleasure passed just visibly through it. The truth was that Dallington loved to make Polly Buchanan laugh; he had been something like in love with her ever since they had discovered she was the mysterious Miss Strickland, nearly two years before.

Did she return his love? At moments Lenox

would have sworn she did. For a while, that summer, he had awaited the news of their engagement daily, and once he had very nearly even *asked* Dallington, before stopping himself. He had seen them laughing and walking hand in hand down Hampden Lane together one evening, and there had been moments in the office when they seemed so close that they barely needed to speak to understand each other.

But Dallington had had a strange run of it— widely condemned by the aristocratic world in his early twenties, nearly disowned, a denizen of every bar and casino and brothel in London, before finding a second life, a passion really, in detection. That passion didn't stop him from slipping back into drink occasionally, however, and the effect of his continuing notoriety was to make him unusually reticent. It would be just like him to pine after Polly for years while keeping enough ironic distance from her never to truly convey how he felt. What unhappiness had made him this way? Lenox sometimes wondered. There was nobody he would rather have seen settled.

Nor was there anybody he would rather work a case with. Polly, in fact, might have been the best of the three of them at their work—or would be, when she was less raw. She had wonderful instincts, combined with a terrifically practical mind; it was because of her that they had several specialists on call for the agency, in botany, in weapons, in forensic science. But Lenox and Dallington worked so well together.

At any rate. They probably wouldn't propose to each other at this meeting, the two of them. Lenox looked at his watch. "I should try to organize what I can, then."

Polly nodded. "It's also a shame you have to go, because—I can't believe it, but I nearly forgot—because of your visitor."

"Visitor?" said Lenox.

"I've been out all afternoon, or I would have told you sooner. It was while you were at lunch."

Dallington looked at her curiously. "A case?"

She smiled. "Yes."

"What was it?" asked Lenox.

The answer that Polly gave occupied Lenox's mind all the way back to Hampden Lane, later that evening. He would get to his desk at seven the next morning, just in case the gentleman called again—good Lord, how he hoped the chap would call again!

Lady Jane must have seen on his face that he was preoccupied. "Hello, Charles," she said, kissing him on the cheek. "What is it?"

"Nothing—a matter of work," he said, taking off his light coat.

They were in the front hallway of what had once been his house. For many years, Charles and Jane, close friends from their childhood in Sussex, had been next-door neighbors here on Hampden

Lane, a narrow, leafy road, blessed with a decent bakery and an excellent bookseller's. When they had married, they had joined their two houses together—to almost universal exasperation, the architect's, the servants', their friends', their own, though the result was comfortable.

"A case?" she asked.

"Perhaps—but listen, I had lunch with my brother today."

"I know you did. How is he?"

Lenox shook his head. Who could say? "I've promised us down at Lenox House for ten days," he said. "From Wednesday. He's going down alone, and it simply won't do. It won't."

They'd been walking toward the dining room, gaslights along the hallways low and flickering, the house quiet. She put a hand on his arm to stop him. "Charles, have you forgotten?"

"What?" he said.

"Our luncheon. Wednesday week."

He widened his eyes and ran a hand through his hair. "Oh, hell."

"There's nothing on earth I wouldn't do for your brother, you know, but—"

"No, of course," he said. "If I weren't so busy I would have thought of it."

Lady Jane occupied a more rarefied sphere of London society than Lenox himself did, a late-morning intimate of the most illustrious house-holds, which would scarcely have acknowledged him if it weren't for her. She and her friend Violet Clipton were giving a luncheon at Claridge's, on behalf of the Indigent Children's Fund. Three members of the royal family were to be there— and a whisper, a very faint whisper, said that the Queen herself might even have plans to appear, though modestly and, maddeningly, without announcement.

She had been planning it for months. "*You* must go, of course," she said. "I hope you will. But I cannot."

Even this was selfless of her. There would be a tremendous amount for her to do between now and then, none of it easier with a husband away from town. "Is Sophia awake?" he asked.

She shook her head. "Asleep."

He felt exhausted, and now disappointed. He'd only had a few minutes' sight of the small, round-faced, sweet-tempered girl that morning over breakfast, and she had spent those calmly tearing the stuffing out of her doll's feet, until Jane had intervened, cross with Lenox for laughing.

Well; he would eat something; and he would go to Lenox House with his brother alone, if he had to. Nothing could be more important than that. His daughter would survive a fortnight without his presence. Even the visitor—the visitor Polly had mentioned—wasn't enough to keep him from making sure that Edmund endured these horrible days.

Though what a visitor!

"It was a German fellow," Polly had said. "A friend of Muller's. He told us he had an idea about the disappearance. Left no name. Refused to speak to anybody but you."

CHAPTER FIVE

Early that Wednesday afternoon, Charles and Edmund arrived at Markethouse by train. Edmund's groom was waiting for them there in the dogcart, but it was such a beautiful autumn day—the sky bright and clear, the trees, reddish in their upper reaches, still green in the lower, swaying in the light breeze—that the two brothers decided they would rather walk. They sent their luggage on the cart and set out.

"And he didn't return yesterday?" said Edmund as they walked.

They had been talking about Muller. "No," said Lenox. "I waited for him all day."

"I wonder who he might have been."

"Yes, so do I. I daresay he's a crank. But if he's not! It would be a very great glory to find Muller—not for me," he added, when his brother gave him a knowing look, "but for the agency."

The train station was a half mile from the village, alongside a softly rippling millstream. They had to climb stiles to cross the countryside. As they reached the top of a ridge, the spire of St. James's came into view, the village church.

About three and a half thousand souls lived in Markethouse; Edmund was their representative in Parliament, and they knew it, and all felt free to call him to task when they saw him coming. Even before the Lenox brothers reached the village, they met a young boy driving cows, who touched his cap carelessly and called out "Fine day, Sredmund!" before passing across the stream on a narrow footbridge.

The Lenox family and Markethouse had arisen from the misty depths of time at the same moment, roughly, the better part of the current millennium ago; the family was not Scottish (that would be the Lennox family, with another *n*), though people often made that mistake. In 1144, an esquire named Alfred Lance, always presumed because of his surname to have descended from some kind of knight, within the family, had settled in this part of Sussex, and subsequent generations had spelled their name Lanse, Lanx, Lencks, and, finally, some time around the 1400s, Lenox. Since then there had been two royal ships named after members of the family—both sunk for breakwaters now, rather ignominiously— and they had won a baronetcy, too, which gave Edmund the right to be called "Sredmund" by boys driving cows. As for Markethouse, it had been the site of the central Saturday market for eight local towns for seven centuries or so now—the same stalls of turnips and chickens and onions and trinkets, that whole while, every seven days. Rather remarkable to consider.

They reached the edge of the town, where

wildflowers were still growing along the stone houses, and parted ways with the millstream. Within a few moments they saw someone they knew—the costermonger, Smith, pushing a barrow of apples. He and Charles were roughly of an age and had played cricket side by side in village games all throughout the summers of their youth, and they exchanged a friendly greeting. Not twenty steps later, as they came to the edge of the bustling, cobblestoned town square, they came upon Pringle, the local veterinarian. He was an old, white-haired, stone-deaf personage; he stopped upon seeing them, beaming.

"CHARLES LENOX!" he shouted, arms crossed, face very complacent. "KNEW YOU'D MOVE BACK ONE DAY! TOLD YOUR BROTHER SO FOR YEARS!"

"I'm only here for a visit," Lenox said.

"TOLD MRS. PRINGLE AS MUCH, TOO, JUST ASK HER!"

"I'm only here for a visit!"

Pringle, who still hadn't heard, nodded happily to himself at the contemplation of his prescience. Then he shook his head. "WELL, THERE'S WORK TO BE DONE, MOVE ALONG, MOVE ALONG, YOUNG LENOX. GOOD DAY."

"Good day," said Lenox, giving up.

Pringle was, at least, an excellent veterinarian, called over much of the county for his skill with horses particularly. The only time he dropped the pretense that he could hear was when there was an urgent case, and then he would ask to have the complete facts of the matter written down. If the farmer who had called him couldn't write, as was often the case, he had to do his best. Fortunately he was very knowledgeable.

By contrast the next person they saw, the chemist, Allerton, was an unrepentant inebriate, considered trustworthy to make up only the most wholly basic medicines and salves. His sideline in homemade brandy kept him in business. For any complicated matter of chemistry, the whole village fled one town west, to a reliable, bespectacled young fellow named Wickham.

Allerton was delighted to see Charles. "Knew you'd be back!" he said.

"Hullo, Allerton," said Edmund.

"Sir Edmund."

"Is someone minding the shop?"

"I'd be surprised if they were!" He chortled and then carried on past them but managed to add, sotto voce, "Knew it!"

They passed the baker, Wells, who touched his hat to them, and then Mad Calloway came ranging by, pipe clenched in his teeth, hair flying out from under his hat—an old man with an age-cracked face, who lived out just at the end of the last street of the village in a small overgrown cottage with a dense garden by it. He survived selling the medicinal herbs he grew. He hadn't spoken, to anyone's certain knowledge, in at least a decade.

"Hello, Mr. Calloway!" said Edmund in a pointedly loud voice.

Mad Calloway didn't bother looking at them as he passed. Just behind him was Mrs. Lyons, a very nice woman who sang loudly in church. She looked worriedly after the hermit, then shook her head, as if to say what-can-one-do, and greeted them with a smile. "Mr. Charles Lenox," she said, "and not at Christmas, nor summer neither! Well, I always did tell your brother you'd move back, was I right?"

"No," said Lenox.

She didn't hear, and went on, chattily, "Nobody could stand London for a minute longer than you have, either, the whole place smells exactly like brimstone—which I consider a very strong sign that it's the devil's own, though I *will* admit that my cousin Prudence had a fine time at the exhibition, in that great crystal palace, even if twenty-five years does seem a long time to be talking about it, and of course, as I told her, the—"

And so on, the social round of Markethouse for a Lenox, half exasperating, half humorous, half enjoyable, half exhausting, all of it home. They walked on a little ways through the square, and then Edmund, hands in pockets, said, shaking his head, "I knew you'd move back to Markethouse."

"Oh, shut up."

It was Edmund's fault. In other towns the squire was a figure of terror, scarcely to be approached, from whom a nod after church was considered an unsurpassably graceful social generosity. But Edmund, like their father, felt a strong sense of duty to the village and its inhabitants, a strong sense of love, too.

Still, it was with some relief that they passed through to the opposite side of town and found themselves on a familiar old dirt road. Soon they came to the wide stone gate of Lenox House, and as they passed it the house itself came into view.

It was a lovely Georgian building, white stone, with three long sides around a courtyard, and a vast black wrought-iron gate on the fourth side, standing open as it usually did. Lenox felt a skip in his heart. This was where he had grown up. Its flower beds, along the avenue as they walked, were as familiar to him as the faces of his friends, and off to the left he could see the pond where he and Edmund had fished and swum as boys, and rising on a gentle upslope of grass beyond that, the steps that led up to the small circular family chapel. To the right of the house as they faced it were the gardens, and framing them a great deal of lovely green springy Sussex turf.

The dogcart stood by the gate, and after a moment there was a commotion at the door, and four dogs came tearing out, falling over each other, barking with happiness. Three of them were little black-and-tan terriers, the fourth (much slower) an old retriever that dated to Edmund's children's childhood. Edmund and Charles stooped to greet them, and as they walked the last hundred yards to the house the dogs milled around their feet, urging them to go faster.

In Edmund's tired smile as he greeted the dogs, Lenox felt the whole sorrow of the past five weeks. It was so difficult! Lenox dealt in death— it was his stock-in-trade, as surely as tin was a tin peddler's. And yet, strangely, when someone died that he had known personally, this familiarity didn't decrease the surprise of it. If anything, the surprise was greater. It was as if he had annexed death strictly to the professional region of his mind, over the years; when it crossed back into his own life it seemed a bizarre thing, terribly sad and wrong. How was it that Molly was dead? A few months before, they had played piquet all through one evening in Hampden Lane, chattering about what it was like to have children. Where could that person have gone?

Heaven, perhaps. He dearly hoped so; there were people he would like to see again. For all his faith, though, it was hard not to experience a feeling of loneliness when he thought of his sister-in-law.

And given that, what must his brother, trying not to trip over the dogs, hands in his pockets, be feeling?

At the door to the house, they met Leonardson, a stout middle-aged man who came each week to do the blacking in the kitchen. He touched his hat to Sir Edmund, congratulated Lenox on moving back to the countryside from London ("a terrible place, v'always said so"), and then waved good-bye as the brothers went inside.

CHAPTER SIX

T he next morning, just as they were finishing their breakfast, the bell for the front door rang. Edmund looked up from the papers he was perusing—matters of the estate—and Charles from his newspaper.

"Are you expecting anybody?" Lenox asked.

Edmund shook his head. "No."

A moment later the butler came in. Waller was his name, a young man, just past thirty years, the best part of them spent in some capacity here at Lenox House, until finally two years before he had ascended to his current august position. He was part of a new guard; with one thing and another there were no old staff left from their youth. Lenox rather preferred it that way. It meant there was no fust of olden times upon life at the house, as there was at so many country houses. To be sure, their father's steward—the older Mather—lived in the village, as did the astonishingly ungifted cook of their childhood, Abigail, upon whom Lenox called every Christmas with a goose. (She was probably the last person alive who called him "Master Charlie"—though she did it with mischief in her eye, an astute older woman, seated every day of the winter by her daughter's fire, knitting and telling stories to her

48

grandchildren, emphatically not cooking.) Otherwise the people had all been here only since Edmund had inherited the house and the title.

"A Mr. Arthur Hadley, to see Mr. Charles Lenox, sir," said Waller.

Edmund and Charles exchanged glances. "I don't know anyone by that name. And I don't think I've told anyone I was coming to the country, either." He looked back at Waller. "What is his business?"

"He has not said, sir."

"What sort of fellow does he look like?" asked Edmund.

"Sir?"

"Does he look likely to point a pistol at us and ask for our money?"

"Oh, no, sir. A respectable-looking gentleman, sir."

"Charles?" said Edmund.

"Show him in, by all means."

After the butler had left, Edmund said, "You have more faith in Waller as a judge of character than I would," then turned his eyes back to his tenant rolls.

Mr. Arthur Hadley was, though, a very respectable-looking gentleman, it was true. He wore a twill suit of clothes, the cloth an ideal weight for this brisk autumn day, and had in his right hand a walking stick with a brass knob on its end. The bottom was covered with fresh mud—from the look of it he had walked here. Lenox put his age at about fifty. He was clean-shaven, with a strong, square face. Under his right arm was a folded newspaper; his left hand was in the pocket of his jacket.

Lenox rose, and after a beat so did his brother. "How do you do, Mr. Hadley?"

"Mr. Charles Lenox?"

"Yes, that's me."

Hadley, still standing in the doorway, said, "I hope I don't call upon you at an inconvenient time."

Lenox smiled. "I suppose it depends on the purpose of your call. Are you collecting taxes?"

Hadley's open, good-natured face broke into a smile, too. "Not at all, sir, no. In fact, I was hoping to gauge your professional opinion of a small peculiarity I have experienced."

Lenox was astonished. "My professional opinion?"

Hadley unfolded the thin newspaper he had been carrying, and read from it. *"In residence at Lenox House,"* he quoted, *"Mr. Charles Lenox, eminent consulting detective of Chancery Lane, London, for an undetermined amount of time."*

"Is that this morning's paper?" asked Edmund. "May I see it?"

"Yesterday evening's," said Hadley, handing it over. "The *Markethouse Gazette*."

"My gracious," said Lenox. "They do move quickly."

Edmund laughed. "Here's cheek," he said to Charles. "It concludes, *Mr. Lenox happy to take on any new business that may present itself.*"

"I admit I felt a powerful relief when I saw that, Mr. Lenox," said Hadley. "The *Gazette* gave us all the reports about your triumph at the Slavonian Club, that terrible business of the women being stolen and brought into England, and I knew at once that I must come see you. It's been a week now, you see, and I haven't been myself—have barely slept."

"But I'm afraid I'm not actually here in a professional capacity, Mr. Hadley. Perhaps you might consult with the local police."

Hadley shook his head. "That's the trouble. Nothing definite has happened. I couldn't trouble them. Yet it's all preying on my mind so constantly."

Lenox had encountered this attitude again and again in his work—the impossibility of "troubling" the official police force, who were of course handsomely paid precisely to handle possible crimes against all members of the citizenry, and yet the utter ease of "troubling" *him,* who was almost invariably expected to take the greatest pains and seek no remuneration. If he had one criticism of his age, Lenox thought, it was this: too holy a respect for governmental institutions. Many of

51

them, hospitals, orphanages, records offices, had gotten away with bloody murder for year on year, simply by residing in imposing buildings and having superintendents with side-whiskers.

He was intrigued, though.

"Edmund?" said Lenox.

Edmund gestured toward the table where they had been sitting, next to a wide window with a particularly lovely view of the rolling countryside to the south, and said, "Please, Mr. Hadley, sit."

"Oh, I couldn't possibly, sir."

"Nonsense. Do you take coffee or tea?"

At last they cajoled Hadley—whom momentum had gotten through the door, and awe paralyzed once he was there—to sit down, and Lenox said, "Now, please: What has happened that has you so concerned, but is so insignificant that it would be of no interest to Constable Clavering?"

He awaited the answer, feeling awake and energetic. The first thing he liked to do when he returned to Lenox House was get on a horse, and that morning he had taken a fine tobacco-colored bay filly, new to him, not yet two years old, on a thundering gallop across the turf. Her name was Daisy, and she rode as well as you liked, he had reported to his brother when he returned.

Arthur Hadley, sitting opposite Charles, took a steadying sip of tea, set down his cup, and began his tale.

"I have lived in Markethouse for nearly two

years now," he began. "I am one of six vice directors of the Dover Limited Fire and Life Assurance Company, and most of my business is in Lewes, but I have a retiring disposition, and upon my most recent promotion, I bought a small house for myself here in Potbelly Lane. I have known Markethouse from my youth. My mother grew up in the village, and her sister, my aunt, remained here until her death, twelve years ago. You may possibly know her—Margaret Wilkes, as kind-hearted an aunt as anybody could have.

"I have been very happy since moving to the village. The place is just as I expected when I came, friendly but quiet. I live alone, with a charwoman who does cleaning and cooking for me from seven to five each day, excepting Sundays, which she takes as her day off. She leaves a cold collation out for me on Saturday nights—or I occasionally visit the Bell and Horns, in Markethouse Square, if I feel a hankering for Yorkshire pudding.

"I am very regular in my work schedule. Each Monday, Tuesday, and Wednesday I travel to several of the larger towns in Sussex—it's 'my' county, as it were—and sell policies for fire and life insurance, or meet with existing policy holders who require my assistance. Incidentally, if either of you require a policy for . . . the peace of mind—"

Lenox shook his head, and Edmund, with a trace of coldness in his voice, said, "I have one already, through the House of Commons, thank you."

"Ah, of course," said Hadley. He soldiered on. "On Thursday and Friday, I remain here in Markethouse and draw up the papers of the week's work. They go by train on Saturday to our head office. In an emergency, I can be contacted here by wire. The local postmistress, Mrs. Appleby, knows that I receive telegrams at odd hours, in the event of a fire or sudden death, and is alert for them even in her sleep, in exchange for which I pay her a small standing fee each month. If there *is* an accident, I make a point of traveling to see my clients immediately, wherever they may be."

Lenox wondered if all this was material—hoped it was. "Go on," he said.

"Well, such is my life, gentlemen. Nothing out of the ordinary has happened to me in the past two years, until last Wednesday night."

"What happened then?"

"I was returning home from a trip to Lewes. It was past nine o'clock. I was very tired—and happy to be back, for while I work on Thursday and Friday, Wednesday is effectively the end of the hardest part of my week, when I am traveling. At my age, the rails are a grueling master.

"By eight o'clock it is dark out, of course, at this time of year. I reached my house and saw two things at once, despite the dark: first, that on my stoop was chalked a strange white figure, and second, that in a downstairs window there was the light of a candle. I keep my curtains closed when I am away, but there was a small gap in them, and I was sure I saw the light.

"I was surprised, as you can imagine, but it was nothing compared to my surprise at what I saw next: A face appeared in the same downstairs window, for scarcely an instant, and then vanished."

"A face?" said Lenox. "A woman or a man's?"

Hadley shook his head. "I cannot say. It was very dim, and my eyesight is not what it once was. All I know was that it was pale, and looked to me . . . well, I cannot say, exactly."

"You must try," said Lenox.

"I suppose it looked very upset," said Hadley. "As if its owner was experiencing great emotion."

"It was the charwoman," said Edmund.

Hadley shook his head. "That was what occurred to me, but I asked the next day, and she swore up and down that she was out of the house by five, that her whole family could attest to it. And then, why wouldn't she have stayed to see me?"

"She didn't want you to know she had remained in the house," said Edmund.

"I take it, if you went to the trouble to inquire with your charwoman," said Lenox, "that you did not find anyone inside the house?"

"I was astounded, as you can imagine, and barely able to keep my wits about me. Almost immediately the light went out. I turned on the gas lamp outside my door and considered what to do. First, I looked at the chalk figure on my step."

"And what was it?" asked Edmund, who was leaning on the table with his elbows now, eyes curious, papers forgotten.

"I shudder to think of it, gentlemen," said Hadley, and indeed he looked pale. "It was a figure of a girl. A small girl. Only a simple drawing, but I hope you will believe me when I tell you that there was something very strange about it—uncanny. I felt my stomach turn when I saw it."

"A girl," murmured Lenox.

"After bracing myself, I went inside. I took up a heavy paperweight that I keep by the door for outgoing post, and went from room to room— well, there are only four proper rooms in the house, a forward sitting room, a dining room, and two small bedrooms upstairs. Everything was entirely as I had left it. The doors of the kitchen and washroom, just off of the dining room, were both locked from the inside, and empty. I checked each room and each closet a dozen times."

"And found?"

"Nothing, and nobody."

"Is there another entrance?"

"Only windows—but there are many of those, front and side," said Hadley. "And I do not keep them latched. Or did not, for now I do."

"Was anything missing?"

"Nothing at all."

"And this is the mystery you hope to solve?" Lenox asked.

Hadley shook his head. "Not all of it. I went to bed that night very afraid, with the door locked from the inside; but the next morning, when I woke, it all seemed rather foolish to me. As I said, I have weak eyesight. Was it possible that I had seen the reflection of a light across the way, and even, perhaps, a face? In the light of day it seemed just possible—though if I call that face to mind now, I know, feel certain, that it was inside my house.

"No, if it had simply been that experience, I might have been disturbed, but I doubt I would have sought any help. It was what happened the next day that has forced me to think something greater must be afoot—and in truth, gentlemen, to fear for my safety."

CHAPTER SEVEN

L enox's coffee had gone lukewarm as he attended to Hadley's account. He took the last sip, always so superbly sweet and milky, and then poured himself half a cup more from the chased silver pot at the center of the table, leaning back in his chair. A feeling of contentment and interest filled him. He'd feared a very gloomy trip, but now he had a pleasant fatigue in his muscles from the ride that morning, a fine breakfast in his stomach, a breezy and warm day awaiting him outside, and here, entirely unlooked-for, something to divert his attention.

And possibly Edmund's, too, he thought.

Edmund had always been fascinated by Charles's work. For years they had joked that they ought to trade jobs, during the period of his life when Charles had been so absorbed from afar by England's politics. Then he had entered the Commons himself. After his election Charles had suggested that Edmund take the reverse course— set out his shingle as a detective—though of course only in jest. In all these years he had never done more than speculate from his armchair, hectoring Charles for ever more detail about his cases.

The look on his face now, intent and absorbed,

was, if not exactly one of happiness, at least one of distraction. "Your safety?" he said to Arthur Hadley.

"I was at my desk the next morning at nine o'clock," said Hadley, "a bit later than usual. That morning I had gone out to the front steps with warm water and scrubbed off the picture of the girl in chalk. I admit that I felt better when it was gone, though it is not rational. That, too, I could account for in the daylight—local children, and what had seemed like eeriness the night before no more than an accident, the inexpert effect of a clumsy hand.

"At about ten o'clock there was a ring at the door. It was Mrs. Appleby, the postmistress. Since you have both lived here, perhaps you know her. A very intelligent, closemouthed, and respectable person—certainly not someone who would be willing to participate in a joke."

"A joke," said Lenox.

Hadley nodded, face grim. His back was straight and his gaze level; he made for a very convincing witness even to strange events, a fellow utterly English, probably without a very great deal of imagination, certainly not prone to exaggeration or whimsy.

"According to the telegram Mrs. Appleby brought me, there was a fire at the corn market in Chichester. I don't know if either of you knows Chichester, but the corn market is cheek by jowl with many of the finest houses on the town square there, half of which, perhaps more, I insure. You can understand my alarm.

"I hired the coach at the Bell and Horns to take me the twelve miles there, at no inconsiderable expense—but there are many insurance companies, and reliability and friendship in a crisis is what I have always felt distinguishes Dover from the others. We are not always cheaper, but we are always better, I tell my clients. Moreover, frankly, to be on the spot of a fire as soon as possible guarantees that we are not defrauded by our customers—that they do not overstate their claims, or what they have lost. Both for selfish reasons and for ones of professional pride, therefore, I was in haste to get to Chichester.

"The horses felt that haste on their backs—I offered the driver an extra half crown if he could cover the ground in less than two hours, and he did it, though we nearly turned over at a ditch near Pevensey.

"We arrived at the corn market, then, and what do you think I found? Nothing. Absolutely nothing—or rather, a normal day's business, without so much as an upset firepot on the premises, or an ember that had flown out of a hearth and onto a piece of hay."

Hadley's indignation was very serious indeed. "Who sent the telegram?" Lenox asked.

"It was signed by the mayor's office."

"Did you not think that peculiar?" asked Lenox.

"No. I'm well known in Chichester, and in the case of a fire they know to call me straightaway. As it is, when I knocked on the door, they were as surprised to see me on a nontraveling day as if I had appeared at their front doors after working hours. Nobody there had sent me the telegram."

"And at the post office?"

"I hadn't thought to ask there." Hadley frowned, then brightened. "That's why you're the detective, though, isn't it?"

Lenox allowed himself a dry smile. "Perhaps it is, though. Is that the end of your tale?"

"It's a very unusual one," said Edmund.

"Nearly," said Hadley. "Thank you both for your patience."

"Not at all."

"I returned home—much more slowly, and much perplexed, as you can imagine. I hadn't yet connected this false report to the incidents of the night before, which had vanished from my mind in all the commotion, and indeed, at home everything was as I had left it. I returned to my papers, confused about the events of the day and regretful about the lost time, but determined to finish with the most essential parts of my work.

"After an hour at my desk it was five o'clock, and the woman who does for me, Mrs. Watson, said good-bye, and that there was dinner waiting for me under a cover. I thanked her, and when she was gone sat back and, with a feeling of great relief, packed my pipe. I changed into my slippers and my robe, found the newspaper that Mrs. Watson had left on my hall table, and thought that I would have a drink to soothe my nerves before I ate. I was looking forward to a good night's sleep.

"I should add that everything in the house, upon my return, was exactly as I had left it that morning. There is no lack of things a thief might take in my house, either. I enjoy collecting small gems, and a few of the finer ones are laid out very prominently on my desk, including one ruby that I flatter myself does not have a superior from here to the doors of the British Museum. Needless to say, I have now stowed them away with the bulk of my collection under lock and key. To think, that I should have to take such a precaution in sleepy Markethouse!

"All of the liquor in my house is kept on a small mahogany stand in the sitting room. I went in to pour myself a drink—I enjoy a brandy—and noticed, to my amazement, that one of the six bottles that had been there, a bottle of sherry, was gone."

"The charwoman took it," said Edmund.

Hadley shook his head. "Yes, it must seem that way—but you are quite incorrect, with my apologies for contradicting you. She has been with me since the week I arrived in Markethouse, and her duties are quite clearly understood between us. She never touches my liquor stand. What's more, I asked her the next day, and she gave me her word that she hadn't taken it."

"Or thrown it away? Was the bottle of sherry empty?" asked Lenox.

"On the contrary, nearly full."

"How can you be sure that it hadn't gone missing the night before?"

Hadley nodded excitedly. "Precisely the question, sir, precisely the question! I am very particular in my habits, and the night before, after seeing that pale face, and that ghastly drawing, I had taken a glass of brandy. I am absolutely certain—would swear it upon my parents' eyes—that all six bottles were there when I went to bed. The same six bottles I always, always keep on hand."

There was a long pause. "Curious indeed," said Edmund.

"I felt a chill run down my spine. I tried to shake it off, tried out just the explanations you have both offered, but I couldn't, and in the end I walked across town and knocked on Mrs. Watson's door, which interview's results I have already conveyed to you. She did not touch the liquor table, did not take the bottle of sherry. And yet it was gone. For the second day in a row, someone had been inside my house."

Now Lenox frowned. "Had Mrs. Watson

allowed any visitors into the house while you were away?"

"None."

"Was the door to your house locked?"

"I generally leave the door and the windows unlocked while Mrs. Watson is there, and I believe I did that day, too. Since then, of course, I have taken to locking everything—and, I don't mind saying, checking twice or three times that I have done so, before I have the courage to fall asleep."

"Someone could have entered the house without her noticing, then?" asked Lenox.

Hadley grimaced. "I would have doubted it, if it hadn't happened. Somehow they must have, I suppose. It's true that Mrs. Watson passes a great deal of her time in the kitchen, which is at the back, and to some degree segregated from the other rooms in the house. By her own account, she was there for several hours in the afternoon while I was gone."

Lenox pondered for a moment all that he had heard, and then, leaning back in his chair, he said, "You have come to ask me my professional opinion—well, you may have it."

"Ah, that's a relief."

"I think that these are very strange circumstances indeed, and I think that the police would unquestionably be interested in them. I am happy to assist them or you, of course, but they know the village better than I do, they have your welfare at heart, and I should certainly, in your position, place the matter in their hands."

Hadley nodded but said, "Without intending any disrespect, Mr. Lenox—I think you are perhaps accustomed to the *Metropolitan* Police, which is of a very different order than our local police forces, here in the country. I deal with loss and fire and theft for a living, and you cannot imagine how hidebound, how immobile, how very contrary, a small village constable can be."

Charles looked to his brother, hoping to appeal to him for a better account—but saw, to his surprise, that Edmund was nodding. "It is quite true. Clavering's a very good fellow, but not one of your cunning London sharps."

"Indeed?" said Lenox. He thought for another moment. In truth, he was intrigued. The pale face, the drawing of the girl, the bottle of sherry. He turned to his brother. "Edmund, you know my days here are yours."

Edmund nearly smiled. "In that case, I happily transfer ownership of them to Mr. Hadley, at least temporarily—and hope that he will accept mine as well, for I am exceedingly curious about what on earth all of this can mean. In Markethouse, too, as he says!"

"Very well," said Lenox. "Mr. Hadley, I will take the case."

CHAPTER EIGHT

Mrs. Watson, the charwoman, lived with a family of six in two rooms on Drury Street. This was one of the small lanes toward the western end of town, near Markethouse's only factory, which manufactured tallow. It was the poorest part of the village—there was an unpleasant smell from the factory at most hours, much worse in the summer—but it was still nothing like the poverty of London. Penned in front of most houses were a few chickens or a pig, and more often than not a small vegetable garden grew alongside them.

The charwoman was not at work in Hadley's more middle-class street, closer to the square, because one of her children was ill; Hadley had given her permission to take the day.

"It's only the second time it's happened these two years," he'd told them in Edmund's breakfast room, speaking in a forgiving tone, and Lenox's ears had pricked up at that. Anything out of the ordinary was worth noting.

"Has she been behaving peculiarly at all, your Mrs. Watson?"

Hadley had furrowed his brow. "Mrs. Watson! Not at all. As reliable as the church bells, she is."

Now they arrived at the house where she lived. The young boy who answered the door didn't look sick. "Do you want to buy a toad?" he asked.

"No," said Edmund.

"What about two toads?"

"Can they do anything interesting?"

"They'll leap something tremendous," he said, with fervent sincerity. "I can give you both for sixpence."

"George!" cried a voice behind the boy, before they had the time to answer. It was Mrs. Watson, hurrying forward. "Gracious me, Mr. Hadley, how sorry I am—George, get out of the house this instant—with your brother ill, no less—go!"

The little boy ran off without looking back at them, and Mrs. Watson, though flummoxed by the appearance of her employer and two strangers who were obviously gentlemen, made a fair show of guiding them into her small, extremely warm kitchen. Another boy was lying in some straw in the corner, a long string bean of fifteen or so, his face waxy, his eyes fluttering. Mrs. Watson put a kettle on for them without being asked.

"Is he all right?" asked Edmund, frowning.

Mrs. Watson glanced down at the boy. "Him? He'll be well enough soon, I hope."

"Should he see a doctor?" asked Edmund.

The charwoman looked at him for a moment, and then realized that her face must have betrayed how stupid the question was, because she said,

"It's a very gracious thought, sir, but not just yet, I think."

Only if the boy was actually dying, of course, Lenox realized, maybe not even then. "I know that Dr. Stallings would come visit if we asked him," he said. "Edmund, why don't we send a note and ask him? It's not ten minutes' walk."

"I call that a capital idea."

So the note was written, and the boy next door enlisted to take it to Stallings, and they sat in the boiling hot kitchen, sipping flavorless boiling hot tea—and waited. Mrs. Watson, a rough, raw-faced, but kindly woman, was too polite to inquire why they had come, and the three men didn't wish to disturb the boy. At last, Lenox suggested they remove themselves to the next room for a moment.

Here they were able to interview the char-woman.

She offered an account that mirrored her master's: She had worked for him for two years, six days a week, Sundays to herself, cooking, cleaning, mending, sewing, shopping, no, the duties was not onerous, sir, yes, she was quite happy in her position. With these initials out of the way, Lenox was able to pose a few more probing questions.

"Can you cast your mind back to last Wednesday?"

"Certainly, sir."

"What time did you leave Mr. Hadley's house?" he asked.

"At five o'clock," she said. "Same as every day, sir."

"When you left, was there anything chalked on the steps of the house?"

She shook her head, face firm. "No, sir. Absolutely not. I would have seen. I always sweep the steps, last thing, before I go."

"Was the day unusual in any way?"

"None at all, sir."

She had so far evinced no desire to know who they were, or why they were questioning her—apparently Hadley's presence was enough to vouchsafe them—but now Lenox said, "We're hoping to get to the bottom of this missing bottle of sherry."

She quite mistook his tone—and perhaps felt herself worried that she would have to pay the bill of the doctor, who was known to travel in a coach led by a horse, too, and she flushed red and said, "I never took it! I swear it before Jesus Christ our savior himself!"

"Mrs. Watson, be calm, please," Hadley said. "These gentlemen don't think you stole anything."

"I didn't!" she said.

"I'm very sorry," Lenox said. "I ought to have phrased it differently: We believe someone stole the sherry, not you, and hope that with your help we might find the person."

"I didn't steal it."

"We have no suspicion whatsoever that you did," said Lenox, though from the corner of his eye he could see that Edmund did.

Ah, that was different, Mrs. Watson said; she would be only too happy to help. She poured more tea into Lenox's cup.

It was at this moment that the sound of hooves came clicking up the small street, and a moment later a small fly led by a single horse arrived at the door. Dr. Stallings dismounted from the conveyance. They waited for him in the doorway, and he inclined a deep bow toward Edmund.

"Sir Edmund," he said. Then he turned to Charles. He was a round, very well dressed man, bald but for a fringe of hair around his ears, with half-moon spectacles. He gave Lenox a slightly shallower bow. "Mr. Lenox. I hope that the reports in town are correct, and I may be the first to congratulate you on your permanent return to the county. For your health, you could not have chosen more intelligently."

"I'm only here for a visit," Lenox said, but Stallings had already turned toward Hadley and was addressing him.

Mrs. Watson, driven to distraction by this accumulation of distinguished visitors (Had the physic said *Sir* Edmund? she muttered to herself, to herself but audible to all), spoke in a long, ceaseless, meaningless rattle, whose gist eventually

70

shepherded the doctor into her overheated kitchen.

Lenox knew that Stallings was a fair physician. He radiated the complaisant good cheer of a man whom life had treated kindly—who hadn't missed a meal in many years, nor lost a bet, nor thrown a shoe, nor shed a tear.

The doctor approached the patient very gravely, sat in the chair next to him, and proceeded to make a considerable examination of him, as they all looked silently on: pulse; temperature; responsiveness of the eyes; examination of the gums; test of the reflexes; and much more beside.

At the end of his inspection, he patted the boy on the arm, stood up, turned toward the adults in the room, and said, in a loud, clear voice, "He's faking."

"Faking?" said Edmund.

"Yes. Faking, shamming, putting it on. However you prefer to put it. He's in more or less perfect health. His most serious ailment at the moment is the castor oil I believe he may have swallowed. Was it as an emetic, young man? Well, never mind. I hope you have managed to avoid whatever you wished to avoid. I will wish you good day, Mrs. Watson . . . Mr. Hadley . . . Mr. Lenox . . . Sir Edmund."

"Good day," Edmund said. "The bill to me, mind you."

"Of course, sir."

Mrs. Watson, amidst these pleasantries, had

shifted from confusion to incandescence—she was cuffing her son on the ear, dragging him up out of the straw, telling him how little he was good for, and how stupid he was, and that he had wasted the time of *four* gentlemen that day, and she had missed work for the first time in two years (she had apparently forgotten the first time, even if Hadley hadn't), and did he think money grew on primrose bushes. Gradually Lenox came to understand that the young man had been scheduled to return to the village school that day for the first time since spring. Unusual, rather, for a boy of fifteen and his class. He made a gentle comment to that effect. Mrs. Watson turned and proudly declaimed to him, Edmund, and Hadley—without any apparent concern for consistency—on the subject of her son's extreme brilliance, overwhelming cleverness, unsurpassable goodness.

Meanwhile the boy was quietly eating a piece of bread—having apparently gone without, while his *ruse de guerre* to avoid school was in action, but having given up now. He did indeed look to be in fine health, now that he was upright. Mrs. Watson rushed him out then, saying that he could at least make the afternoon lessons—and he went, hair flattened, a slate and chalk tied to his belt, and a sprig of mint in his hand to sweeten his breath when he made his excuses to the teacher.

At last, this comedy of errors concluded, their interview could resume.

CHAPTER NINE

P lease tell us what you did on Thursday of last week, then, the next day, Mrs. Watson," said Lenox, "beginning when you arrived at Mr. Hadley's house in Potbelly Lane. Was it at seven o'clock?"

Mrs. Watson, who looked as though she had never experienced a more eventful hour in her life, fanned her face, took a deep breath and a long sip of tea, collected her thoughts, and then nodded, trembling slightly. "Yes," she said. "It was seven o'clock in the morning, as usual, sir."

"And you found Mr. Hadley in a state of some consternation?"

"Sir?"

"Mr. Hadley was upset?"

She shook her head. "Not that I noticed at first, sir. I banked the coals, you know, sir, and fixed his tea and breakfast—he sleeps late on a Thursday, after traveling the previous three days—and when he came downstairs at half past, he was very friendly-like, sir, which is just as usual, you see."

Hadley, a peaceable soul, smiled at her encouragingly. "Go on, Mrs. Watson," he said.

"As I was cleaning the sitting room, where he sits and works at his desk, sir, he mentioned that he thought he had seen someone in the house last night—but I said to him quite honest that I had gone at five as usual. Then, of course, he was called away to his fire at Chichester."

"You remained in the house," Lenox said.

She nodded stoutly. "I did. Immediate upon him leaving, I locked up every door and window in the place, because I was not quite happy to be left there alone."

Lenox shot a meaningful glance at Edmund, upon whom this new fact was not lost. Hadley, too, frowned. "Then how could someone have entered the house while I was gone?" he asked.

"It certainly would have been much more difficult, and suspicious, than if you had actually left all the doors and windows unlocked while you flew to Chichester, as you thought you had," said Edmund.

"Mrs. Watson, you heard nothing? Nobody entering?" asked Lenox.

"No, sir."

"And the first you heard of the missing sherry was that evening, when Mr. Hadley came to see you?"

"Yes, sir." She grew defiant. "And you may search the house up and down—and it may please you to know that I do not even care for sherry! And nor does Mr. Watson, and the boys are too young to drink spirits, except on Saturdays."

"We certainly don't think you took it," said

Hadley. He looked perturbed. "I wish we knew who had."

Lenox ran through several more questions. He asked Mrs. Watson if the chalk figure was familiar to her (Hadley had replicated it upon a piece of paper), which it was not, and in detail about the construction of the house, which he presumed she knew as well as her master, if not better—specifically if there was anywhere that might have concealed a person who wished to hide. She was adamant that there was not.

Hadley looked horrified. "You think someone might have been in my house *the entire time?*" he asked.

"I don't know," said Lenox.

"I tell you it's not possible," said Mrs. Watson, *sirs* forgotten in her certitude. "After I locked the doors and windows I looked the house through and through. There's nowhere a person could have hid, not under the beds, not in a closet. Nowhere."

Lenox went on to ask her in detail for her activities Thursday, so that they might try to estimate which hours she had been in the kitchen, and therefore less likely to hear someone enter by the front door. She thought she had gone back there at around noon, perhaps a little earlier, and come out to clean the front rooms at one o'clock. Nothing had been disturbed or altered in that interim. The front door had still been locked—she had checked, some of Mr. Hadley's nervousness

75

having rubbed off on her before the telegram drew him away to Chichester.

At last they left, with their thanks. Mrs. Watson told Mr. Hadley that she would be to Potbelly Lane directly, now that her son's health was "improved," which seemed a rather inaccurate word to Lenox, though he made no comment upon it.

"I hope that was of some assistance to you, gentlemen," said Hadley.

"It was entertaining, at any rate," Edmund answered.

"May I ask what course you now mean to pursue, Mr. Lenox?"

Lenox checked his pocket watch. It was just past one o'clock, and after so much exercise before breakfast, he found that he was famished. "I would like to look at your house," he said, "and then speak with your neighbors. But first, I think I may need to eat something. Is it convenient for you if we call at your house in an hour's time, Mr. Hadley?"

"More than convenient. I wait upon your leisure, Mr. Lenox."

"Thank you."

"The house is number seven, with the blue shutters. I will be there."

Soon the brothers were alone. "Well!" said Edmund, as they walked down the quiet streets of Markethouse, in the direction of the Bell and

Horns. "You have brought me a far more interesting morning than the tenant rolls would have."

Lenox shook his head, doubtful. "I cannot say I like it."

"I'm surprised to see you look concerned," said Edmund. "From what I understood, you missed this sort of thing, with all of your administrative duties."

"I meant that I don't like a case I don't understand," said Lenox.

"How do you mean?"

Lenox shrugged, then said, "What facts do we have? To begin with, how many crimes have been committed? One? Three? None? A missing bottle of sherry—there are a dozen innocuous explanations that present themselves for that. Would Mrs. Watson sincerely have wished us to search her house? Because *I* think Mr. Hadley is a gentle employer—very easy to take advantage of.

"And then, can we even be sure that the bottle was there in the first place? Mightn't he have been primed for some oddity by the evening before, and forgotten that he finished it?"

"I found him very convincing," said Edmund.

"Well—yes. But the chalk figure, the face in the window. Nobody except Hadley saw them. He has no witnesses to confirm his story. Are we to believe it without any cavil? He might be losing his grip on reality."

"Hm."

"Then again," said Lenox, as they strolled onward past a small churchyard, its trees pleasantly orange and red, the whistle of wind in them just audible, "there is the matter of the call to Chichester. That, at least, is verifiable. Indeed, I think we must verify it for ourselves before we proceed."

Edmund nodded. He was taking tobacco from a small pouch in his coat pocket as they ambled, and packing it in a pipe with two fingers, face full of thought. "There are three possibilities, then," he said. "First, that Hadley is mad, or badly mistaken. Second, that one of these things is suspicious—the face in the window, say—and the rest are easily explained, the chalk figure a child's drawing, the sherry mislaid or stolen . . ."

"And third," said Lenox, "that it is all connected, and something very strange indeed is afoot in your little town."

Edmund smiled. "Our little town, I think you are entitled to say, Charles, given that you have permanently returned. Tell me, is it wrong that I hope for the third possibility to be true?"

"Ha! No, of course not. It is exactly always what I hope for, you know—secretly."

As the brothers walked on, talking about poor Hadley's troubles, Lenox almost thought he saw a look of peace in Edmund's face—the absence, anyway, of that carefully managed anguish that had drawn it inward for the past five weeks.

They ate a pleasant lunch at the Bell and Horns (Lenox was congratulated on his return to the parts by three different people), and after they had scraped their plates clean of the delicious spongy cake with which they rounded off the meal, and sipped their pint pots of ale down to nothing, they betook themselves to Hadley's house.

"Are you sure you can spare the afternoon?" asked Lenox of Edmund on the way. "I'm happy to proceed on my own—or drop it altogether."

"There's nothing on earth I would rather be doing," said Edmund. Then, a shadow passing over his brow, he said, "Other than spending time with the boys, obviously."

"That goes without saying," said Lenox, and then added quickly, in the hopes of distraction, "We're skipping over the most intriguing question of all, by the way."

"What's that?"

"Hadley's collection of gemstones. How much is it actually worth? And how carefully did he look to see that none of them were missing?"

CHAPTER TEN

Hadley's neighbors on Potbelly Lane were an unfortunate combination: useless and extremely talkative. All of them knew Edmund by sight, as their Member of Parliament, and more than one had some issue they thought ought to be brought before the Commons—the Land Act, taxes, suffrage, in one instance a missing cat. They all admitted cheerfully that they had seen nothing, not the previous Wednesday nor the previous Thursday.

With one exception. Opposite Hadley's small, well-maintained house, which was white with a handsome blue trim, there was a ramshackle place, the remnant of an earlier architectural era—not a row house, but a gingerbread cottage with smudges of green garden on either side of it.

Here they discovered a retired solicitor named Root. He hadn't seen anyone entering Hadley's house on the previous Wednesday or Thursday. Intriguingly, however, he had seen the chalk drawing.

"You did?" said Lenox.

Root nodded. "Yes. I spotted it coming out of my house on Wednesday evening. It was still light out, so probably not after a quarter to seven.

Awfully peculiar, you know. I wasn't likely to miss it."

"Could you draw it for us?" asked Lenox.

"I'm not much of a hand at drawing."

"Even a rough approximation would help."

Root accepted a scrap of paper and a nub of charcoal, then spent a careful forty seconds at the table next to his door, tongue in the corner of his mouth. When he showed them the result of his work, Lenox felt excitement. It was nearly identical to the image Hadley had provided them. Something concrete, then, something to confirm that Hadley wasn't simply going mad. If anything, Root's figure had slightly more detail to it.

"Braids in the hair," murmured Lenox.

"Yes," said Root. "There weren't many distinguishing marks to the drawing, but I recall that one. And the mouth—that was what gave me rather a jolt. It wasn't a smile, as you would expect. Nor a frown. A straight line."

"Expressionless," said Lenox.

"Yes. There was something unsettling about it."

"What did you think of the drawing at the time?" asked Lenox.

"Well, I thought enough of it that I stopped and looked at it for a moment before going on into town. I suppose I assumed some children had done it."

"Even though Hadley doesn't have children?"

"I didn't give it all that much thought, you

know, not enough to inquire of myself what children would have done it."

"And now? What do you think?"

Root frowned. He was an older, acute man, contemplative. He had come to the door with his finger holding his place in a book. "If I consider it again," he said, "though I'm not certain, I think perhaps it seems too . . . too expert for a child to have drawn it. Of course, I may only be ascribing that impression to it now, since two gentlemen have come to my door and asked me about it, including my representative in Parliament!"

Lenox nodded. "I understand. And you're sure you saw nothing else—nobody unusual loitering in the area of Mr. Hadley's house?"

"Only Mrs. Watson, whose family I have known sixty years."

"Are you that long in this district, sir?" said Edmund, sounding surprised.

"I grew up here—left for London for thirty years, where I had offices in High Holborn, and now am back, in my mother and father's old home, though I spend the coldest months of the winter on the Continent, for my health. I know you by sight, however, Sir Edmund. It is a pleasure to meet you in person."

Edmund put out his hand. "The pleasure is mine," he said.

Root took the hand and dipped his head deferentially. They spoke for another few minutes, but the solicitor wasn't able to add any information to that which he had already given them. Nevertheless, as Lenox and Edmund walked across the street toward Hadley's, they were both animated—a clue, confirmation of a clue.

"Is this what it's always like?" Edmund asked.

"It's usually a good deal more frustrating than this. And there are a great number of doors slammed in your face, and occasionally slop thrown after your feet. And curses behind your back."

"I say, that would be thrilling."

"Well, I doubt Hadley is the man to do any of that, and here we are at his door," said Lenox, "so you will have to wait your treat out."

The chief impression Hadley's house gave was of unimpeachable tidiness. If he said there had been six bottles of liquor in the liquor stand, Lenox believed that there had been six bottles of liquor in the liquor stand. In the compact entry hall, there was a table with a clock on it, polished to a gleam, an empty calfskin card stand (no visitors that morning, at least), a paperweight, and a stack of precisely a week's newspapers, the *Times*. Lenox counted them surreptitiously with his finger. Here was another signal, like the collection of gemstones, that, while Hadley's house was small and he kept only a part-time servant, he was well off; the *Times* cost nine pounds a year, not an inconsiderable sum, and most men even of the middle class merely rented it for an hour's use each day, which cost a little above a pound per annum. (Lower down the scale, it was possible to rent the previous day's paper for about a quarter of that price.) Money: always something to keep in mind when a crime had taken place. Hadley's could have made him a target.

They walked with great care through each of the house's four rooms and its small rearward kitchen. Lenox had Edmund go back and enter the front door as he and Hadley stood by the stove, quiet. They couldn't hear him come in. So it was possible that a person could have slipped inside while Mrs. Watson was in the kitchen, though obviously it would have been a risk.

Mrs. Watson had been telling the truth, too—there was nowhere in this house where a person larger than a child could reasonably have hidden, by Lenox's reckoning. He knocked at the back of every closet, listening for the hollow sound of a false compartment, inspected the floorboards, asked whether there was an attic.

It was growing rather late now. "We have mastered the facts of the case today, at least," said Lenox to Hadley. "Tomorrow I hope we may make further progress."

A shadow of panic crossed Hadley's stolid British face. "Do you think I am in danger?" he asked.

Lenox shook his head. "I think that if anyone intended you harm, they wouldn't have gone to such lengths to draw you *away* from Markethouse, by reporting that fire in Chichester." Hadley and Edmund made identical faces then, some realization dawning on them. Lenox felt a discreditable little moment of superiority and covered it with a frown. "On the other hand, I think something unusual is certainly occurring."

"And you advise?"

"Giving us a little more time," said Lenox. "If you feel uneasy, I would be sure to let your neighbors know before you retire for the night. A street full of inquisitive neighbors is often the most powerful deterrent to crime in my experience."

Hadley nodded and, as they gathered up their cloaks and went to the door, thanked them profusely, telling them that he would be home all the next day, their servant whenever they might have the time free to see him again.

"An interesting day," said Edmund, as they walked down Potbelly Lane and through Cow Cross Street. From a thousand summer afternoons, they both knew without saying it that they would take the shortcut across the old grazing pasture home—much quicker than the long road. "Why didn't you mention the gemstones, may I ask?"

"I'd like to know a little more about it all first."

"About the crime?"

Lenox shrugged. "The crime, the criminal, the telegram—and Hadley, too."

At Lenox House, Waller greeted them in the entrance hall, where their footsteps sounded loudly on the black-and-white checkerboard floor.

At this hour, the light falling gray through the windows, lamps still unlit, there was something peculiarly sad in the air, to do with Molly— something silent, almost more silent because of their own small sounds in this empty little hallway, with its vestiges of another, fuller life, gloves on the front table, umbrella stand poised to receive hats and sticks. In a frame next to the front table was a small line drawing of the dogs.

Waller coughed discreetly. "One of your tenants, Martha Coxe, is at the servants' entrance, Sir Edmund, enquiring for"—he looked distinctly uncertain as he said the next words—"for the late Lady Molly, sir."

Edmund hesitated before he responded. "She doesn't know . . . no, evidently not," he said. "They're very isolated down in the valley, I suppose. Please, lead the way."

Edmund followed Waller. Lenox, alone, sighed and walked into the drawing room.

Things were a little bit more cheerful here, at least. On his mother's sideboard there was a rounded china urn of hot tea, with plates of biscuits and sandwiches near it, and gratefully he poured himself a cup, spooning in a small noiseless snowfall of sugar, then pouring a bit of milk in to follow it. Ranged across the long wall, opposite the windows looking out at the garden, were the old familiar portraits he had ignored so intimately in his childhood, when he spent hour upon hour in this room, especially on rainy days. One of the old Lenoxes—Sir Albion Lenox, 1712–1749, a small brass plate said—looked exactly like a cross between Charles's father and a large frog.

He took his cup over to the piano and found on the deep black shine of its surface a letter and a telegram waiting for him. (This was where Edmund always had Waller leave his post, and Lenox followed suit when he visited.) There was also a large stack of official pouches from Parliament, and he smiled, remembering the ceaseless flow of documents and constituents' letters and blue books from his own time in the House, and feeling glad that this cataract fell upon Edmund now, not him. He picked up the wire with his name on it and read it.

His eyes moved quickly. When he was finished, he said, in a low voice, "Well."

He tossed the telegram down onto the piano. Down here, sadly, he'd be at least half a day behind in hearing any news of the missing German, even if Dallington wired, as he had now.

Anyone who really wanted to take a hand in the Muller case had to be in London.

The young lord's telegrams had a unique style, for he tried to be economical with his words since they cost a halfpenny each, but could never quite manage to contain himself. His message said:

> Scotland Yard admitting stuck Muller STOP have called in agency STOP not us blast them STOP LeMaire STOP Polly advises independent investigation STOP urges you return STOP all here vexed in extreme STOP hope all well STOP Dall

CHAPTER ELEVEN

L enox woke up very early the next morning, with the first dark blue light. After taking a cup of strong coffee, he unstabled and saddled Daisy, gave her a handful of oats, and then set out with her across the country. Yesterday had been sunny, but this new day was wet and dark, a thin mist hanging over the open green landscape. He rode very hard. The horse responded beautifully, though he learned that he had to angle her off on downslopes, where she might easily have tumbled heels-over-head, for she didn't slow her pace at all. During their whole gallop his mind was an utter blank: the noise of the horse, the air in his face, the sensation of the thousands of pounds of muscles working beneath him, the close control he needed in his hands and his legs to stay safely astride her.

At last they stopped at a small brook, where he ladled water from the stream for both of them, first himself and then the horse. The soft rain was wonderfully cooling. After his breath had slowed, Lenox looked back and saw the house, only a small rectangle on the horizon. He ate a hard rind of cheese he had brought, chewing almost automatically because he was so hungry, and fed Daisy first an apple, then a few cubes of sugar, both of which she took with snorting joy.

He thought of Sophia; she could sit on a small stool in the stable for hours, feet swinging above the ground, watching the horses as they were combed and fed—indeed, watching them do nearly anything. He felt a thud in his heart, the sensation of missing his only child, sad but not unpleasant.

In his breast pocket he had Jane's letter, and as he caught his breath he took it out and read it again. Not very much news, since she had written it only a few hours after he left.

My dear Charles,
Does the post arrive there only four times a day, rather than six? Now I cannot recall, for some reason. Still, this should be with you tomorrow, with <u>any</u> luck—with it my love and Sophia's. You will be no doubt content to hear, since you are pleased to indulge her worst vices, that she pulled the hair of a little boy on the street when he wasn't looking. He shouted terribly. She said that she knew him—<u>didn't</u> like him, he had done the same to her earlier. I had to apologize abjectly to her mother, who looked fit to roast me over a fire.

Toto arrives in ten minutes to help me plan the seating for the luncheon. If HM does come, of course, every plan will be shot straight to pieces. Then again, nobody will care, because she will be there. Then again again, even if she comes I will feel as if I have done wrongly, for Edmund's sake. I am glad that you are there at least.

Will you see my brother while you're in Sussex? Do call on him if you remember. More tomorrow morning—I will send cuttings of the news on Muller, as you requested. Write me by next post, would you? Love always,
Jane

Muller. Lenox, sitting on a rock by the brook, restored now but waiting to be sure that his horse had caught her breath, too, contemplated the missing German. The night before, after he had gone to his bedroom (the blue room, the best in the house they'd always thought, and strictly out-of-bounds in their youth), he had stayed up with a candle and examined his own small private file on the case. There was something slightly unbecoming—to be kept private, at any rate—in this collection of paper clippings, notes on chronology, scribbled thoughts. It was the pride of it. He had a great deal to do, and many, many men were already focusing their efforts on finding the pianist, LeMaire now among them, a wily old hand.

Yet Lenox found that he couldn't quite resist

making his own surmises. Then again, neither could Pointilleux, nor Dallington, nor Edmund, nor probably HM herself, if it came to that. So it was without too much self-recrimination that he'd sat up later than he had intended, pondering every facet of the case anew, trying to circle in closer to the truth. If Polly thought the agency ought to be involved, she was no doubt correct. Of the three of them she had the best head for business.

He was nine-tenths of the way home, riding at a canter, when to his surprise he saw Edmund, walking down the slender path that led west away from the house. "Have you had your breakfast?" asked Charles. "It's very early."

"I have," said Edmund.

"I was expecting to see you over coffee. There's Hadley."

"Yes, of course! I shan't be more than an hour or two. I just liked the sound of a walk."

"With your valise?"

"Blue books, in case I sit."

"Do you want company?"

Edmund shook his head soberly. "You'd better stable her. It's only getting wetter. I'll be back soon."

Lenox watched his brother go, then shrugged and turned back toward Lenox House. He wouldn't be able to distract him indefinitely, that was the trouble. With a twinge of memory he recalled Edmund referring to "the boys" the day before.

This was among the cruelest aspects of Edmund's grief: that his two sons did not yet know of it.

The older of them, James Lenox, who'd become baronet one day himself, would learn of his mother's death soon. He was an adventurous, handsome, fast-living young person, who had decided after he graduated from Harrow to forgo the slow rewards of university education and instead try his hand in the colonies, specifically Kenya. The letter Edmund had written him with the news a month before would arrive shortly, if the mails ran as they ought to.

But then there was Teddy, Edmund and Molly's younger son, who had been particularly close to his mother. He was at sea aboard the *Lucy*, a senior midshipman of Her Majesty's Navy. There was no way at all of knowing when he might return, or even what latitude he was currently sailing upon.

Lenox rode into the stables, gave his horse to the groom after a pat on her neck, and went into the breakfast room through the glass doors that looked out on the garden. To his surprise, a figure was seated there.

"Houghton, is that you?" said Lenox.

The fellow turned in his chair. "Ah! Hello, Charlie. How do you do, how do you do?"

This was Lady Jane's younger brother, Clarence, the Earl of Houghton. "What a pleasant surprise!" said Lenox.

Houghton stood, tucking his newspaper under his plate, and smiled warmly, putting out his hand.

They had never been terribly close. Houghton was an inscrutable sort, even to Jane. He was very old-fashioned. As a boy, an heir born after his father had nearly given up hope of such a thing, he had always been a marvel within the family, cosseted and beloved, and there was some air of permanent distance or detachment in his bearing now, as kindly as his manners were. A nursery air. He was deeply conscious of his position, both its perquisites and its responsibilities. He was married; had two sons himself; had no passions to speak of other than the administration of his enormous estate and the maintenance of his position. He probably hadn't opened a book in twenty-five years, but he read certain parts of the *Times* without fail—the court circular, the chess problem, the weddings and deaths, and the crime reports from London, though it was rare that he spent more than three days a year there. Jane managed him very well. She chaffed him, pushed food on him, mothered him. It was what he wanted, perhaps. In the end, Lenox thought of him as still half a boy, for all his frowning sense of duty. His wife was a cold, impeccably lineaged, proper woman, Eliza. The closest Lenox had ever felt to Houghton was after an unpleasant dinner with Eliza, when the two of them played cards in his library together alone; in silence.

"There's a ball next Friday night. I'm to invite you," Houghton said. "Jane wrote."

"That was decent of her."

"I would have come straight across anyway, had I known you were here. Why the devil didn't you write to say you were going to be staying?"

"I had planned to write this morning. I only decided at the last moment, when my brother needed me to come down. It all happened in a rush."

Houghton nodded. "I was very sorry about Molly."

"We were glad to see you at the funeral," said Lenox.

"Oh, of course."

"Did you ride across today?"

"I? Oh, no, I took my carriage. Is your brother here?"

"He is out on a walk upon the estate," said Lenox.

"Ah, is he! Capital, capital—so much to do with that sort of thing. You have it easy, Charlie, larking about London. Only he and I know all that can go wrong in places such as ours."

This was polite of Houghton. Lenox House was not one of England's great stately homes—a hunt, riding hard, could cross its acres in five or six minutes, whereas Houghton's land would have taken them the best part of an hour, and two river fordings at that.

Still, Lenox had always felt with pride that it was one of the prettiest of country houses, a small jewel of its kind, the pond serene and fringed in each season with different lovely green shoots and flowers, primroses or cowslips or cyclamen. Being back now—the ride that morning, and indeed seeing Houghton, whom he associated so strongly with the country—gave him a wistful, loving, affectionate feeling for the place. He was very fortunate to have grown up here. He was conscious that in Edmund's absence, just for this moment, he must play its host. It was a duty that birth, to his great fortune and occasional sadness, had precluded him from ever truly performing. He could do it momentarily now. He rang the bell for hot coffee, gestured for his brother-in-law to sit down, and asked what the chess problem had been that morning, and whether the skies looked likely to clear.

CHAPTER TWELVE

Hello, Sir Edmund!"
This was the bright greeting of Mrs. Appleby, the postmistress for Markethouse, later that day. "Hello, Mrs. Appleby," Edmund said.

"Ah, and Mr. Charles Lenox. I thought I saw a letter addressed to you last evening. Only here for a short visit, I take it?"

"No, I'm—" Lenox stopped himself. "Yes, in fact! Only a short visit. How did you guess?"

"Oh, London rarely spits 'em back out."

She was a stout, rosy-cheeked, white-haired woman, who worked from a windowsill in her house with a small ledge in front of it. There she gathered parcels, letters, and, most importantly, behind the counter, telegrams. There were only two telegraphs in the village.

It was nearly noon; Edmund had taken a longer walk than he anticipated. "We're helping Mr. Hadley, of Potbelly Lane, with a small private matter," Lenox said. "I understand from him that you two have an arrangement about telegrams."

"Certainly we do. Always shut the window and bring 'um to him straightaway. Him and the doctor. I s'pose I would do the same for you, Sir Edmund, if the Prime Minister was to write."

"No fear of that," said Edmund.

"You brought Mr. Hadley a telegram from Chichester last Thursday?" said Lenox. "A week ago?"

"I did. Only it wasn't from Chichester."

"Excuse me?"

Mrs. Appleby looked at him as if he were slow-witted. "It wasn't from Chichester."

"Where was it from?"

"Massingstone."

That was a village four miles north of them. "That's the opposite direction of Chichester," Edmund said.

"So 'tis!"

"How many people work at the post office in Massingstone?"

"Four," said Mrs. Appleby.

"They deal with more telegrams than you, then?" said Lenox.

"Oh, many more, dozens more a day."

Another mystery.

Charles and Edmund put a few more questions to Mrs. Appleby—she hadn't kept a copy of the telegram but would swear that it came in from Massingstone, she could see the initials before her eyes even now; no, the figure of the little girl in chalk they showed her didn't mean anything to her, though she couldn't rightly say that she liked the look of it—and then left her window with thanks.

"Very curious," said Edmund.

They were walking across the square. "Mm."

"I'm beginning to believe that Mr. Hadley is in danger."

"Something rotten is going on, all right," said Lenox, studying the ground as he walked with a knit brow. He looked up at Edmund. "But if you wanted to harm a fellow, would you clear him out to Chichester? No, it's something in the house, I think."

"The bottle of alcohol?"

Lenox shook his head. "Would it surprise you at all if this pale-faced man or woman had swiped the sherry to steady their nerves? And kept the bottle, not guessing it would be missed so quickly?"

"That's plausible."

"No, it's not the sherry that concerns me. For my part, I keep returning to the gemstones."

They were going to see Constable Edward Clavering. "Here we are—turn here," said Edmund.

Clavering was Markethouse's sole police officer, although in times of trouble he could enlist the help of several volunteers, and there was also a night watchman who walked the streets and had the power of arrest in exceptional circumstances. Lenox wanted to talk to him, too—and as luck would have it he was with Clavering, a beanpole named Bunce.

Lenox had only a passing impression of

Clavering, who was a tall, bristle-mustached, thick-faced, stupid-looking fellow, standing at attention now outside of the sole jail cell in Markethouse. He took off his hat immediately upon seeing them, deference to the local squire's presence.

"How do you do, Sredmund?" he said.

"Very well, Clavering, very well—and you?"

Clavering frowned. "*Not* well, I don't mind telling you, sir, since you're back in town, and glad we are to have you. *Not* well."

"No?" said Edmund, concerned.

"May I ask who this gentleman is?" asked Clavering, nodding to Lenox.

"This is my brother, Constable. His name is Charles Lenox. He's a consulting detective in London, though at the moment he's working on behalf of Mr. Arthur Hadley."

Lenox nodded. "How do you do?"

"A detective!" said Bunce wonderingly.

"Is Mr. Arthur Hadley having a trouble now, too?" said Clavering. He brushed his hand across his forehead, looking overwhelmed. "Add him on the list, then, for he ain't the only one."

"Why, what's been happening?" asked Edmund.

"All sorts," said Clavering. "All sorts. Day on day. And starting at the market, worst luck yet."

Charles and Edmund nodded somberly. The market was essential to life at Markethouse— what had given the town its name, of course,

many centuries before, and what kept it prosperous now. The market occurred every Saturday,
fifty-two times a year, without fail, whether
England was at war or peace, without regard for
who had left or entered the world, as regular as
sunrise. It was the closest market for the citizenry
of eight villages and their environs, and drew
sellers from farther away still. You could buy
anything there: a bag of walnuts, a Spanish guitar,
a herd of cattle, a tin pot, a painted cabinet, a glass
of stout.

It ran on Saturday because that was the day
when employers paid wages, and many of the
attendees of the market shopped for the week.
For that reason it stayed open well into Sunday
morning, hundreds of stalls humming through
the night. Markethouse's church had always had
erratic attendance.

"What happened at the market?" asked Edmund.

"And what's been happening generally?" Lenox
put in.

"Theft," said Clavering pointedly, shaking his
head.

"Theft," Lenox repeated.

Bunce nodded, and Clavering removed a small
notebook from his breast pocket. "Which it is
this, sir, in the last ten days, the following have
gone missing: two chickens, from a house in Cow
Cross Lane; four shillings in change, from three
various market stalls; a half wheelbarrow of

carrots, also from the market—a half wheel-barrow!; a springer spaniel, name of Sandy, belonging to a farmer who had stopped to wet his whistle at the Bell and Horns; several blankets and a cloak, from the church basement; a box of candles, from Mr. Woodward's stall at the market; and just this morning another chicken from a yard in Victoria Street."

"My goodness," said Edmund, and the concern on his face was real.

"The dog may have run off," Clavering added, "but the owner thinks not. It were a very obedient dog."

"Is this an abnormal amount of crime?" asked Lenox.

Clavering's small eyes widened slightly. According to Edmund, he was a conscientious but not dazzlingly gifted officer of the law. Then again, the chief qualification for the job he held was to stand under the hot sun in a thick uniform without looking uncomfortable each year during the school prize-giving, and evidently he was an eminent hand at that.

"Is it an abnormal amount of crime? Well, put it this way: It's as much as we had in the whole entire preceding year all together," he told Lenox.

"Are there not often thefts at the market? That surprises me."

Edmund interjected here. "Never. The vendors of long standing have a strong interest in self-policing. No forgiveness. Permanent expulsion, fines and jail if they can manage it. They'd use the gallows if we let them."

Clavering nodded. "And as for chickens, they roam more or less free in Markethouse, and nobody dreams of stealing them."

Bunce agreed. "Can't recall the last time a chicken went missing."

Lenox felt an idea percolating in the back of his mind. "The blankets and the cloak in the church, whose were they?" he asked.

"The blankets belong to the church. Itinerants occasionally sleep on the porch there in winter, though we encourage 'um on their way with a hot meal and a penny or two. The cloak belonged to the pastor himself, Reverend Perse."

"Very interesting indeed," said Lenox. "Have you observed anything else peculiar happening?"

Clavering shook his head. "No. That's enough for me, mind."

"More specifically," Edmund said, "we were wondering if either of you had observed anything in Potbelly Lane, last Wednesday or Thursday, perhaps, though really any day at all."

Clavering shook his head again, but Bunce said, "I have."

"Have you never!" said Clavering, turning to look at him indignantly. "And you didn't saw fit to tell me?"

"I forgot."

"Forgot! Haven't I enough on right now, without secrets? My *goodness*," said Clavering, with cutting disdain in these last two words.

"What did you see?" asked Lenox.

Bunce's answer shouldn't have surprised him, but it did. "There was a chalked drawing on a stoop there. Tolerably odd one, too."

Lenox raised his eyebrows. "Was it this?" he asked, pulling from his pocket the drawing Root, the solicitor, had made.

"That was it," said Bunce.

Clavering looked unhappy. "Now what?" he asked. "Was something else stolen?"

"A bottle of sherry," said Edmund.

"Dear me, dear me," said Clavering. He took out his notebook and wrote that down. "A bottle of sherry, too. From Mr. Hadley?"

"Yes," said Lenox.

"Heavens."

"Tell me, this is a small village—has anyone returned recently, or has there been any new face people are talking of?"

Clavering and Bunce looked at each other and smiled grimly, a passing moment of amusement in a serious day. "What?" asked Lenox.

"None except you, sir. You haven't been stealing chickens, have you now, Mr. Lenox?"

CHAPTER THIRTEEN

L ate that afternoon, the two brothers sat in the drawing room, Lenox on the sofa under old Sir Albion, Edmund in an armchair by a window, which was running with rivulets of rainwater. Each brother had a cup of tea, and each was reading. At the far end of the room a steady orange fire burned in the hearth, its susurrating crackle a homely, comfortable pleasure. Occasionally one would recite something out loud to the other— Lenox from a pile of cuttings that had arrived for him from Lady Jane about the disappearance of Muller, Edmund from the evening edition of the *Markethouse Gazette*, which Waller had brought in not long before.

"Nothing on the thefts in it?" asked Lenox. "Or on Hadley?"

Edmund shook his head. "The leading story is about the market tomorrow. Apparently it is 'scheduled to run as per usual.'"

"Seems a bit thin for the top news story."

"The whole newspaper is only four pages long," Edmund pointed out.

"I don't know how they fill that many."

Edmund, cutting the second and third pages with a penknife, smiled. "Well, then, tell me what's happening in London, where you can fill a newspaper just with stories of murdered musicians."

Lenox shook his head. The cuttings were interesting but inconclusive. The newspapers, especially the *Telegraph*, blared the news of LeMaire's entry as a new assistant to Scotland Yard, all of them giving summaries of his experience and qualifications, as well as making prominent reference to his detective agency. Invaluable publicity.

In fairness to him, he had already, perhaps, chased down one lead: A cabman swore that on the night of Muller's disappearance he had taken a man in a dinner jacket, just such as Muller had been wearing during his performance, from the Cadogan Theater to Paddington Station. He recalled it clearly because the gentleman had been wearing no hat and no coat. Nor had he carried any luggage, which was odd for someone well dressed and on his way to Paddington.

It did sound like Muller—and Paddington Station had trains at that hour that could carry him all over the Isles, and from thence by boat to Europe, certainly. LeMaire's men were currently interviewing the employees at Paddington and felt confident of further success.

"And they are kind enough to inform us," said Lenox, "in an irritating little boxed note, that LeMaire—well, I shall read it to you. *Monsieur LeMaire is no doubt familiar with the word 'cabriolet,' which in the language of his native shores means 'a little leap,' the precise sort of motion that a British carriage of one horse, or 'cabriolet,' makes—and whence, as a result, the word 'cab' has descended to us, in one of the many portmanteaux of our two nations. Perhaps this knowledge gave him the special insight needed to find the cabman who may have driven the German pianist to Paddington Station."*

"Ha!"

Lenox shook his head. "No doubt it was that—he was pondering the word 'cabriolet' in his office for a few leisurely hours, and finally it inspired him." Edmund snorted. "Daftest thing I've ever read."

"I do wonder where he is, though. Muller, I mean, not LeMaire. Fancy, just disappearing like that."

"It's got me foxed," admitted Lenox.

"What would be your best guess? If you *had* to guess, without hedging, I mean?"

That had been Edmund's favorite method of inquisition for his younger brother since childhood (*If you* had *to give up either toffees or licorice forever, which would it be?*), and Lenox smiled.

He glanced down at the other cuttings. There were vanishing, evanescent little fragments of information in them: that Muller had asked for a second sandwich wrapped in a napkin just before he played the concert, for instance, indicating that he might have been planning to travel (though of course he could have just been hungry); that he had quarreled with his manager before the first recital in London. An enterprising young journalist had traveled to Dover and reported that at least one gentleman answering to Muller's description and, crucially, traveling without luggage, had been on the evening packet to Lille the night of his disappearance.

Still, none of that answered the basic question: Where had the German gone directly after he finished playing?

A thought occurred to Lenox. "I suppose if I had to guess," he said, "I would hazard that it's all for publicity. Muller's sitting right now in a room in the house of the owner of the Cadogan Theater, reading penny novelettes, eating cakes, and waiting. The owner of the theater is rubbing his hands together gleefully, planning how to spend all of the money he'll rake in next week when Muller makes his triumphant return from the dead."

Edmund thought about that for a moment. "Interesting. Yes—what price wouldn't people pay to see him after such an absence?"

"There you have it."

Edmund lifted his paper again to cut it and said, "I can tell you that I would pay a pretty steep price to meet whoever left that chalk drawing on Hadley's stoop."

"Mm."

After speaking with Clavering earlier that day, they had walked through the rain to Hadley's house. Mrs. Watson had answered the door, greeting them in a low tone. "He's not well, Mr. Hadley. His nerves."

"Is he in bed?" asked Lenox.

"In his sitting room—but wearing his slippers."

She'd said this as if it meant he were next door to death. In fact, Hadley had indeed seemed somewhat broken down, and when Lenox asked after his state of mind, he confessed that he had barely slept.

"I keep seeing that face in the window," he said. "I know that somebody has been in the house. That's the problem. I have half a mind to check in at the Bell and Horns and stay there until this is all over."

Edmund and Lenox had nodded sympathetically and asked a few questions. Was Mr. Hadley aware of the other thefts in the village? Did he have anything at all to do with the market? The answer was no in both cases. They went over what he remembered more slowly then, though nothing useful came of it, except, perhaps, that Hadley was more inclined to think that it had been a woman's face that he'd seen in the window than a man's.

"Do you remember the person's hair?" Lenox had asked.

Hadley had shaken his head. "Nothing so distinct, Mr. Lenox. It's only a feeling, you understand. I would never swear to it."

At last they had come, gradually, to the subject of Mr. Hadley's gemstones. Charles had suggested that Edmund be the one to bring it up, and he had—a surprisingly capable assistant. "You're certain the sherry was the only thing that was missing when you returned from Chichester last Thursday?" he had said.

"Yes, quite sure."

Edmund had nodded. "Good, good. I only asked because I know you mentioned your collection of gemstones. I am pleased to hear that it is intact."

For an instant of an instant, Lenox thought he saw something flare in Hadley's eyes—something possessive, something angry—but when he looked again, it was gone, as surely as if it had never been there. "They are all as they were," Hadley said, "though it is not such an astonishing collection as all that, only a hobby."

"Are they under lock and key?" Edmund asked.

"They are now, though the cabinet is not very—not a citadel, if you take my meaning, not impenetrable. Fortunately, I don't advertise their presence, so it would take a thief some time to discover them."

"I might suggest removing them to a bank," said Lenox.

Hadley nodded. "Yes, perhaps."

But it was plain he was only being polite. "What is the collection, precisely?"

"They are rough gemstones—uncut, unpolished—some very valuable, some, many of my favorites, in fact, entirely forgettable, at least from a monetary point of view. Such stones have been my passion since I wandered over the cliffs with a chisel as a boy, Mr. Lenox. I am fortunate enough to have attained some expertise upon the subject. Indeed, I have published articles in several small journals, and been in communication with leading scientists in London."

Hadley's ardor wasn't at all uncommon. Theirs was an age of fanatical amateur geologists, who roamed the countryside in clubs, covering twenty and thirty miles in a day with ease. (Prince Albert himself, Queen Victoria's late husband, had been one of these men.) Many of them, recently, had taken to visiting the quarries near Oxford, where they were uncovering most remarkable fossils, unknown to science, with elements common both to birds and lizards; the eminent naturalist Richard Owen, an acquaintance of Lenox's, whom many of these amateurs revered, and to whom they took any bones that they struggled to identify, had given these ancient animals the collective name *Dinosauria.* The press—abjuring Latin—called these strange beasts "dinosaurs."

Gemstone collectors were a subset of this cultishly zealous group. If Hadley was a known figure in that particular field, he might well have attracted the wrong sort of attention.

Lenox nodded, understandingly. "That's excellent," he said. "But I would consider removing them to a bank, as I said, or failing that precaution I would at least consider buying a safe. I am far from persuaded that the crimes of which you have been a victim are at their end."

CHAPTER FOURTEEN

The next day was Saturday: market day, which might as well have counted as two days of the week here. In the morning, Lenox rode again, his muscles loosening slowly as he went, for he was sore as the devil from the previous two mornings' rides. It was gray and wet still, though bracingly open. He wished Jane and Sophia were here to take the air. He might miss any number of things about London—his office, his friends, his clubs, the noise, the light—but he didn't miss the soupy fog that rolled through the streets this time of year, troubling every pair of lungs in the street.

When he returned to Lenox House, Edmund was again gone, though it was scarcely eight o'clock. "Where is he now?" Lenox asked Waller.

"Out upon a walk as he was yesterday morning, sir. He gave me to understand that he does not expect to return for a period of one to two hours."

Lenox was vexed; he wanted to get to the market early, before it grew too busy, and interview the stall-holders who had been the victims of the thefts Clavering had described. After lingering over breakfast, checking the window every other minute for Edmund's return, he decided he would go on his own. He asked Waller to tell his brother to meet him in town.

To save time, he borrowed an old dray horse from the stables, Matilda, a gentle, lolloping beast, fifteen years old and still just about faster than a man on foot. She carried him to the square, nuzzled him when he patted her mane, and gracefully accepted an apple from his pocket. He found a boy in the square—a local, who spent market day hanging around the central square to do odd jobs—and gave him a penny to take her back to Lenox House.

"Don't hire her out to your friends for rides on the way, either, or I shall hear about it," said Lenox. "There's another halfpenny if you find me within the hour with the news that she is home."

With that finished, he stood at the top of the square, gazing down at the gentle slope. Dozens of stalls were crammed higgledy-piggledy into it, the noise and smell already impressive.

"Lo there, oysters?" called a fellow passing him, with a yoke around his neck and a tray hanging from it full of cracked oysters. A pepper box and a salt cellar hung from his belt.

"Later, perhaps, thank you," said Lenox.

There were other wandering vendors of this type, selling ale in flagons, coffee in tin pots, apples, flowers, long braided strings of turnips and onions. A teenaged boy had rock sugar for a farthing. A bargain: As Lenox knew from his boyhood, with careful husbandry a medium-sized piece of rock sugar could be made to last through a full market day.

Then there were the stalls. Cockerels, more substantial varieties of fruit and vegetable, trout (from Edmund's and Houghton's waters, almost certainly), fat pheasants, white sugar in twisted brown wax paper. What an infinity of things to buy! Down the west lane were the patent medicine sellers—all fraudulent, McConnell had assured Lenox, and most of the medicines simply alcohol, though many in the lower classes all across England swore by their effects with sacral fervor—and down the east lane were stalls selling jewelry, muslin, bombazine, perfume, soapstone carvings, slippers, sponges, cloaks, squares of glass, penknives, anything you could imagine. Out in front of these stands, knife-cleaners and tin-menders sat on low stools, the tools of their trade close at hand. Down near the fountain, a barber was warming water over a small covered fire to give his shaves and cuts.

"Mr. Lenox?" said a voice.

Lenox turned. "Constable Clavering, how do you do?"

Clavering looked overrun of his capacities, but he nodded bravely. "Hoping for uneventful, sir," he said. "Uneventful would be ideal."

"I wonder—could you point me in the direction of the sellers who were stolen from, the last two weekends?"

They spent the next hour going from stall to stall, Clavering walking with the assurance of a man who knew precisely where every stray potato in this marketplace had fallen.

None of the vendors could explain the thefts. Lenox asked them to describe any customers who had stood out, but the crowd was too various and bustling to allow for such recollection—yes, there were regulars at each stall, and among the irregulars most of the faces at least were familiar. That still left two or three in every ten who were strangers, or whom the vendors had only seen once or twice.

The most audacious of the thefts had been the half wheelbarrow of carrots. "Gone," the fellow who had missed them said to Lenox, his astonishment undiminished by time. "Gone! Simple as that. Talked to a customer for a moment or two, turned back to the barrow I'd been unloading, and it was gone."

"You didn't see anyone lurking about?"

"There are always boys in and around the market. But we've never had a problem—always deal very severely with anyone caught stealing, several months in jail from the magistrate, 'cause we all know Markethouse needs the market, don't we?"

Clavering nodded emphatically at that.

It made Lenox think, this. The two sets of crimes were very different. On the one hand, there was the simple theft of necessities—food, blankets. On the other, there was the rather uncanny victimization of Arthur Hadley, including the telegram, the chalk drawing, and the sherry.

Were these crimes necessarily related? he wondered.

He spent the next half hour moving around the market. He saw a great many people he knew. There was Mrs. Nabors, who had been the housekeeper at Lenox House some years before, but had been fired when she'd been found selling the house's food from the back door; apparently she had continued in that business, for she had a stand full of meat pies and gave Lenox a very dirty look as he passed it. He saw Mad Calloway again, wandering with his herbs, simples, dandelion greens, mushrooms, and nettles, stopping occasionally to accept a coin for a bunch of them. And he spotted Mrs. Watson's older boy, in full health apparently, sprinting up an alleyway with a group of children around his age.

He found Edmund near the Bell and Horns at a little before eleven o'clock. He was with the mayor of Markethouse—a slender, staid-looking man whose name was, for some reason that had gone into the ground with his parents, Stevens Stevens. It was really the only notable thing about him.

"Hello, Mr. Stevens," said Lenox.

"Hello, Mr. Lenox. Wet day, isn't it?"

"Clearing, I would have said."

The mayor looked up doubtfully. Lenox had known him for forty years, since he was a swottish, pedantic boy at the village school, and more or less the same look of circumspection had been on his face the whole time. He had never in that time evinced any vivacity except a complete, joyful absorption in numbers. Markethouse—a market town, after all—liked that, and his rather stooped figure, permanently hunched forward from a lifetime of peering over his glasses at balance sheets, inspired a fond confidence. He'd run unopposed several times in a row now.

"I don't know—it could be more rain," he said. "I find these Saturdays exhausting, though of course necessary, too. Louisa, could you run inside and fetch me a glass of sherry with an egg beat up in it, and a sandwich if they have it?"

The young secretary next to him, a girl of fifteen or sixteen with thick spectacles, clutching a stack of loose papers, said, "Roast beef or cheese?"

Stevens pondered this question as if a great deal hung upon it, hemming and hawing, were they the same price, they were, interesting, before deciding upon roast beef.

The glass of sherry Stevens had asked for reminded Lenox of Hadley, and he said to the mayor, "Do you know a man named Arthur Hadley? He lives in Potbelly Lane."

Stevens shook his head. "Sir Edmund has just been asking me the same question. I do not. I fear that my work has kept me indoors much of the summer, when I ought to have been out, behaving sociably. In politics, as you gentlemen know, that common touch is vital."

"He's been a victim of a theft," said Lenox.

"So Sir Edmund told me." Stevens shook his head, looking, like Clavering, overwhelmed. "And beyond that there are the chickens, the carrots, the books, the blankets, the—"

"Books?" said Lenox sharply.

Stevens nodded. "Yes, books have been stolen."

"Clavering didn't mention that," said Edmund.

"Four, stolen from what is already a very small lending library here in town. I started it with a surplus of funds we had—sixteen pounds—because of a rather elegant legerdemain, if I say so, that I was able to perform, with the budget of the—"

"What were the books?" said Lenox.

Stevens narrowed his eyes, trying to recall. "One novel, I believe, perhaps by Mrs. Gaskell, and . . . but Louisa will know, when she returns with my food and drink. I wonder if I suddenly wanted a sherry because of Edmund's telling me about Mr. Hadley. Funny, how the brain works. Do you know, I often think that—"

But Lenox, who was not very eager to hear Stevens Stevens's speculations on the nature of

119

the brain, interrupted him again, saying, "When were the books stolen?"

"Last week."

"Could they have been stolen to resell?"

Stevens shook his head proudly. "Upon every page of every book we acquire, there is stamped the name of Markethouse Library, and at random throughout the book there is a stamp informing any potential buyer that the book is not for sale, nor ever will it be. They did the same at Massingstone. Rather a clever idea."

"Very, very curious," muttered Lenox.

Stevens's young secretary came back with his food, blushing as she intruded upon their conversation to hand it to the mayor, and after a few minutes Edmund and Charles bade him good day.

When they were alone together, Edmund asked, "Why were you so fixated on the books?"

Lenox shrugged. "Because they change the whole complexion of the matter, at least as far as I'm concerned."

"How is that?"

"How many men in England who are desperate enough to live upon stolen chickens, and sleep under stolen blankets, can even read—let alone care so much about reading that they'd steal books, too?"

CHAPTER FIFTEEN

They remained at the market until one o'clock. Then they went into the Bell and Horns—the village's main inn, gathering point, public house, stables, a large, flourishing place of two stories—and had a lunch of roast, potatoes, and peas, served inside a golden Yorkshire pudding.

As they left the pub, they nearly bowled over young George Watson, the smaller of Hadley's charwoman's two sons. He was covered in mud and offered to sell them a toad, as he had before. Edmund said no thank you, and George said what about a songbird, they were dead cheerful, and Edmund said no thank you again, but he would give him half a penny if he went and fetched a cup of water from the bar so Edmund could rinse his hands off. George was back in a jiffy and had disappeared down into the welter of the market with his halfpenny before Edmund's hands were dry.

"I cannot see how you plan to proceed," said Edmund, shaking out his wrists. "We've spoken with anyone who might know anything about the intruder at Hadley's house, and we've looked it over for ourselves. It's all dead ends as far as the eye can see."

"Yes. It's bad. This is generally the point where I give up," said Lenox.

Edmund's eyes widened. "I never! Is it really?"

"No, of course not. Don't be preposterous."

Edmund looked abashed. "Oh."

"There is always somebody else to speak with, of course. Just now I think we ought to talk to the milk and egg man of Markethouse, whoever he may be."

"Pickler."

"Is that his name? Yes, then, him. In my experience, nobody knows a village more intimately than its milkman. He crosses every line of class, respectability, geography—he knows the inhabitant of every house by name—he's called Pickler, you say?"

"Yes," said Edmund.

"It was Smith when we were young."

"So it was. This is his son-in-law," said Edmund. "In fact Smith is still alive. His daughter Margery married Pickler, and together they took over the business. They buy some of our milk at the house."

"Then sell it back to you?"

"In bottles, and half-skimmed, and on the doorstep, with a pint of cream, too," said Edmund.

"I see."

"And furthermore, we don't miss out on having milk if our cows fall sick or don't feel like giving any. It would mean hiring a whole other fellow to be sure of all that myself."

"Ah, I see."

"Of course, Molly always said we ought to have more than two cows, but she was more faithful to the country than I am. I couldn't be bothered with the trouble of it. Give me horses any day."

"Horses are much more interesting than cows. Less milk, however."

Lenox had said these words quickly, hoping to push the conversation ahead, but his effort at distraction was unsuccessful. Edmund's face hadn't exactly changed as he mentioned Molly, but he had somehow nevertheless seemed to fade, to exist a little less. It was terrible.

"I probably ought to have done it," he said—not quite to Lenox.

"Come on, let's see if we can find Pickler."

"Right-o," said Edmund, shaking his head sharply, as if to clear it out.

They found the milkman shopping for himself, as it happened, near the cattle pen to which local farmers had driven their calves for sale. He was happy to step away from the pen and speak with them for a moment, he said, tipping his cap respectfully to Sir Edmund.

He was a man of about five foot five inches, with a sportingly angled houndstooth hat. Apparently he and old Mr. Smith's daughter scrimped all they could in order to buy a cow every two months or so, because of course the more milk they provided themselves, the greater their profit.

"Nor do we feed them on the spent mash out

the breweries," he added, "though it would be cheaper in the short run. But they make more and better milk on real grazing."

Pickler himself lived in a small pair of rooms; the cows were all stabled on a local dairy farmer's land, where they could graze to their hearts' content for a small fee.

Lenox and Edmund asked him if he had heard of the thefts. He laughed; he had, the implication being that you would have to search much farther than him to find someone who didn't know about the thefts.

"Have you seen any unfamiliar faces around town?" Lenox asked the milkman.

He shook his head. "Not recently, no. Mrs. Hargrave had a nephew visiting, but he's been gone this week and more. Other than him, nobody."

"In that case, I am wondering if there is any particular spot in Markethouse that might serve as a bolt-hole—where a person might conceal himself, sleep at night, lurk during the day."

Pickler frowned. "It's not the village I would choose for it," he said.

"That's true," Edmund put in. "It's very tight."

"I suppose the churchyard is the only place I can think of," said Pickler. "Every other room in every other house is occupied, and my missus and I would know it in a heartbeat if someone was in our cellar, for instance. You wouldn't last long trying to hide in any of the streets here. No, I don't think it's Markethouse you're wanting, for that kind of thing—unless it's the churchyard, as I say."

"Every village must have an abandoned room—a little lean-to—where a person could hide?" said Lenox.

Pickler shook his head. "Not in Markethouse proper, sir. The town is overinhabited as it is, sir. Folk are very jealous of their space here."

Edmund affirmed this. "There's a law on the books against putting up two continuous buildings or more within a few miles of the town limits. Agreed long ago by the local landowners. Everything's very compact as a result, just as Pickler says."

"I see."

A few minutes later, as they watched the milkman walk back toward the cattle pen, Edmund said, "You think it's an itinerant, then, someone living rough?"

"I really don't know. The blankets and the food would seem to indicate as much. But then there are the books, and Mr. Hadley's peculiar experience."

"Mm."

"It can't hurt to look at the churchyard, at least. Come, let's go there now."

But at the churchyard they found only another dead end. They walked the whole length of it, then looked in all the nooks and crevices within the church itself, but there was no sign at all of inhabitation. And as Lenox thought of the town, he realized that Pickler and Edmund were right: There were very few places in Markethouse where one could hide out. Its most affluent residents lived in Cremorne Row, in a long line of alabaster houses, its prosperous burghers round about the area of Potbelly Lane, and its lower inhabitants toward Mrs. Watson's end of town. In all that space, as he thought of it, he couldn't call to mind a single dark alley, or a stableyard that wasn't hawkishly watched. If the town said Mrs. Hargrave's nephew had been the last stranger to visit before Lenox himself, the town was right.

And yet, and yet . . .

"I have an idea," Lenox said.

Forty minutes later both brothers were on horseback, Lenox on Daisy, who was cantering with a sprightly gait, and Edmund on an eight-year-old chestnut he loved better than all but a handful of human beings, Cigar.

They rode in a perimeter around Markethouse. They started very close in, along the fields at the edge of town. There were several small buildings near a small public garden, but all of them were locked; when they came back to where they had started, they went a half mile farther out from the town and started the circle again.

This was precisely the way Lenox always approached a corpse: moving away from it in concentric circles, studying the body and its environs from farther away with each one. Scotland Yard had officially adopted it as a standard method two years before.

Now the corpse was Markethouse, and they circled it three times, at a half mile, a mile, and a mile and a half, stopping at every small building they saw, jumping easily over the fences they passed. On the main road a few people were starting to leave Markethouse, their goods all sold, evidently, traveling by donkey or by foot.

They came again to the head of the stream where they had started, longitudinally, and Edmund said, "Another circle?"

"If you don't mind."

"With all my heart. It had been too long since I was on a horse."

Lenox broke into a grin. "I told you! There's nothing like it."

"Yes, I remember now that you know everything. Come along, catch up if you can!" cried Edmund, and put his heel into the horse's flank.

Neither the next circle nor the one after that showed them anything. There were a few small buildings in various attitudes of crumble, but none looked as if its threshold had been crossed in years, never mind the last few days.

It was growing dark when they reached a

small, tumbledown gamekeeper's cottage. They were about three miles outside of town now, and another three west of Lenox House. Both of the brothers were breathing hard. Markethouse was in the distance from them on the eastern horizon, smoke rising in thin columns from a few dozen different chimneys on this brisk day.

"Whose land are we on?" Lenox asked in a low voice.

Edmund looked at him curiously. "Alfred Snow. We have been for the past seven or eight minutes. A farmer in these parts. He keeps a good deal of livestock, too. A rough sort, but very smart—worked his way up from the orphanage in Chichester, you know, wholly on his own in the world, to very great wealth indeed. I have a good deal of time for him. He bought the property from Wethering when Wethering went bankrupt, poor sod. You remember Wethering. Why? Do you see something?"

Lenox pointed at the ground. There was tobacco ash in a pile next to the door, as if someone had been leaning there and refilling a pipe. It might well have been nothing—another rider, stopping by, or the gamekeeper.

But. "Does Snow keep game?"

"No. Wethering did, and his forefathers, of course. That's why this building is here."

"Let's look inside," said Lenox. "Quietly."

They dismounted, tied their horses to a tree,

and walked silently toward the door. Lenox put a few fingers to it, and it swung open easily.

Within the small stone cottage there looked to be two rooms. The door to the rear room was drawn to, but in the first it was obvious someone had been resident recently. There was a make-shift pile of twigs and branches in the fireplace, half burned, though it had been extinguished by the rain. Lenox went to it and felt the stones of the hearth—warm.

He turned back to Edmund and raised his eyebrows. There was a blanket here, too. One of the church's?

And then his blood went cold. In the next room there was a sound, a footstep.

Edmund looked at Lenox, who rose very, very slowly to a standing position. "Stay," Lenox mouthed to his brother, holding up a hand.

He walked as softly as he possibly could across the stone floor and put his ear to the door.

There was certainly someone in the next room. He could hear the fellow's breath, rather heavy, as if he'd been running.

Then there was the sound of another door opening and closing.

"Quick!" said Lenox. "There must be a back door!"

He and Edmund burst through and saw the back door of the gamekeeper's cottage flung

open. Nobody was in this second, smaller room—
a kitchen—and Lenox ran to the door.

He pulled up short there. "Look," he said,
pointing out into the field.

Sprinting into the gloaming there was a small,
sturdy dog, barking happily.

"A spaniel," said Edmund.

"Sandy," Lenox said.

Edmund shook his head. "Damn it."

They walked back around toward the front
of the house, each wishing that it were a little
brighter out, careful where they stepped, both
wary of someone who might be lurking there,
waiting to do them harm.

When they reached the front of the house, they
saw two leather lines hanging loose from the
trees. Their horses were gone.

CHAPTER SIXTEEN

It was a very long walk home.

As they were nearing Lenox House, with its low glimmer of domestic light shining in the darkness of the evening, Edmund said, "You know, it occurs to me, we might easily have gone up to Snow's and asked him to lend us a couple of horses."

Lenox stopped in his tracks. "It occurs to you, does it?"

Edmund smiled good-naturedly. "Yes, I'm sorry. But listen, there's no need to be cross with me. You didn't think of it either."

Lenox smiled wearily and clapped his brother on the shoulder. "No, you're right. What a pair of flats we look, I'm sorry to say."

The rain had pasted fallen yellow leaves to the smooth marble steps of Lenox House, and they walked up to the door carefully. Two of Edmund's footmen came out to hold umbrellas over them, Waller hovering in the doorway and watching. "Thank you, thank you," said Edmund. "Yes, thank you. Waller, have our horses come back?"

"Your horses, sir?"

Edmund, despite his light tone, was desperate to have the horses back, particularly Cigar, and had forced Charles to a breakneck pace on their walk home. He had fire in his eyes now. "Send for Rutherford, please."

That was the man in charge of the stables. "Yes, sir. Immediately sir."

"After that, get the cook to make us some kind of hot drink, please."

"Make it stiff as a poker too," Lenox put in.

"Very good, sir."

They were in the entrance hall, and despite being wet and cold, despite having lost the horses, Lenox felt a kind of good cheer. This was the same hall, with its black-and-white checkered floor, its curving staircase, that had seemed desolate the day before, but now, with the dogs and the servants around them, it reminded him of long-ago days, coming home after a traipse in the country with Edmund, or on occasion with his father.

"And I could use something quick to eat, too," he added.

"By all means, sir," said Waller, though looking overwhelmed by this succession of requests.

"Rutherford first, though," said Edmund. "We'll change in the meanwhile."

A few minutes later they met Rutherford in the hall, both changed, with their hair toweled dry.

He was a cagy-looking outdoorsman in his fifties with bushy gray eyebrows and a matching mustache. He said their horses hadn't returned—and he took the news that they were gone very,

very hard, particularly because of Daisy, whom he had been training. He couldn't understand how Charles and Edmund had lost them.

"Never mind that," said Edmund. "Ride into town and put the word about among the other groomsmen. Will they recognize the horses?"

"Every groom in Markethouse knows Cigar."

"Good. And while you're there, fetch Clavering for us, please."

"Constable Clavering, Sir Edmund?"

"Yes—this is a crime. Quickly, if you please. And tell the stable lads to get two or three other horses ready for a longish ride, too—several miles."

Rutherford frowned darkly but said, "Yes, sir."

Before they had begun their walk back toward Lenox House, they had looked over the game-keeper's cottage carefully. "He must have heard us from the start," Edmund said after they had stood dumbly for a moment, looking at the tree to which their horses had been tied. "He took the dog to the back room, let him loose to distract our attention, and then slipped around to take the horses."

Lenox had nodded. "Yes. I think that sums it up."

It had been twilight by then, dark falling fast, and though they had scanned the fields all around the house, they hadn't been able to spot the horses riding away—too dark. It didn't help that the cottage was low in a swale, surrounded by hilly land.

When they returned to the cottage they found candles ("a box of candles, from Mr. Woodward's stall" had been among the missing items, Clavering had said). Lenox was carrying matches, and they lit two of the candles, then set about sifting through the loose, lived-in contents of the little dwelling.

It was a clever place for a fellow to hide himself: isolated, but warm and close to the village. As Lenox had suspected, it didn't seem at all as if a mere itinerant had been living here, waiting to be discovered before he moved on. The blankets and cloak on the floor were made into a small, tidy bed; in the kitchen, meanwhile, there was a tin pannikin full of water, a group of wild apples, and a small slate cooking stone, which had the remnants of a blackened chicken leg on it. A stolen chicken leg, presumably.

What had interested Lenox most, though, was the collection of things that sat close to each other near the head of the makeshift bed: first, a lovely bundle of loosestrife, an entirely pointless decorative touch; second, a book from the Markethouse Library, the fourth volume of *Robinson Crusoe*; and third, a knife.

"I've always been very fond of loosestrife," said Edmund, coming over to stand next to Lenox.

"I wonder if this thief has local knowledge."

"Why would he?"

"Did he know that Snow doesn't have a game-keeper, whereas Wethering did, and that therefore this building has been lying empty?"

"Mm."

"Tell me, can you see this place from Snow's house?"

Edmund shook his head. "Certainly not. It's a mile and a half away over uneven terrain."

"Then he could have safely lit a candle here at night, even had a fire, without worrying about the smoke from the chimney."

They looked and looked by the candlelight. When they were done, Edmund stood tall and stretched his back. "Shall we walk back to Markethouse, or the house?" he said.

Lenox knew they ought to fetch Clavering immediately—but home sounded irresistible. "The house is a bit closer, isn't it?" Lenox said.

"Yes, I think so, if we cut across my fields. Our fields."

Lenox smiled. "Yours, certainly! James's, too, if anyone's. Yes, let's head home. There is no urgency to go over the cottage before daylight tomorrow. I doubt the fellow's returning to it tonight, after seeing us, and the horses are a pretty enough prize in exchange for his loss of a roof."

So it was that they had walked back across the

country in the driving rain. Now, as they sat drinking warm cider in the short room—that was Edmund's private study, a satisfyingly untidy book-lined cherrywood refuge, with beautiful large windows looking out over the pond—Lenox said, "Do you know what was interesting about the cottage?"

"What?"

"All that we didn't find there."

"What's that?"

"A bottle of sherry, for starters."

"Hm. Nor any chalk, for that matter."

"We'll have a closer look in the morning," Lenox said, shaking his head. He thought deeply for a moment, then added, "It's an unusual case. I'm glad Hadley came to us."

Edmund's face, glowing rather pink after the exertion of the walk and the switch from cold air to warm on his cheeks, looked tired but engaged. "I'm very glad you've come to visit," he said, glancing through the window.

"Though it's lost you your horses?"

"I don't know that I could have faced dinner alone on a night such as this."

Lenox followed his brother's gaze outside, to where it was storming, the trees mauling each other at the edge of the pond. Grim, indeed. "Do you ever eat triples any longer?" he said.

Edmund laughed. "Oh, yes."

"I still say you got them more often than I did."

"Not likely."

Triples were a reward of their youth; any time one of them received a good mark, or finished chores early, their mother would give him a piece of candy she (and nobody else on the earth) called a triple, which was a striped piece of burnt sugar. They were horribly chewy. "After that walk we deserve a triple," Lenox said.

"I doubt Father would have thought it particularly commendable to lose the better part of three hundred pounds' worth of horseflesh."

"Well, Mother was an easier touch, it's true," said Lenox. "You were somehow able to convince her every Christmas that you had saved me from a bullying at school the term before, though I was perfectly fine, and she would give you extra pocket money."

"A fair stratagem," said Edmund. "I used the money to buy picture-cards of the seaside, I remember. I hung them up above my sink in sixth form. Everyone envied me."

Clavering arrived. He joined them in the study; they told him what they had found, and about the theft of their horses. Perhaps because he didn't feel the happiness they did simply to be inside and dry, his consternation was very much greater than theirs.

"There was nothing there what to identify him, sir?" he said to Edmund.

Edmund shook his head. "Not that we found. I

suppose you'll go around to look for yourself in the morning?"

"Yes, and tell Snow, too," said Clavering, shaking his head. "He won't like it a shred, he won't."

"He's still got his house—we haven't got our horses," Lenox pointed out.

"That's true. He'll be deep in for it now, though, whoever this fellow is. The assizes take horse theft very seriously."

"Was anything else stolen at the market today?" asked Lenox.

"All sorts, I don't doubt, sir," said Clavering, with a despairing look. "And who'll hear about it come the morning? Me, that's who."

CHAPTER SEVENTEEN

It was finally bright again the next day, a soft autumn wind shaking a few leaves from the trees now and then, the sun mild but warm. Downstairs early, drinking his coffee and sifting through the new cuttings about Muller that Jane had sent by post, it occurred to him that the horses were actually gone. He had half expected to wake and find that they had wandered home overnight, as horses were wont to do.

Lenox rode nevertheless. Not far this time—the walk the night before, in combination with the unaccustomed exercise of the previous mornings, had left him very sore—but it was too pretty a day to miss out.

Edmund was again out upon his walk when Lenox returned, the third day running. He came home sooner now, though. He greeted Charles with a smile, took a piece of toast, and said, between bites, "Shall we go down to church in the village? The service is at ten o'clock."

"Will I be noticed if I give it a miss?"

"Oh, yes, certainly," said Edmund. "Without a doubt."

"Very well."

"What do you say to visiting the chapel before we go?"

The Lenox family chapel had been built sixty years after the house itself. It was a small round building with a fine ivory dome, situated on a hillside beyond the pond, where you could reach it by a series of stone steps laid into the ground.

Inside was a single room, full of natural light from the series of windows ringed just above eye level. There was an altar at one end. Along the walls were busts and statues of previous baronets, as well as flat marble stones inscribed with the names, dates, and achievements of various second sons, cousins, wives. Two large medieval swords were crossed under one window.

There was a fresh bust now—on a plinth near the door, Molly's face. The sculptor had captured something of the ease with which she laughed. Edmund went instead toward the busts of their parents, saying, "Mother, Father," with a dry smile, which seemed at once to indicate the absurdity of such a greeting, and therefore apologize for it, while also allowing him to deliver it—for he paid his respects sincerely, Lenox did not doubt that. He did, too. He touched the figures with a feeling of loss. He had loved them both. They would meet Sophia in the next life; indeed, perhaps they already knew that the pretty, sharp-eyed Houghton girl had become his wife, the love of his life.

Edmund was sitting with one leg crossed over

the other, an arm along the back of the bench, staring at the altar. At last, he said, "They didn't do the beard very well on Jesus."

"Have it touched up."

"Are you mad? It's three hundred years old."

Lenox smiled. "Leave it, then. I suppose we could light a candle?"

"Yes, certainly," said Edmund, and he stood up. "Where are they? I know for a fact they were in this room the last time I was, so they can't have gone. I think they're in this little box." He tried to open the box, but it was locked. "Who on earth would have locked this?"

"Waller, of course."

"That seems like an excess of caution," Edmund muttered, patting his pockets. "I can't think where the key is—unless—"

He hopped onto the bench and reached behind a carved wooden scroll on the wall, which bore the Lenox coat of arms and the family motto, *Non sibi*, "Not for one's self." Had he lived by that? Here and there—nobody could do it comprehensively, nobody but a saint, and they weren't very common in Lenox's experience.

Apparently there was a small latched cubby concealed behind the wooden fanwork, because Edmund opened it and came out triumphantly with a key.

When they were young, they had come to the chapel very infrequently—two or three times a year, on special holidays, to light a candle. Otherwise they'd gone to St. James's in Markethouse, sitting in their pew there. Of course, when a family member died, the service was held in this small chapel. It was a matter of understanding within the family that no matter how far the person had strayed, no matter how many years it had been since he or she had come to Lenox House, no matter what enmities had existed in life, no matter the person's character, a Lenox was entitled to a service here.

Lenox's mother had also spent a fair amount of time in the chapel, particularly after her own parents died, it seemed to him now, as he watched Edmund take a candle from the box he had unlocked, light it, and place it in front of the altar. She had treated the chapel very casually, bringing a book up to read there, or even her sewing.

They sat in silence for some time, until Edmund said, "Shall we go down into town, then?"

"Yes, all right," said Lenox. "I suppose after the service we could call on Clavering and see if he's made any headway."

"By all means."

The two brothers went to church and listened to the sermon, stood on the steps afterward and shook a great many hands, and then walked over to the station house, where Clavering was filling paperwork.

His one jail cell was occupied, but he said he hadn't made any progress.

"Who is this, then?" asked Edmund. "Not related to—"

"No, no, it's young Adams, sir, that's all. He got himself black drunk and fetched up a brawl. Thirty days in jug, I reckon." Adams's punishment sounded as if it had already begun—he was groaning. "I took him in some water. Not a bad sort before his eighth pint, you know."

"Have you been to Snow's cottage?"

Clavering nodded grimly. "Bunce and I went this morning. Exactly as you described it, sir. We brought back all of the stolen objects and left the rest. I'm waiting to hear if they're the church's blankets, but I reckon they are. Bunce is over checking with Reverend Perse now.

"As for Sandy, the springer spaniel, I saw his owner last night at the Bell and Horns, Mickelson. He said he would keep an eye out for the pup. Didn't reckon he would find his way home, though. Not a smart creature, he said."

"Mickelson. Why do I know that name?" asked Lenox.

Edmund shook his head. "He was involved in a bad business a few years ago. He's a farmer in these parts. He was at a coaching inn near Whitson and quarreled with a fellow, a gambling debt—"

"I believe it was over a woman, if you'll allow me, sir," said Clavering.

"Was it, though? I certainly heard it was a gambling debt, but these stories get distorted. Anyhow, he struck the man with a cane and blinded him in one eye. He only avoided prison very narrowly, if I recall."

Clavering nodded. "Not a friendly fellow."

Edmund frowned. "Could he be involved?"

"Anybody could be involved, unfortunately," said Lenox.

"Could he have been the one staying at the cottage, though?" said Edmund. "With his dog?"

"But why would he, if he's local?"

"There you've got me."

Pondering that, Charles and Edmund bade good-bye to Clavering and then returned to Lenox House, planning to ride out again to see the gamekeeper's cottage; Lenox wasn't satisfied with the thoroughness of their inspection the evening before.

When they returned, however, there was a telegram from Dallington that caused him to forget Markethouse's problems, at least momentarily.

Dreadful news STOP three clients gone over to LeMaire STOP somehow has gotten our client list Polly thinks STOP planned assault STOP lower fees and now name in every paper STOP all in a jumble here STOP please advise STOP best

Dallington

Lenox read over this twice. Then a third time, as if upon rereading it might give up some secret he hadn't spotted yet.

Three clients! This was cataclysmic news. They kept their list of clients jealously guarded, knowing that LeMaire and his ruthless backer, Lord Monomark, would be willing to operate at a loss to put them out of business.

He showed Edmund the telegram, and Edmund shook his head. "That's very unfortunate."

How unfortunate his brother didn't quite understand. The ground that had felt so firm under Lenox's feet two days before—their new detectives, their new clerks—was all at once shifting. If they lost three more clients, they might have to let someone go. Three more than that, they might have to let two more go. Three more than that, they might have to close. And Monomark's pockets were very, very deep.

Lenox forgot about the trip back to the gamekeeper's cottage; he sat in the long room brooding on the problem, wondering whether he ought to go back to London. There was no solution that came to him, though. If LeMaire had the agency's list (and how had it gotten out?) and was willing to undercut them on prices, he would be able to pick off their clients one by one. It was as simple as that. A few might remain out of loyalty, but they were mostly businessmen, accustomed to the exigencies of competition, used to seeking out the lowest prices for the best services.

They would still have Polly's clients, and Dallington's intermittent ones. But those weren't enough to keep them afloat in anything like their current form. Things had grown precarious very, very suddenly.

Lenox closed his eyes, feeling rotten. Sooner or later he must have fallen asleep—the room was drowsy, with the fire burning quietly, the sofa soft beneath him—because when he woke it was with a feeling of disorientation, and with the thought that he was in his house in London, but that it didn't look right.

After a moment he realized where he was, and his breath slowed again. He blinked his eyes several times to open them—and then it came to him, with breathtaking clarity.

"Edmund," he said, "I have to get to London immediately."

"Because of these clients?"

"No, no. Because I know where Muller is."

CHAPTER EIGHTEEN

He spent the ride back to London thinking not about the German pianist, whose whereabouts he thought he now knew, but about who had betrayed the firm. That was the question that had carried him through the trip, from the silken fields of Sussex to the bright din of King's Cross Station.

It was so hard to say. The names and files of their clients were all held securely in a safe in Lenox's office. Only the three partners had access to that safe and therefore the list, though obviously each of the agency's detectives, Atkinson, Weld, Mayhew, and Davidson, knew some of the names on it, since each was responsible for the day-to-day needs of four or five of the companies who retained the agency's services.

Of the three clients that had taken their business to LeMaire, one had belonged to Mayhew and two to Davidson, the new fellow.

Could it be that Davidson had turncoated them? He had come with impeccable references; had an honest, open face; worked very hard.

He was also close with Mayhew, however, and despite his best precautions, Mayhew might have let a name slip.

Or Davidson might have—two names, and

Mayhew, who was talented but mercurial, a bit of an enigma, perhaps too smart for his own good, could have sold them to LeMaire . . .

In a way, that would be the best thing. It would mean that the damage was contained. What was really frightening was the idea that someone had the entire list and was selling it piecemeal to LeMaire, or his backer, Monomark, the cross-grained, eagle-eyed old lord.

As his train pulled into King's Cross, Lenox was so deep in contemplation of this question that it took him several minutes to notice that they had arrived and to disembark, one of the last men on the platform. He nearly directed the cab he hailed to Chancery Lane, and the office—then thought perhaps he would go straight to Dallington's, in Half Moon Street.

But home won out.

Soon he was pulling into Hampden Lane. In the upper windows of the house there was the yellow flicker of gaslight, and upon the door a pretty garland of evergreen boughs. Through the front curtains he could just see the pale blue wallpaper of the forward drawing room, and the edge of the dainty spruce pianoforte that stood near the window there, surrounded by armchairs and sofas of light green velvet.

He slipped inside. "Hello?" he called out.

"Charles!" said Jane. She happened to be close and came into the front hallway, her reading glasses folded in one hand, a book beside them.

He kissed her on the cheek. "Hello, my dear. How are you?"

She looked uncertain. "Is there any trouble? Is Edmund well?"

"Oh, perfectly, yes. I wired before I left—didn't you receive it? I'm back for twelve hours, no longer, alas."

She shook her head. "I was out. I only arrived home a few minutes ago. I was just about to look in on Sophia before she goes to sleep, in fact. Come along, let's go upstairs. But why have you come back?"

As they walked upstairs he told her that he thought he had an idea about Muller that he wanted to look into ("I knew I selected those clippings beautifully," she said) and also about what Dallington had wired.

They came to Sophia's buttercup yellow nursery. At the unexpected sight of both her parents, her plump face broke into a smile of delight, and she waved her arms up and down furiously and cried out their names. The nurse gave them a severe look. They lowered the volume of their greetings apologetically, but Lenox couldn't help lifting Sophia up and kissing her, giving her warm little body a squeeze to his shoulder.

When he and Jane left the nursery twenty minutes later, he felt happy. They walked downstairs together, talking, for while they had only been apart for four days, there was an infinite amount to discuss—what each of them had been doing, Edmund's state of mind, Jane's forthcoming luncheon, whether the Queen might come, all the hazy news on Muller, Sophia's hair-pulling activities. Lady Jane kept Lenox company as he ate a quick supper, and then they moved into the drawing room, where there was a little fire against the chill on the windowpanes.

He poured himself a whisky. "Then there's this mysterious business down in Markethouse, though I only wrote you about it yesterday, so you may not know about it yet, depending on the mail."

She shook her head. "I don't know anything about it. I can't think what the postman has been doing. Burning your letters in a grate, I suppose, the moment they reach his hands. What mysterious business?"

So he told her about Hadley, about the gamekeeper's cottage, and about Edmund's absorption in the problem, which Charles hoped was a useful distraction. "It's better than the two of us moping around the house."

"Which is what he will do while you're gone," Jane pointed out.

"I rather hope not. I asked him to go to Snow's cottage again tomorrow morning and see what he can find. That will at least occupy his time—and who knows, he may find something. I have little enough faith in Clavering, the constable in

Markethouse, though he's a well-meaning fellow."

Lady Jane shook her head doubtfully. "I don't like it. What is the meaning of that drawing chalked on Mr. Hadley's step?"

"There you have me. Child's mischief?"

"And the gemstones," said Jane. "And the knife you found in the cottage. No, I don't like it."

"Nobody has come to any real harm in Markethouse since the Glorious Revolution. Anyhow, whoever was staying in the cottage left the knife behind, which must surely be a good sign, mustn't it?"

"What if he has a pistol?"

"What if he has a unicorn?"

"You laugh, but he has your two horses."

Lenox shook his head. "Really, I give you my word that I think you may rest easy about us."

She was curious about his thoughts on Muller—it was still the talk of every drawing room—but he told her only that he wanted to have a look at Muller's dressing room for himself, that LeMaire's involvement had raised his competitive hackles. It was true, too. Of course, he also didn't want to tell her his idea—in case he was wrong. If he was right, she would know tomorrow, a few hours before the rest of the world, and then he could return to Sussex triumphant.

What a thing it was, vanity!

The next morning, when Lenox woke up in his own bed, he was again momentarily confused as to his whereabouts, that old feeling. Then almost in the same instant he remembered that he was home, and he would therefore be able to breakfast with Sophia, which was great fun as long as you managed to dodge the flying porridge.

It was at around nine o'clock, when his daughter was asleep for her morning nap, that Lenox, dressed in a woolen autumn suit, his beard shaved close and his cloak over his arm, went down his front step and in the direction of the City. As he often did when he had thinking to do, he felt the urge to stroll—what Dickens, that most inveterate and observant of London walkers, had joyfully called "a little amateur vagrancy."

It was a half-hour walk to the City, the tiny scrap of London that was in fact the only place that could technically be called "the City of London"—the other boroughs having their own names, Westminster, Hammersmith, and so forth. The City was London's center of business, and to say that someone worked in the City meant that he was in one of the professions: law, business, the stock market.

Chancery Lane, for instance, where the agency's office stood, was in the City.

The City was divided from the idler sectors of the West End by the Temple Bar, a narrow stone gateway that had been widened but nevertheless always had a long backup of carriages waiting to pass through it, what locals called the traffic-lock.

He came to this gateway after twenty minutes or so. Sometimes, as Lenox passed through it, he felt a strange little emotion: one foot in the West End, his old, aristocratic life, and one in the City, his new, money-centered one. Would his father be disappointed? Time bulled its way forward, of course. Lenox saw more familiar faces than he would have expected in this side of town nowadays. The Earl of Allingham's third son owned a stockbrokering concern two doors down from them. It was true that two or three men in his clubs had snubbed him since the agency was founded, though few people with any social ambition could afford to alienate Lady Jane. His good fortune, that.

He walked on. The season was changing, he saw. For the first time since April, the pea soup vendor was selling hot elder wine, too, in halfpenny and penny measures. Lenox touched his hat to the man, who was doing a brisk business, then moved with expert agility between the ale sellers and the horses spattered up to their blinkers with mud, touching his hat to a different fellow, this one something of a local celebrity, named Joz, who always stood on the same corner selling pamphlets, stationery, newspapers, and "the smallest Bible in the world."

Finally, this gauntlet run, Lenox turned down Chancery Lane, eager to find Dallington and Polly and tell them his suspicions.

CHAPTER NINETEEN

Two hours later he stood in the unprepossessing doorway of Muller's dressing room, backstage at the Cadogan Theater.

Just behind him were his two partners, accompanied by Thurley, the manager of the theater; just ahead of him, opening the door and going into the dressing room, were two men from Scotland Yard. One was a friend, Inspector Nicholson, tall, hook-nosed, and gangly. The other was Nicholson's superior, Broadbridge, a froward, scowling individual in his fifties, with close-cut white hair, smelling strongly of a morning visit to the barbershop. He wasn't pleased to have Lenox there. Then again, he wasn't pleased not to have found Muller, either, and for the moment at any rate it appeared that that displeasure outweighed this new one.

Nicholson looked nervous. "I'm not even on the case," he had said that morning, standing at a coffeehouse near the Yard with Dallington and Lenox, as they attempted to persuade him to intervene on their behalf.

Dallington shook his head. "I must say, I call it pretty shabby to bring in that fraud LeMaire, after all the help we've given the Yard over the years, from the murders in Fleet Street to—"

"But I've told you that I'm not even—"

"To that terrible business about the prostitution ring in Regent Street, to Mrs. Wilkin's missing pearls, to—"

"They were under her dresser!" said Nicholson. "Anyone could have found them! And as I said, I'm not even on the case!"

Dallington took a sip of his coffee. "You could have put in a word."

"I think you have an inflated sense of my importance, my lord."

Dallington laughed. "Once you've been shot at together, last names will do, I think. Call me Dallington."

At last, Nicholson had consented to take them to Broadbridge. The chief was seated at his desk, with his back to a splendid view of the Thames, signing papers. A constable was next to him— "My nephew, Bailey," he said, not joyfully—and he put his pen back in its inkstand and crossed his hands over his fat taut stomach, giving them his exclusive attention.

"Thank you for seeing us."

"Nicholson says you have an idea about the pianist," said Broadbridge.

"I'm Charles Lenox. This is my associate, John—"

"Yes, I know who you are. What about the German?"

"Hardly call that proper German music,"

said the nephew, Bailey, in a cockney accent.

Dallington snorted. There were two types of street bands in London, English and German. The German ones rarely had any Germans in them; the name only meant that they played brass instruments, as opposed to string ones.

"Quiet!" thundered Broadbridge at his nephew.

"I don't rightly call it German when—"

"Quiet, I said!" Broadbridge looked as if he would happily murder the lad, who had an obstinate frown on his face, as if he were ready to debate the issue. By way of explanation, he added, "He's my wife's nephew, the young fool."

"From what I understand, Muller's wineglass was empty," Lenox said.

"Yes."

"Who filled it?"

Broadbridge glowered. "This isn't a twopenny quiz game, it's a criminal investigation."

Nicholson stepped forward. "I believe the two stewards, as was customary," he said, sounding anxious to keep the peace. "I'm not on the case myself, but word goes around."

"It shouldn't," said Broadbridge, "and that's incorrect. Muller himself poured the wine, at intermission. Now, Mr. Lenox, spit it out, quickly."

"I need to see his dressing room before I fully explain my theory," said Lenox. "It's essential."

"Out of the question. It's not a stop on the day tour of London."

"If I am wrong, you will have lost half an hour, and you will have my sincere apology. If I'm right, this will be over—solved."

Broadbridge hesitated. Lenox sensed through his gruffness his desperation to find Muller and get the Yard out of the morning newspapers. Pressure from the Palace itself—Broadbridge's superiors must have been hounding him hourly for answers.

"Very well," he said. "Bailey, fetch my hat. Mr. Lenox, these answers had better come pretty sharpish once we're there, you understand."

Now they were there, in the dressing room.

It was a small, square chamber—though perhaps large in proportion to the crammed warren of the average theater's backstage area—dominated by an immense vanity mirror on one side, which had a row of gas lamps above it, and a table and chair in front of it. The wineglass itself stood upon the table, a small red smudge of wine dried in its bottom. In the center of the room were two sofas, and in the corner there was a stepladder, stacked with books. Lenox leafed through them— all German. Apparently Muller had been a reader.

Above them was an immense chandelier, shimmering with crystals. Lenox studied it for a moment thoughtfully. "This is very fine," he said.

"We often use it in our performances, actually," said the theater manager, who was still in the doorway. "Comes right down, only glass. It hooks onto a gaff above the main stage."

Lenox knelt and grazed his fingers across the rug that stood between the two sofas. He pressed down.

"McKee has done all that," said Broadbridge, impatient. "LeMaire too, now that we've been told to bring him aboard, the sod."

A look shot between Dallington and Lenox. *Told* to hire him—Monomark's influence again, in all likelihood. That was a piece of information to stow away.

Lenox lifted the rug. The floorboards were solid, seamlessly joined. He tapped on the floor in a few different places and heard a thick, dull sound. Well, that was no less than he had expected.

He was just knocking the floor in the corner of the room when there was a noise in the doorway. "What's this!"

Lenox turned and saw McKee. He was Scottish, an inspector at the Yard, a small man with freckles and bright orange hair. With him was LeMaire. Lenox, from his crouched position between the sofas, inclined his head toward the two men in greeting, but neither returned the courtesy.

"We have already checked the floor," said LeMaire. He turned his gaze to Broadbridge. "I have been trusted with the consultation of this matter, sir, but now I find a competitor of mine on the scene—tampering with the work I have done. Who is to answer for this?"

McKee looked disposed to voice a similar objection, though Broadbridge was a station above his own, so he remained silent—clearly outraged, but silent.

Broadbridge seemed to puff up. "I would hear out a goat-boy from the circus if he had a plausible idea about where this blasted German has got himself to. Mr. Lenox—is this all mere showing away? Or can you help? My patience is running short."

Poor Nicholson, who knew he would have the consequences of that impatience to deal with, looked at Lenox. "It's certainly not showing off, Mr. Broadbridge, I will vouch for that. But Lenox, I hope you have something, however. Do you?"

Lenox rose to his feet, dusting his hands off. "Four things," he said. "First, where is the wine bottle from which Muller poured his glass? Second, why is there a stepladder in this room? Third, why has it been moved out of the corner and moved back to the corner in the past week?"

"And fourth?"

"And fourth, who would like to help me use it now?"

The room was silent. Dallington smiled, and Nicholson, looking relieved, glanced at Broadbridge. Broadbridge said, "Use it now?"

"What makes you think the stepladder's been moved?" asked McKee.

Lenox looked at it. "There are four rectangles in the dust, in the shape of its feet, where they must have rested for a long time previously—just slightly off from where it currently stands, you can see for yourselves."

"Muller himself moved it, then," said McKee.

Lenox smiled. "I don't think so."

"Why?"

"Look closely at the books on the stepladder. It has three steps, as you can see. On the first, all of them are alphabetized by their authors' last names, from *G* to *R*. On the second step, from *A* to *F.* On the highest step, from *S* to *Z.*"

"So?" said McKee.

"They are Muller's books—most have his name on the flyleaf. Clearly he was scrupulous about how he ordered them. But these are out of order. Someone, I think, took the three stacks, put them on the sofa, used the stepladder, and then replaced the books—with the three stacks in the incorrect order."

There was a pause in the crowded room as everyone absorbed this.

"Well done, Lenox," said Dallington.

"Someone other than Muller used the stepladder, then," said Broadbridge. "Why do we care?"

Lenox looked up at the chandelier. "You say this comes down easily, Mr. Thurley?"

The manager nodded. "Yes."

What Lenox's slumbering mind had told him, back in Sussex, had been simple: if everyone was agreed that Muller hadn't left the room, then it must be the case that *Muller hadn't left the room.* Mustn't it?

He took the books off the stepladder, setting them carefully on the floor, and brought it underneath the chandelier. This he removed. It was surprisingly light, only glass, as Thurley had said, and easy to hand down to Dallington, who stood beneath him. Lenox looked up at the ceiling with narrowed eyes.

"There's a latch there!" said Nicholson.

"I'd no idea that was there," said Thurley, voice astonished. "No idea at all. I've been here nine years."

McKee looked ill. "Hm."

Broadbridge shot him a look of disbelief. "A door in the ceiling!" he said. "McKee, of all the hellish incompetence!"

Lenox allowed himself a moment of sympathy for the fellow. McKee had tried the floorboards, which showed some resourcefulness. And a chandelier is such a grand object that it would have been hard to imagine it moving. This one, however, made of cheap glass and brass . . .

He tried the small black handle, which was embedded in the door but pulled out. There was a lock in it.

"Do you have a key?" he asked Thurley.

The manager shook his head. "I don't think so. Here, you can try my skeleton key. It works in most of the locks in the building."

It worked in this one, too.

Lenox, heart racing, pulled down the door. Nothing fell, as he had half expected. "Hand me a candle, would you?" he said.

Having taken it, he stepped onto the highest footing of the stepladder and popped his head above the ceiling.

What he saw confounded him, and he inhaled deeply, pondering it—a mistake, because there was the beginning of a smell.

"There's a body up here," he called down.

"Muller?" shouted Broadbridge.

"No, I'm afraid not. A woman."

CHAPTER TWENTY

That afternoon it began to rain, and when the employees of Lenox, Strickland, and Dallington gathered in the large central room of their offices, leaning aginst the various slanted clerks' desks, or sitting in their chairs, their chatter was matched by the steady thrum of the drops on the window.

The three partners of the agency stood at the door, facing them.

Fourteen men in all. There were the four hired detectives, Atkinson, Davidson, Weld, and Mayhew; six clerks; Pointilleux, who occupied a position somewhere between clerk and detective; Anixter, the immense, dark-browed, and ominously mute ex-seaman who had accompanied Polly wherever she went as long as Lenox had known her, and presumably made it safe for a woman to be a detective in a city that could be unfriendly to both detectives and women; and two boys, Jukes and Chadwick, each around thirteen years of age. Both had been more or less urchins, well known in Chancery Lane for running errands for small change. With the regular pay of the agency, each had ascended to the highest sign of social acceptability he could imagine, the ownership of a hat—a gently used black bowler for Jukes, a wide-brimmed soft cloth cap for Chadwick. Neither had removed his in Lenox's sight since obtaining it, indoors or out. Hats mattered a great deal, of course. Lenox had once seen a man being released from Newgate prison refuse to acknowledge his family, who were eagerly awaiting the reunion, for fifteen puzzling minutes, until a friend found and handed him a hat. Then he turned to them and embraced them all, as if he had just spied them and it was the most natural and spontaneous thing in the world to say hello.

It was Lenox who cleared his throat, waited for the chatter to subside, and then spoke. Though the partnership was equal, he was the eldest of the three, and perhaps for that reason the employees paid him the greatest deference.

"It has come to our attention that someone may have passed proprietary information belonging to the agency to an outsider," said Lenox.

Everyone looked at him blankly.

"More specifically, the identities of at least three of our clients have been passed to LeMaire and Monomark, we believe."

That drew a stronger reaction. "How do you know this?" asked Pointilleux.

"All three clients have defected. Lower fees, LeMaire's name constantly in the paper. It's not surprising."

Without staring at them too closely, Lenox was

trying to keep an eye on Mayhew and Davidson, the two friends. Davidson stood upright, his bearing fastidious; Mayhew leaned against a desk, one hand in his pocket, occasionally drawing his other languorously to his mouth to have a puff of his small cigar. Neither had betrayed any surprise. Perhaps it was natural that they should just listen, however.

"Good Lord!" said Pointilleux, outraged, using one of the British expressions he often leaned on as he limped through the language.

In truth he ought to have been the first person they suspected—he was LeMaire's nephew—but as the partners had walked back to Chancery Lane from the Cadogan a few hours earlier, all had agreed that it couldn't be him. It seemed impossible, that was all.

"He's too . . . too unimaginative," Dallington had said.

"I think it's more than that," put in Polly. "I think he has honor. We've come to know him, haven't we?"

Lenox had agreed with both of them. Now he went on, describing new security precautions to the employees, urging them to come forward if they had any idea about the crime, and finally promising whoever had done it that if he had the full list and returned it now, he could avoid criminal prosecution—a promise that would not hold should the partners discover the person's guilt independently, which they believed they were within a day or two of doing.

After the meeting was over, a chattering buzz had broken across the room.

"One other thing," Dallington said.

Everyone quieted down and stared at him, including Lenox, who wasn't sure what his young protégé intended to say.

"This morning, the agency made a major breakthrough in the Muller case. The Yard has officially hired us to investigate it, at one and a half times our normal rate. All three partners will be dedicating at least some of their time to it in the coming days, so there may be a bit more work for everyone, later nights. I don't expect to hear any grumbling about it, or I'll have Anixter drag you under the keel of a ship."

There was a laugh, and immediately a louder, more insistent conversation. What was the break-through? Had they found Muller? That had been smart of Dallington. Better to leave them on a note of optimism than doubt.

Dallington, Polly, and Lenox went to Polly's office, where there was tea on the desk, and closed the door. Dallington poured three cups of tea, dashed some sugar into his, and then sat back heavily into an armchair, crossing his legs and stirring his tea moodily. "We're in for it if someone has that full list," he said. "No chance they'll come forward."

Polly, stirring milk and sugar into her own tea with the precision of a chemist, said, "We have to hope the person who stole it is a coward, and fears jail more than the loss of his job." She sat down on the front edge of the seat behind her desk, thinking. Her hair was pulled back with a gray ribbon.

Lenox smiled at the two of them, so well mismatched. "We can only wait," he said.

Dallington shook his head. "I hate waiting. I've never had any patience."

"Do we find it odd that Mayhew and Davidson are so close?" asked Polly in a low voice.

"Yes," said Lenox. "They're very different."

"They eat at the same slap-bang every day, down Cursitor Street." Slap-bangs were popular among law clerks and other penurious professionals in this part of London for both their cheapness and speed—many only took fifteen or twenty minutes for lunch. They took their name from the sound that the busy waiters made dropping off the food. "I see them there every time I pass it on the way to the Beargarden for my own lunch."

"Could they be conspiring then?" asked Polly.

"We simply can't know yet," said Lenox. "At any rate, our trap may work."

Among the precautions for security that Lenox had enumerated before the employees was a new safe in Dallington's office. It contained a sheet with the name of a lawyer and the password

("Chancery") that would allow him to release their client list. In fact, it was Lenox's own solicitor; anyone who approached him with that password would be held there by the bailiff under presumption of guilt.

"Leaving this aside," said Dallington, "my question is, what do we do next on the Muller case? If we could only solve it, clients would line up to India for us."

"We must be close now," said Polly. "If only McKee and LeMaire weren't working on it, too."

"But Broadbridge must give us first whack, after this morning," said Dallington.

Lenox shook his head. "I don't think he cares who solves it."

The three partners looked at each other in silence for a moment.

Lenox thought back to that morning. Theaters were odd places, full of lost rooms, winding backstage corridors, unexpected closets. Above the main dressing room, apparently, there was a small tunnellike space.

They had taken down the woman, as carefully as they could, Broadbridge's nephew assuming the bulk of her weight, and laid her on the sofa.

Thurley, the theater manager, had gone pale. "That's Margarethe," he'd said immediately.

"Who?" asked Broadbridge.

"Margarethe. Mr. Muller's sister."

"What in damnation—did we even know she was missing?" said Broadbridge.

Thurley shook his head. "She was here on opening night—she traveled with Muller as his assistant. But after the first performance, she went on to Paris, his next destination, to book his rooms and make sure everything was in order there."

"Christ alive, man, are you telling me that we may have a *pair* of dead Germans?" Broadbridge said, a look of despair on his face. He glanced over at McKee. "You've had this room for a week."

"Yes, sir," said McKee—and then, because blame runs downhill, he shot a sidelong glance at LeMaire.

Lenox was examining the body. "Nothing on her person, no money, no identification. No signs of violence either," he added.

"Poison, perhaps," said Dallington.

"Do you think Muller killed her?" asked McKee.

Lenox shrugged. "I couldn't guess. But your constable ought to fetch the medical examiner—and then, gentlemen, I propose that we investigate this tunnel that passes above Mr. Muller's dressing room."

CHAPTER TWENTY-ONE

B roadbridge had been reluctant to climb the stepladder and investigate the tunnel himself. McKee, meanwhile, had been the opposite, raring to lead the inspection. In the end, Bailey, Lenox, Dallington, and McKee climbed through the small square in the ceiling, in that order. Each had a candle.

They entered a dim corridor, just barely high enough to walk down, not wide enough for two people to have passed each other. At its distant end, Lenox could see a spark of light—some kind of exit.

First they looked around the area where Margarethe's body had lain. They didn't find anything there until Bailey's large boot made a hideous crunch.

They crowded around and saw, beneath his foot, broken glass.

"A wineglass," said Dallington. "You can see the stem."

"Blimey," said Bailey.

"A second wineglass," Lenox murmured.

There was a moment of silence, and then McKee said, "Let's move along, unless there's anything else."

Slowly, they proceeded away in a single line down the corridor.

"Is this the only entrance from above or below?" Lenox asked.

"It's all uncommon smooth so far," said Bailey.

"One entrance, one exit," Dallington said.

Indeed, as they had gone down the corridor, Lenox had looked closely for another drop door, anything rough or uneven along the four walls, and found nothing.

There was a moment of nervous laughter when Bailey tripped again, but they walked, hunched, without too many missteps, until the light grew brighter.

They came to a wooden panel with slats. Lenox felt a fluttering in his stomach. It was not large, barely big enough for a thin man to slip through. In fact, Bailey's shoulders were nearly too large to pass through it.

But he thought he would just be able to squeeze himself, he said. "Shall I go first?"

"By all means," said Lenox.

"Any guesses where we are within the theater?" asked Dallington.

"I don't know it well enough," said Lenox.

"We've been going in the direction of Took Street, the side street," said McKee. His voice was tight and unwilling, but apparently he had decided their help was worth having. "I can't say exactly where we'll come out, though."

Soon they knew. They emerged into the light, one, two, three, four, to find that they were standing in an office—and staring into the dumbfounded face of the theater's owner.

"Gentlemen," he said. "How in heavens have you gotten into the aeration system?"

"Aeration?" said McKee.

Fifteen minutes later they had reunited with Broadbridge, Polly, Thurley, and the others, and told the theater's owner—his name was Greville, a handsome broad-chested man with a brown beard—how they had come to be in his office.

He came and looked at the drop door himself, leading them back to the dressing room through the backstage area. "I didn't have the faintest idea it was there," he said. "I didn't build the place, of course."

Lenox looked at him sharply. "No idea at all?"

Greville shook his head. "None. I have thought for five years that the wooden panel in my office was part of the theater's aeration system, which I was assured when I bought the theater was the most modern thing going. No risk of disease among the actors or stagehands."

"Where were you for Muller's final performance, may I ask, Mr. Greville?" Dallington said.

"I have told these gentlemen a dozen times—I was in the audience! It was the finest concert I have ever heard, I've told them that, too! I never went backstage."

McKee nodded. "Yes, we've confirmed it. He

was in the owner's box the whole time, with a party of fifteen."

"Mr. Muller never played more sensitively, more beautifully," said Greville. "It was transporting, gentlemen, the beauty of his gift—I could have listened to it forever. What a loss, if he is gone. And Margarethe, a quiet but sweet—I am at a loss, I am terribly perturbed, gentlemen, terribly perturbed." He looked it. He ran a handkerchief across his pale brow, and sat down in a chair near the door.

"And after the concert?" said Lenox.

"And here she is upon this very sofa! My God. The poor woman. In my own theater." Greville shook his head. "What were you asking, though—yes, the concert. After it ended, I stayed for a moment in my box, joining in the applause, and then I made my way backstage, to add my congratulations to those of the other people present. Of course, I was never able to see Mr. Muller."

Lenox nodded. It seemed clear, now, that the German had left his dressing room through the corridor, gone to Greville's office, and from there gone directly to the street by the theater owner's own door, which led outside.

Muller could have slipped straight in among the departing crowds by such a stratagem. Lenox saw Broadbridge realizing that he had received both a solution and another problem: Why on earth would anyone wish to kill Muller's sister? And where was Muller now?

Back at the Yard, they discussed this for a long while—a conversation that had culminated in Broadbridge hiring them on, and Polly shrewdly holding out for a higher rate, since, as she pointed out, the case would draw them from their usual work. Broadbridge had agreed to her terms without protest.

"Just find this blasted German," he said.

"Certainly we will try," Polly had said.

"I can scarcely bear to think about tomorrow's newspapers. Margarethe Muller? They'll turn her into a saint within the next eight hours, and her death into the bloodthirstiest thing this side of the Crusades. Damn them all, Fleet Street."

Now, in Chancery Lane, Lenox, Dallington, and Polly sipped their cups of tea, rain still beating loudly against the windows. Hadley seemed miles and miles away, both literally and figuratively—Lenox had scarcely been back in London eighteen hours, and yet he was wholly absorbed by the two puzzles here, the one at their office, the other at the Cadogan Theater.

He considered this and felt a wave of guilt: Edmund. He didn't want to linger in the capital while his brother needed him. The days were shortening; dinner would be terribly lonely at Lenox House, Edmund and his papers and the portraits, the awful small talk with the servants, somehow more solitary than solitude.

Still, Muller, the agency, another few days, two or three days . . .

As if reading his thoughts, Dallington said, "How shall the three of us proceed, then? Charles, will you stay in London? For my part, I can abandon all of my other work. The one case that needs urgent attention I'll give to Atkinson."

"Yes, it's the same with me," said Polly. "Anixter can keep everything in hand for a day or two. Honestly, I cannot imagine anything better for the agency than solving this case, short of us laying our hands on the treasure of the *Flor de le Mar*, and that's in Sumatra, and probably doesn't exist."

"Which makes it harder to find," said Dallington.

Polly smiled. "Precisely, my fair fellow. The point is that it's worth more than money to us to solve the case. With any luck it will be in the evening papers that the Yard has hired us."

Dallington looked at her quizzically. "How?"

"I've written to the reporters I know, that's how, you gull."

The young lord laughed. "Well done."

"I'll stay," said Lenox, "and I have an idea of where to start."

"Oh?" said Dallington. "Where?"

"With Greville and Thurley."

"They both have alibis," Polly pointed out.

"That's fine," he said. "What I want to know, then, is why both of them are lying. And who else knew that you could remove that chandelier in Muller's dressing room so effortlessly, and what was above it?"

CHAPTER TWENTY-TWO

There was a thick fog the next morning, the kind you could find only in London; Lenox thought of Esther Summerson in *Bleak House*, arriving in the city and asking whether there hadn't been some enormous fire. It was somewhat wistfully that he told Jane over his soft-boiled egg about all the fresh air he had inhaled, riding upon the heaths of Sussex.

When he had finished his breakfast, he checked his watch. He was due to have coffee with his friend Graham at ten o'clock, at the latter's invitation, and had fifty minutes until then: just enough time to take Sophia to her favorite place in London. He stole her away—wrapped in about thirty layers of wool—from the nanny, and they walked toward Green Park.

"Where are we going, Papa?" she asked.

"Where do you think?"

She looked ahead, frowning with thought. "George's," she said at last.

That was her friend Georgianna, who was older than Sophia, five—the daughter of Thomas and Toto McConnell. "No," he said. "Guess again."

"I can't guess."

He pointed ahead. "What does that green thing look like?" he asked.

"The park."

"And what's there?"

Her eyes widened. "The circus?" she said, scarcely daring to hope.

"Yes, the circus."

She whooped happily (and not very demurely) and dropped her piece of gingerbread, but was in such ripping spirits that she didn't care.

A few minutes later they came to Green Park— and here he was, the fellow in the red-and-white striped shirt, with the straw hat, standing over a tiny little proscenium made of cheap wood. It was nothing to the grandeur of the Cadogan, but Sophia wouldn't have traded.

"THE CIRCUS," she bellowed as she broke into a run, and Lenox, laughing, had to shush her, catching up with her and holding her hand.

He passed over a shilling, and she sat upon a tiny stool. The owner of the circus drew back the curtain, and a small crowd gathered—watching for free, or at any rate on Lenox's coin, though the hat would be passed around when it was over.

Sophia was rapt, her hands clutched together in anticipation. Soon it began: Two small bright yellow canaries (for it was the *canary* circus) in military jackets hopped out onto the stage, chirping. Their owner placed a miniature cannon between them, and instantly they went to work with their beaks, first dropping a small ball in the muzzle, then running back to the breach and lighting it with a tiny match. After a moment of breathless expectancy, the ball popped six or eight inches forward, and everyone applauded.

The circus continued, the canaries walking along a tightrope, dancing with each other formally, and, for a finale, playing an inexact but fairly convincing game of billiards.

As they walked back toward Hampden Lane, Sophia described the entire thing to Lenox in minute detail, as if he hadn't been there, becoming so absorbed in the telling that occasionally at some important moment ("and then the other bird hopped on one feet") she stopped and stood stock-still to concentrate, staring into the distance. Her father listened very carefully.

After he restored her to her nanny, he took the short drive to Parliament, where Graham met him at the Members' Entrance, which of course it had been Lenox's prerogative to enter himself until the previous year. He looked tired, a compact, sandy-haired man about Lenox's own age. He shook his former employer's hand warmly, though.

"What's it now?" asked Lenox.

"Ventilation," said Graham shortly.

Lenox sighed and shook his head in sympathy. His own experience within these grand, honey-colored walls had taught him that "ventilation" was a word that politicians could use to exact almost any cruelty upon the poor, such was the fear of disease spreading by "bad air." Buildings might be leveled, tenants evicted, children parted from their parents—all of that and more had been done under Lenox's gaze in the name of ventilation, though in actuality that word was most often merely a fig leaf for the moneyed interest that wanted a certain building torn down, and a different one put up . . .

Meanwhile, nobody had any interest in the ventilation of some of the tenements he and Graham had seen in their tours around the slums of Clare Market, where dozens of abandoned boys and girls lived side by side, each renting a few feet of space at night, few in anything more than underclothes, all far too many dozens of hours from their last real meal.

Graham had entered Parliament the year before, after having spent two decades as Lenox's butler, or more accurately as his butler, assistant in detection, confidant, and friend—an astonishing rise, but one for which his intelligence and strategic nous made him signally qualified. In the last few months, he had made the tenements of East London his primary concern, despite representing a district in Oxfordshire, the county from which he hailed; in British politics, Members in the Commons were often only tenuously affiliated with their constituencies, a very different system than say the American one, where one had to be resident in a state to represent it in Congress.

"What now?" Lenox asked.

They had walked through a long hallway and come into the comfortable paneled quiet of the Members' Bar. A few men nodded toward them, and a fellow named Baltimore came and shook Lenox's hand warmly.

"Your brother has been kind enough to support my Tenement Act," Graham said when they were seated, "but I fear it may not pass. We haven't the northern vote."

"Too many factory barons?"

"That's precisely it."

Lenox smiled. "I don't miss those headaches. But what can you give the Tories for their support? What do you have to trade?"

"That's the trouble—nothing. I have already voted on their side three times this year. I cannot do it again."

"You're a man of your word. Promise them you'll vote with them next session."

"They do not count on me still being here. You know that they're running a strong candidate against me, Armitage."

"Yes," said Lenox. "Edmund told me."

Graham waved to a passing waiter and asked him for coffee—and in that transient gesture Lenox perceived that his friend was finally comfortable here, finally felt as if he belonged. "Even if I am forced out, I hope I will pass this bill before I go," he said. "It would be worth the defeat."

"Then promise them the world," said Lenox. "And either give it to them next session, or apologize that you cannot."

Graham brightened slightly. "Yes. Perhaps that's right."

They fell quickly back into their old, familiar ways. There was still just a hint of deference in Graham's speech—a silent "sir" at the end of his sentences—but it didn't prevent them from having a lively exchange, about Muller, about Hadley, about Graham's long evenings in the House, leavened with gossip about Disraeli and Victoria and the next vote.

When their coffee was cold, Graham seemed to hesitate. "What is it?" Lenox asked.

Graham leaned forward in his armchair and said, "I wonder if you would give me your advice upon a personal matter."

"You needn't even ask."

Graham looked troubled for a moment—paused—and then said, "The truth is that I am contemplating the estate of marriage."

Lenox smiled. "This is wonderful news. You contemplate it not conceptually, I take it, but as regards a specific young person?"

Graham nodded. "Miss Abigail Winston. I believe you know her. She lives in Hampden Lane."

"The housekeeper at Dawkins's house?" Lenox knew her by sight, a pretty, amiable woman of around thirty-five, with a beautiful smile. "I think it's a wonderful idea."

"I am concerned that my current position . . . that perhaps it is less suitable, on either side, than it might have been once."

"Perhaps you ought to quit and come be my valet again."

Graham smiled. "Do you think so?"

Lenox leaned forward now, too. "Since you have asked my advice, I won't pretend that I don't have any," he said. "If you feel that this marriage would make you happy, I think you ought to declare as much to Miss Winston without waiting another minute. Life is long, but it's short, too, you know. I would do it this afternoon."

A wave of relief swept over Graham's generally imperturbable face. "Do you think so?" he asked.

"I'll be there with the silver fish-slice myself, if you'll have me."

"Perhaps you're right," Graham said, looking into the distance, and not as if it were ventilation on his mind. "I don't doubt that you're right."

Their conversation continued for some time. Eventually Graham saw him off, and at a little before eleven Lenox arrived at the office in Chancery Lane, where Dallington and Polly were waiting for him.

"You're late," said Dallington, who was at the door in his overcoat.

"I'm sorry," said Lenox.

"Well, it's usually me who's late, anyhow. We ought to go, though. Polly wants to take Anixter and speak to the people at Muller's hotel. You and I are marked for the Cadogan Theater. Did you see the papers last night, by the way?"

Lenox handed his valise to a clerk, and they turned back for the door of the office. "Yes, I did."

Dallington grinned. "We'd better damn well solve it. Oh, I say, before we go—you had a telegram this morning. No, two telegrams."

"Who from?"

"I'm not sure."

"Let me fetch them, then, just another minute if you don't mind."

They were sitting on his desk. Both were from Edmund. Lenox frowned, wondering what they could be.

He had his answer soon enough, and as he read them he felt a chill run through him. That morning there had been an attack in the village of his youth—in Edmund's constituency—in gentle old Markethouse.

CHAPTER TWENTY-THREE

With Graham's removal to another, more exalted station, Lenox's valet in these days was an extremely earnest young Yorkshireman named Pierson, not more than seventeen years old ("He looks about six," Dallington had commented), who'd previously been a footman of the household. He had short hair and a scrubbed red face. He never spoke a word if he could help it.

As far as Lenox was concerned, however, he was worth his weight in gold, for a simple reason: He moved quickly. After receiving the telegram, Lenox returned by cab to Hampden Lane, and once he was there told Pierson to have his things ready for a return to Sussex as soon as possible. Seven minutes later, barely long enough for Lenox to interrupt Jane and Toto's morning chat and explain why he was going, Pierson was standing in front of the house with two bags, his fingers between his teeth, whistling for a cab.

They just made the 12:01 train, and two hours later they were back at Markethouse.

No dogcart waiting for Lenox this time, nor any warm welcome. Indeed, the station was unnervingly empty—its usual population of coffee sellers, cart drivers, and hangers-about all gone. In town, he presumed. Markethouse hadn't had a violent crime in at least two years, to his knowledge, and then it had been a domestic matter.

Lenox told Pierson to find his way with the bags to Edmund's house; a cart would be by sooner or later. He himself set out on foot for the brick and stone towers of the village, rising not far beyond the treeline. He carried only Edmund's telegrams, which he read yet again as he walked:

> Request return at once STOP attack here upon SS STOP knife wounds STOP hovering nr death STOP stationed Bell and Horns STOP all at LH safe STOP Ed.

And then the second:

> Request again your return STOP see previous STOP Edmund

Edmund's style was more laconic than Dallington's. *LH* was Lenox House, to be sure, but who or what was *SS*? He hadn't bothered to wire his brother back more than a word to indicate that he was on his way.

At the edge of town he finally met someone, a girl of fifteen or sixteen in a bonnet and a dark wool cloak, from her dress and carriage obviously

186

of fair birth, reading as she walked the muddy road.

"Excuse me," said Lenox, "I was wondering if you might tell me who has been attacked in town. My name is Charles Lenox. My brother lives here."

In London he would never have addressed her, and even in the country not with more than a nod, not having ever made her acquaintance. But she seemed to understand that it was an emergency. She had her book at her side, finger marking her place. Lenox noticed that it was from the village's library—Dickens. She said, "The mayor of the town, I'm sorry to say. I'm Adelaide Snow."

Lenox bowed to her out of automatic politeness, but his mind was running pell-mell toward the town hall. The mayor—Stevens Stevens, that was his *SS*. They'd stood together on the steps of the Bell and Horns only a few days before. The abbreviation must have seemed obvious to Edmund.

"Thank you, Miss Snow," he said. "May I assume that your father is Alfred Snow, who lives on the old Wethering land?"

"That's him. And your brother must be Sir Edmund Lenox?"

"Yes, he is. Indeed, I had better go see him now. Thank you very much for your time."

"Good luck," she said, turning to look back

toward the village. "Your brother went over our gamekeeper's cottage with a fine-toothed comb, though the books and blankets and dog were all gone from it. Twice! I always told Father he ought to let the little place, but he said he didn't trust having someone live on his land. Well, he's had that anyway, and without anything in return for his trouble."

"Did he find anything new, my brother?"

"I don't know, I'm sorry."

"Not at all. Thank you very much, Miss Snow. A pleasure to meet you. Good day."

"Good day."

She walked away slowly, lifting her book again after a moment to read. Lenox stopped for a beat to look after her, considering that library book. *Our gamekeeper's cottage.*

He turned his steps toward town again. Soon he arrived at its edge.

It was mayhem. Every sentient person in Markethouse was evidently gathered in the square, and he could hear them even from a few streets off. When he came into sight he realized that all the villagers had abandoned their posts, as if it were a holiday, including both the workers from the factory and their managers. Almost everyone seemed to be roaring drunk. Certainly the Bell and Horns could never have done more business. Two boys in black neckerchiefs were running continually to and from the bar with pints of ale, which they sold faster than they could bring. Just down from the pub, near the fountain, a group of women had gathered, while children too young to be in school darted in and among their apron strings, earning cuffs on the ear if they jostled anyone out of a moment's gossip.

Lenox approached the public house and saw Bunce, Clavering's tall, thin associate, the night watchman, peering out across the square. "Bunce!" he said.

"Ah! Mr. Lenox! Clavering will be powerful happy to see you—powerful happy. I was just sent out what to look for Mickelson, but I reckon they'll be happier when I've brung you. They're all gathered upstairs, your brother, too."

"Mickelson?" said Lenox. That was the owner of the springer spaniel he and Edmund had watched sprint away from the gamekeeper's cottage and across Alfred Snow's meadow. "Why him?"

"The dog still ain't found," said Bunce. "We wondered if he might have had a previous owner, as it were."

Not a bad thought, but Lenox knew from the barman that Mickelson had bred the dog from a pup.

Lenox told Bunce as much. Still, he had an idea. "Do you think you might find him anyhow? I have a favor to ask him."

"Certainly," said Bunce.

"In the meanwhile, they're upstairs, you say?" asked Lenox.

"Yes, we can go there now."

The Bell and Horns was a coaching inn. This meant that downstairs it housed a many-roomed pub, with an enormous blackened fireplace opposite the bar. Every bench around it was crammed at the moment, all of the barrels of ale sure to be gone before five o'clock.

Upstairs were rooms to let for the night, as well as a small private dining room. It was here that the town's leading men were gathered.

"Charles!" Edmund said when Lenox came in. "Thank goodness you've come."

"Stevens?" said Lenox. "How bad is it?"

All the men in the room—including Clavering, the town's banker and solicitor, and perhaps half a dozen of the more prosperous market vendors—shook their heads doubtfully in unison. Very bad, their faces seemed to suggest.

And indeed, Edmund said, "Pretty bad, we think."

"When did it happen? And where?"

"Early this morning, at his office."

"Has the office been disturbed? Can I see it?"

Edmund nodded. "We had to remove him, obviously, but otherwise it's untouched. Clavering, would you like to come with us?"

"Perhaps Bunce should take them," said one of the men, a large fellow with heavy jowls and a white mustache. "Clavering can help us organize these patrols we've been discussing."

Edmund nodded again. "Good idea."

"Patrols?" said Lenox.

"We have to do something to calm the town," the same man said, with his white mustache. Lenox thought he recognized him as a merchant. "People are in a right agitated state."

"Where is Stevens?" asked Lenox.

With Dr. Stallings, several voices told him at once—the same doctor who had seen through Mrs. Watson's son's fake illness.

"Stallings is not very hopeful," Edmund added.

"Understating it, that," said Morrow, the banker. "He's called in Reverend Perse."

Lenox nodded thoughtfully.

He was used to the aftermath of violence— arriving in its wake—and though nobody had exactly said anything negative, he didn't think he had ever been in a room as full of despair as this one.

"Chins up, fellows," he said, voice hard, not sympathetic. "Stevens is still alive. Clavering's patrols will watch the streets. Meanwhile, my brother and I will figure out who did this, and they'll be in a jail cell within a day or two."

"Well said," put in Edmund.

"This will all be over before next market day."

At that moment Bunce came in with a heavy-set, grizzled man—Mickelson. He had a sour face. "You asked for me, gentlemen?" he said.

Lenox introduced himself. "I understand your spaniel is the one that was stolen," he said. "I wondered if you might give us something of his—a blanket he's lain on, for instance."

"Why?"

"We might set a scenting dog after him. There's a chance he's still with the person who stole from the market and took our horses. Not to mention attacking Stevens, of course."

Eyebrows rose around the room: a good idea. Mickelson nodded, grudgingly. "I'll send a boy back home. It may take a while."

"Fine," said Lenox. "Thank you. Now, Bunce— can you take me to the mayor's office?"

"By all means, sir."

Bunce led him out of the room, and soon the two brothers were following his long stride down the slope of the town square, toward the town hall at its base.

With his brother, Charles could be slightly more pensive than he had been in the little private dining room of the Bell and Horns. "What on earth happened?" he asked.

"The devil knows. The attack occurred some time before seven o'clock this morning."

"How do you know that?"

"Stevens's secretary—that young girl in the large spectacles, you remember, the one who follows him like a shadow—found him unconscious when she arrived at seven. He was just barely breathing."

"Did Stevens always get to work so early?"

"No. In fact, the assistant usually arrives at eight, a minute or two before him, but Stevens had asked her to come in at seven. The annual budget is due to be submitted in six days, from what I understand. A busy time of year."

Lenox filed that piece of information away. The budget could be controversial in Markethouse, against all odds—what money went to the market, what money went to the council, the mayor's own salary. According to Edmund, who attended when he could, the meetings had grown heated in the past.

"And what was done to him, exactly?" asked Lenox.

"He was slumped over an armchair. Blood everywhere, and six or seven wounds."

Lenox saw Bunce, ahead of them, wince. "Back or front?"

"Oh, directly to his face and his chest. He saw whoever attacked him. Look, we're here. You can see the office where it happened for yourself."

CHAPTER TWENTY-FOUR

The town hall was a two-story building the width of about four houses, topped with a large black-iron clock that had never worked in Lenox's memory. In days when their mayor had been less able than Stevens Stevens, the villagers had noted that fact as ironic—but Stevens had looked into the expense of fixing it and dismissed it as frivolous within his first year in office, and revisited the issue only to reach the same conclusion every five years since.

That was the kind of mayor he was.

For that reason it seemed almost impossible to Lenox that anyone could feel such violent emotion toward him—six, seven knife wounds, to his head and chest, which meant looking into his face. Early in the morning, not in the drunkenness of midnight. What could their dry, pedantic mayor, whose whole life was bent toward the ledger, have done to inspire such passionate hatred?

Of course, that led directly to the second question he had: What, if anything, did this have to do with Arthur Hadley?

Stevens occupied a large corner office on the second floor of the town hall. Two men were sitting outside his door. One was, judging from his modest black suit and tie, clearly an office clerk, the other was wearing a gray uniform and tall black hat, with a torch dangling from his belt. Edmund explained that these were Stevens's chief clerk and the building's watchman. They had been stationed here since the attack to make sure nobody entered the mayor's office.

"What time do you come on generally?" asked Lenox of the watchman, whose name was Sutherland.

"Ten minutes before eight o'clock each morning, sir, which is when the building is opened."

"Is there a night watchman?"

"No, sir."

"Is the building locked when you arrive?"

"Oh, yes, sir."

"How many people have keys?" asked Lenox.

"Only three—myself, Mr. Stevens, and the charwoman, who stays behind every evening to clean from seven to eight o'clock."

"Who is she?"

"Mrs. Claire Adams."

Bunce interjected. "She's Mrs. Watson's sister."

Lenox and Edmund exchanged a startled glance. "Elizabeth Watson? Hadley's charwoman?"

"Yes. She's housekeeper to the Malone family, but cleans here five evenings a week to make extra money." Then he added, in a quieter voice, "Her husband, you know."

Sutherland nodded knowingly.

"What about her husband?" asked Lenox.

There was a beat of silence, and then Sutherland said, simply, "Gone."

Lenox decided to leave that for later. He said, "And was there any sign of forced entry here this morning when you arrived? A broken window, a jammed door?"

Sutherland frowned. "No, not that I saw."

"Was it locked when you arrived this morning?"

"Yes, sir."

"Peculiar. Perhaps you could check around the building again now for any signs of a forced entry, while I look at the office."

"If you wish, sir."

Lenox turned to the clerk. "And you might tell us what Mr. Stevens's planned meetings for the day were."

"Miss Harville would be better able to inform you of that than I am—but I can look in her desk if you like."

"Miss Harville is Stevens's secretary," said Edmund. "The one who found the body."

"Where is she now?"

"Downstairs in the ladies' lounge," said the clerk. "She is . . . perturbed."

"We must speak with her next," said Lenox.

The clerk, who had on round glasses and struck Lenox as rather like Stevens, a local boy with ambition, said, doubtfully, "You can try. She's a bit frantic. We always warned him that it was no good having a woman for a secretary, but he always did, several in a row."

It was true that this was unusual. "Why did he, then?" asked Lenox.

"He said they were sharper," said the clerk, and then went on, with a trace of bitterness in his voice, "and less womanish than the male clerks he had."

Lenox, father to a strong-willed daughter, smiled fleetingly. "Very well. Please tell her that we mean to come speak to her soon, after we look at the office. Incidentally, where were you this morning?"

"I? With my family—my father, my mother, and six besides. Then I breakfasted at the coffee-house on the corner, Taylor's. I do most mornings."

Lenox hadn't liked the note of animosity toward Stevens in the clerk's voice, but his alibi sounded solid. "And your name?"

"Van Leer, sir."

"Thank you, Van Leer. After you've told Miss Harville we're coming to see her, please come back and resume your watch here, if you don't mind."

"Yes, sir."

Lenox turned back to his brother and Bunce. "Bunce, if you could send a telegram for me, by Mrs. Appleby, I would be grateful."

"Of course, sir."

Lenox scrawled it quickly and handed it over with a shilling—a note to his friend Thomas McConnell, asking if he would consider coming down that afternoon for an hour's work. It was Tuesday, fortunately, McConnell's day off from Great Ormond Street Hospital. Tuesday: Lenox wondered if Hadley was traveling for his work with Dover Assurance or had decided to give himself the week at home since his unnecessary trip to Chichester.

When Van Leer, Bunce, and Sutherland were all gone, and the two Lenox brothers stood alone before the door to Stevens's office, Edmund said, "Lord, Charles, I wonder if you know what a holy terror you are, issuing orders to everyone you meet."

Lenox shook his head unsmilingly. "It's no joke, an attack with a knife. We must move quickly."

"Shall we go in? I'll admit to a bit of trepidation. This will be the first time I've seen it, too—I've been at the Bell and Horns all morning."

"Lead the way," said Lenox.

They went in.

Because Stevens's office stood on the corner of the second story, in a village full of low buildings, it received a great deal of light, nearly blinding them as they entered. A large desk dominated the room. It was covered with tidy stacks of paper. A pair of spectacles sat on the leather blotter directly in front of the desk chair. Opposite, facing the desk, were two large brown leather armchairs, studded with bronze tacks in long trails from leg to arm to back and down again.

One was drenched with a thick, dark substance.

Lenox, who recognized the suffocating smell of it, winced. Edmund took a moment longer, and then he, too, winced. Though the chair was brown, it was obvious from a glance that it was blood pooled on it.

"Look," said Lenox.

He was pointing at the floor. "What? Oh!" said Edmund.

In the deep blue of the carpet, there was a distinguishable darkening. Lenox knelt down and dabbed it with his handkerchief. It came up a brownish red. Blood, too, a few hours spilled. He looked carefully at the carpet and said, "It starts here, at the side of the desk. None behind the desk, at least that I can see."

Edmund watched. "He might have been stabbed behind the desk and then staggered forward, hoping to make it to the door to cry for help."

Lenox nodded. "Yes, it's possible. But it's awkward to stab someone seated behind a wide desk like this, isn't it—to get so close? And then, six or seven slashes with a knife—there would likely be blood sprayed straight on the desk, right away. But there isn't any."

"Mm."

"I would guess that Stevens came out from behind the desk to meet his attacker and was stabbed halfway to the door. The blood sprayed across the carpet; then the poor fellow lurched forward and pitched himself across the armchair."

There was no response, and Lenox glanced up toward his brother, who had turned and was staring at the wall opposite the desk. His face looked pale.

"What is it?" asked Lenox.

But then, turning, he saw what was there for himself.

"It's the same as Hadley's," said Edmund.

Lenox stared for a long beat. "Yes, it is."

It was the stick figure of a schoolgirl—flat line for a mouth, with pigtails. Identical to the one that had been chalked on Hadley's stoop. It was painted on the white wall in the vivid red of Stevens's blood.

CHAPTER TWENTY-FIVE

Almost involuntarily, both brothers looked around the office, making sure there was nobody about to leap out at them. Nobody was—there was nowhere to hide, no closet to slide into or sofa to crawl under. They turned back to the figure of the schoolgirl. It wasn't pleasant to look at, even there in the broad light of day.

"Well," said Lenox, trying to keep his voice steady, "at least our attacker has had the courtesy to link our crimes to each other. That was sporting."

Edmund, whose face had always been so full of good cheer and country haleness until Molly's death, now looked sick, as thinned out as Lenox had ever seen him. He shook his head. Here he was, close to death once more. "I don't know that I like this job of yours," he said. "I didn't realize—well, I don't know."

Sympathetically, Lenox went and put a hand on his brother's shoulder. "Yes, I know," he said. "Dallington had a terrible time with it at first, I suspect, though he never said a word. But one gets used to it—and then, think, hopefully we may be a help, to all of these frightened people in Markethouse. If the porch of the pub is anything to go by, they've lost their wits with worry."

Edmund nodded. "Yes. I'm only telling you that I don't like it. I don't."

"Would you like to wait outside while I look at the office?"

"No, no. Tell me what we ought to do."

They looked over the office very carefully together. At one point Lenox asked if anyone had mentioned the figure on the wall before his arrival, and Edmund said no one had, which was odd—Clavering ought to have.

Then again, Edmund pointed out, it had still been near dawn when Miss Harville had found Stevens Stevens, and everyone's energy had been intent upon moving him safely to Stallings's house. It was possible they had missed it. And since then, Clavering had been with the town's leaders, trying to come up with a plan to ensure the calm and safety of the village. Nobody had returned to inspect the office.

That made some sense, and as Lenox looked through the papers on the mayor's desk he thought about what the drawing might mean. It felt . . . well, it felt *personal,* and yet both Hadley and Stevens were men without any strong personal ties, neither married, both childless, each more engaged with his work (or, in Hadley's case, a hobby, the gemstones) than any individual connection.

Might this lack of connections even be what linked them?

"What do we make of our second Watson sister?" asked Edmund, who was crouched by the armchairs, looking underneath them, at Lenox's instruction. Two sets of eyes on everything in the room—for it was even odds that the motive behind the attack must be in this room, Lenox had been at pains to insist to his brother. "Small-town coincidence, or more?"

"I wish we knew that it was one or the other," said Lenox. "Because I don't like that it might be either. I suppose we must try to speak to Claire Adams."

Edmund chuckled lowly. He had some of his spirit back. "Hopefully she's not preoccupied by a child feigning illness."

"Stallings has real work now, I'm afraid."

"Too true, alas."

The office was a disappointment to Lenox— neat as a pin, the drawers mostly empty other than bits of charcoal and nib ends and spare ink-stands and *SS* stationery, no evidence whatsoever of Stevens's life outside of this room. The papers on the desk were indeed mostly about the budget, along with a few others on village subjects, a report on the refurbishment of the pews in the church, another from the schoolmaster. The closest he found to anything related to the crimes was another report, this one about the thefts at the market from Clavering. It wasn't even clear the mayor had read it yet, however.

Lenox stood irresolutely at the window, looking down at the town square, which rose up toward the Bell and Horns. It was still packed with people. He stared at the long line of horses standing throughout the alleyway, overflow from the stables.

"Graham may be getting married," he said to his brother.

Edmund joined him at the window. "Is he never! I say, that's good news at least."

"It's not sealed yet. Don't congratulate him. He's still contemplating whether to make the proposal, though I think he will."

"She'll need to be a pretty deep file," said Edmund, shaking his head skeptically. "He's one of the sharpest fellows I've met. Sees twice what other men do. I've often told Lord Cabot that I'm glad he isn't a Tory. Well, my. I'll send him the fish-slice."

"I already signed up for that. It will have to be teaspoons for you—nothing more boring than giving teaspoons, ha."

"Let her accept first and we'll race."

They stood in silence for a moment, staring toward the pub—until, out of the blue, Edmund yelped.

"My God, what is it?" said Lenox.

"It's Cigar!"

"Where?"

"There at the Horns! Third horse back!"

Lenox peered at the alleyway. "Are you quite sure?"

"I would know him from twice the distance, with half my eyesight. I would swear it on your life."

"Steady on."

"Come, come, let's go get him. I had given up hope—I promise you I had altogether given up hope! Hurry, Charles! My goodness, for all we know Daisy may be there, too!"

They ran from the office. Fortunately both Sutherland and Van Leer were back. Sutherland stopped them as they hurried past to say that all the doors and windows were as he had left them the night before, no sign of forced entry.

Edmund didn't care. He tore up the square, faster even than they had when they were boys. At the Bell and Horns he looked ready to weep with frustration when a mass of men, standing by the porch, blocked his way back to the alley and the stables.

They made it through after ninety seconds or so of very hard pushing. When they reached the first horse they met, Edmund grabbed a young groom. "That horse there, the chestnut! Whose horse is that?"

The boy, alarmed by the vehemence of Edmund's questioning, said he wasn't quite sure, but Mr. Wapping would be sure to know. Wapping, brother-in-law of the pub's owner, was in charge of the stables. Edmund by this time had made his way to Cigar and was at his neck, talking into his ear. Charles said he would go and find Wapping.

Leaving his brother, Lenox waded into the incredible noise of the stables, which were as overcrowded as the pub and twice as pungent. He spotted Mrs. Watson's older son—one of several boys shoveling the stalls, no doubt hired on just for this busy morning.

"Mr. Wapping?" called Lenox loudly.

A thin, pale-faced, black-haired man turned. "Aye?"

"I believe you're holding a stolen horse. Will you come with me?"

Wapping, apprehensive, came into the alley. His face calmed slightly when he saw that he knew the claimant of the horse—*Sredmund*—and said how sorry he was, that he hadn't known Cigar by sight, but he didn't doubt for a second that His Highness (he seemed to be confused about the titles of the English aristocracy, and neither brother bothered to correct him) knew his own horse. But still, wasn't Mr. Flint, who owned this horse, a very respectable wheat trader from Massingstone? And was he likely to have a stolen horse? It was all very puzzling.

It took no time to find this Flint. He was on the porch of the pub, a handsome man with curly dark hair, dressed in riding breeches. Once

Wapping had made it clear to him that Charles and Edmund were from Lenox House, he was all civility.

"I very much fear that your horse—the horse you've left here—is mine," said Edmund. "He went missing three days ago."

Flint was astonished. "My goodness," he said. "Well, Tattersall's shall give me my money back. I paid forty-five pounds for him yesterday and thought it a snip. He's a very fine beast, and not more than ten."

"He's eight," said Edmund shortly. "Who sold him?"

"The house."

That might mean anything. Tattersall's was an auctioneer of horses, with a central location in London, regional ones elsewhere.

"Why not resolve it now?" Lenox asked. "Edmund, you could go to Tattersall's, with Mr. Flint if he will be so good."

Flint looked doubtful. "I had hoped to stay here and get news of the attack."

"Will you trust me to take the horse?" asked Edmund. "I'll ride him to the auction house. One way or another you'll have your money back, regardless—even if I have to pay it out of my pocket."

"For your own horse!" cried Flint. "No, please take him. You'll find me here until about six o'clock this evening. After that time, anybody in

Massingstone can tell you where to find Juniper Cottage."

"How will you get home without your horse?" asked Lenox. "You must allow us to hire you one."

Flint shook his head firmly. "Out of the question," he said. "There are a dozen men here who will allow me to hitch on with them. Go, please. I look forward to hearing what they have to say at Tattersall's."

"Your servant," said Edmund, bowing his head. Then he looked at Charles. "I'll return in a few hours—with a name, I hope."

CHAPTER TWENTY-SIX

After having seen Edmund off, Lenox decided that he ought to go to the house of Dr. Stallings to gauge Stevens's chances of survival and discover something about the attacker. On his way, he stopped in at Potbelly Lane and knocked on the door. Mrs. Watson answered. Apparently Hadley was away on business, having left at his customary hour, around seven o'clock. He had done the same the day before, too, Monday. He was on his regular schedule again.

Mrs. Watson said she had heard about Stevens, yes. Strangely, she didn't seem very sorry, though she was curious. It wasn't anything she said, exactly, that gave Lenox this impression—more something in her tone. It bothered him.

"Your sister cleans at the town hall, I understand?" he said.

"Claire? Yes, she works like a galley slave, too, sir, keeps it right tidy."

"Does she like Stevens?" asked Lenox. "Do they have much cause to interact?"

"You'll have to ask her, sir. I don't know, do I?"

It was still there, that tone of voice. "She wouldn't have been there this morning?"

Mrs. Watson shook her head. "She gets to the Malones' at six o'clock and leaves at four. Then she makes tea for her three boys before she goes and puts in two more hours at the hall, bless her. We take the boys at ours to eat as often as we can."

Lenox remembered that Claire Adams's husband was—*gone,* that was the word Sutherland had used. "She lives nearby?"

"Two doors down from me. But you won't find her there, she'll be at the Malones'."

"Please tell Mr. Hadley when he returns that I'll call on him this evening," Lenox said.

"Yes, sir, I certainly will."

Next Lenox went to Stallings's. There was a crowd of people in front of it; not unusual. In London one often saw crowds of hundreds in front of the homes of the dying, if they were even moderately well known.

Stallings's butler admitted Lenox after checking with his master. The lights of the house were dimmed. In the front parlor, Lenox met two people, who introduced themselves as Stringfellow and Allerton—the first the deputy mayor (a part-time job, for Lenox knew that he was also prominent in the local grain trade), the second the town's chemist, that notorious drunk.

He looked decently sober now, at least. "How is he?" asked Lenox.

"Fading quickly," said Allerton.

Stringfellow shook his head. "I thought I might be mayor one day when Stevens took his rightful place in Parliament. Not this way."

"Stallings is with him?"

The question answered itself—from a swinging white door, the doctor emerged. He nodded at Lenox. "Mr. Lenox," he said.

"I hear that he's not well."

"No," said Stallings curtly. "His breathing is ragged; his eyelids are fluttering; he sweats profusely. All the symptoms of catalepsy induced by trauma and loss of blood."

"What can you tell me about the attack?"

"That is not my field. He was attacked with a sharp object of some sort obviously, not a powerfully sharp one though, perhaps even something like a letter opener. I cannot hazard anything more than that."

Lenox recalled the letter opener on Stevens's desk. It didn't look as if it had been used in a violent stabbing—but of course it could have been wiped clean. "I see. How long do you think he will live?"

"If he remains in his current condition, thirty or forty hours. Or, if he improves, thirty or forty years."

"I have asked a friend, Thomas McConnell of the Great Ormond Street Hospital, to come down and look at the wounds—not as a medical matter," Lenox hastened to add, lest he offend the doctor's professional pride, "but as a criminal one. Would you consent to him seeing Stevens?"

To his surprise, Stallings agreed readily to McConnell's consultation. He said that he welcomed another opinion; that nobody could call him closed-minded; and so on. Only after Stallings went on for a few moments about the variety of medical insights did Lenox realize that he might be outmatched, this imperturbable village doctor, even afraid, unaccustomed to this sort of patient—seemingly as phlegmatic as usual, but in fact shaken.

Lenox promised to stop by with McConnell later. In the drawing room he said good-bye to all three men, then left the house.

What next?

He trudged in the direction of the Bell and Horns. Though he was pleased Edmund had found Cigar, he wished his brother were here with him; he would have been glad of someone to turn over his thoughts with. He was also curious about what Edmund had found on his second, daylight viewing of the gamekeeper's cottage on Snow's land. That was still their closest encounter with the criminal, after all.

The great matter now was to find the connection between Hadley and Stevens—and more to the point, to discover why Stevens had been attacked and Hadley had not. Was it a matter of opportunity or of motive?

One thing was sure: He would hardly feel comfortable in Hadley's shoes, out roaming the countryside unprotected.

The next few hours were frustratingly slow.

At the Horns, Clavering was still interviewing people—a thankless errand, when everyone in Markethouse had something to say and nobody in Markethouse had anything to tell. Lenox stopped in quickly enough to ascertain that Clavering hadn't discovered anything vital.

He also picked up a piece of flannel that Sandy, Mickelson's springer spaniel, often wore around his neck, according to Bunce—the person who passed it on—to keep fleas off his face. Lenox took it with a smile ("It's been years since I had fleas") and tied it up in a piece of brown paper, which he sent back to Lenox House by one of the pub's boys.

His next stop was the Malone household. There, he had a brief interview with Claire Adams, Elizabeth Watson's sister, who hadn't been in the town hall since the night before, still had her key, and yes, she could show it to him this instant. She produced it, tied on a thin string around her neck. She did seem shaken by the news of the attack—though, like her sister, somehow not quite devastated. She had been at the Malones' that morning from six o'clock. Mrs. Malone confirmed this to Lenox before he left—that Claire Adams had been in the household the entire time—and was all the more plausible because she seemed almost sorry to report the news, a petty, gossiping person, who would have been only too happy to believe that her maid could have killed the mayor.

McConnell, bless him, arrived on the 3:40 train.

He found Lenox at the Bell and Horns, and Lenox thanked him profusely for coming down. "Not at all," said the doctor.

"I wouldn't have asked you so urgently, except that it's very close to home for me. It *is* home, in fact. I hope you can stay over?"

"I have to go back this evening, I think. But you can stand me a local Markethouse dinner first if you like."

"With pleasure."

They walked across the square, back toward Stallings's house. McConnell drew looks from the congregation outside it, a stranger on a day when any stranger was bound to attract attention; he was a rangy, handsome man, with curly graying hair and a face worn by a long decade of drink and unhappiness, but now restored, in some measure, to youthfulness—he was a happy father, finally a happy husband to Jane's effervescent cousin Toto, and most importantly once again a full-time physician, working at the children's hospital.

Thanks to Lenox, McConnell had a vast experience in criminal medicine, and as he leaned over Stevens's body—the victim did indeed look fearfully pale, Lenox saw upon his first glimpse— he examined him with an assured and practiced air, unwrapping his bandages tenderly, feeling his forehead, listening to his heart.

Stallings stood back. "A faint arrhythmia, I believe," he murmured at one point. "Not unusual?"

McConnell nodded. "Yes, quite right."

Stallings looked pleased. "A short knife, I would have guessed?" he ventured now.

"That's a bit more difficult to say. If you'll give me a moment—"

"Of course, of course."

Stallings and Lenox stood in silence as McConnell, with great, great care, examined Stevens by the fading light from the windows. He spent an endless amount of time on each wound; the mayor never flinched, and to Lenox's untrained eye he looked past rescue, four-fifths dead, closer to walking with his ancestors than to walking in Markethouse again.

At long last, McConnell neatly redressed Stevens's wounds, placed a thin sheet over him, and then stepped to the basin in the corner of the room to wash his hands. When that was finished he looked at the two men and nodded toward the door, indicating that they ought to speak away from the patient.

Once they were in Stallings's office, McConnell, his face grave, shook his head. "He'll be gone before nightfall I think."

"Oh, dear."

"He lost too much blood, and it was not a strong constitution to start with—overwork, lack of exercise, alcohol. Dr. Stallings, is that accurate?"

"I would not have called him more given over to alcohol than other men. A glass of sherry with lunch. Overwork, certainly."

"Well—perhaps. I see the signs in a certain venous lethargy. Leave that aside, anyhow, and we can agree that he was singularly ill suited to survive such an attack."

"Would he do better in London?" Lenox asked.

McConnell shook his head. "His whole fate is in his body's reaction now. That will determine whether he lives or dies. There is nothing more that medical attention can do for him. Thus far the signs are not hopeful."

"And what about the attack?"

"Ah. There I can be more definite." McConnell ran his hand through his hair, gathering his thoughts. "I'm sure Dr. Stallings observed that the wounds are mostly clustered well below Mr. Stevens's sternum. There are seven of them. Six are very shallow, one slightly deeper, and all of them were dealt in the same flurry. Lenox, you recall my study of wound patterns in East End stabbing victims. The attacker was right-handed."

"Anything else?" asked Lenox, slightly disappointed at this vagueness.

But McConnell had an arrow remaining in his quiver. "Yes, this: that based on the height, depth, and nature of the wounds, I think it overwhelmingly probable that you are looking for either a woman or a boy."

CHAPTER TWENTY-SEVEN

The country evenings were getting icy now, and as Lenox and McConnell walked from the village back toward Lenox House an hour or so later, both pulled up their collars, shivering when the winds picked up. It was pleasant to stamp their feet on the threshold of Edmund's house and feel the warmth awaiting them inside; they went straight to the long drawing room, where tea was waiting, and took opposing armchairs next to the hearth. Thawing, they drank their tea in appreciative, sleepy silence, both staring into the lulling light of the wood fire.

After a few minutes, when they had poured their second cups of tea and woken up slightly, they began to talk, McConnell first. "May I ask how your brother is faring?"

Lenox shrugged. "I should say, not well, all in all—not well. The case has at least been a distraction."

"Poor fellow. Molly was a lovely woman."

"Yes, she was. I think if only the boys knew, he might begin to—to look forward, at least a step or two. While they don't know about their mother, it's as if it happens again every day."

"I understand."

The conversation wandered back in the direction of Stevens. Lenox had asked that word be sent if he died, and McConnell, not a man usually given to pessimism, had said on their walk that he would wager the news would beat Edmund back to Lenox House. He hadn't at all liked the clamminess or pallor of the mayor's skin.

They had achieved little after seeing the patient. First, they had gone to see Stevens's secretary, Miss Harville, at the town hall, only to learn from the mayor's clerk that she had gone home to rest until the morning. Then they had checked in once more with Clavering, a baleful figure in the pub, still negotiating the aggregated rumors of Markethouse. Hearing nothing new from him, they had returned home to wait for news and for Edmund, in whichever order they came.

Waller came in and topped off their tea, coughing discreetly when he was done and asking whether they knew how many they might be for dinner.

"Three," Lenox replied. "At least, I'm almost sure my brother will be back soon."

He was right: Not ten minutes later there was a noise in the front hall, and Edmund, red-cheeked and watery-eyed from riding in the twilight cold, entered.

There was a minor commotion as the dogs greeted him. He strode forward with a creditable imitation of good cheer to greet McConnell, saying how grateful he was the doctor had come down, how happy he was to see him, inviting him to stay the night, regretting it when McConnell said he could not, expressing his pleasure that at the least he could stay for dinner—his manners still intact even though the spirit had half gone out of him, as Lenox could see more plainly with an outsider present.

"And Cigar?" said Lenox, as they all settled down.

"Well, he's mine again," said Edmund. "I just rode him home. Damnably cold for my troubles, too. Waller, could I have a whisky?"

"I'll have one, too," said Lenox.

"And I," said McConnell.

"So?" said Lenox as his brother sat down. "Who sold the horse to Tattersall's?"

Edmund screwed up his mouth, looking frustrated. "It's a maddening story. No name. At first they were extremely stiff with me—said they didn't deal in stolen horses. I took a pretty high hand with them after that, I must say."

"Did you tell them that you were a Member of Parliament?"

"No, I told them I was going to bring in the police. Finally a fellow named Chapman was able to help me. He said that he had bought the horses from an older gentleman, well dressed, with a gray beard, three days ago."

"And this person didn't leave a name?"

"No. Chapman had the good grace to be embarrassed by that, for of course they usually insist upon a full record of ownership. But that's a stricter rule in London than here, apparently. Chapman said this fellow was well spoken, and he told them he had won the horses in a bet but didn't want to take the trouble of housing them, nor did he want the publicity of having his name attached to them. In the end they struck a handshake deal. Chapman told me that they only paid twenty-five pounds for the pair, by way of explanation. Cash."

Cigar and Daisy were thoroughbreds, together worth probably close to a hundred and thirty pounds at the right auction. Twenty-five pounds for the pair would have been a hard bargain for any horse trader to resist. "How much did they sell them for?" asked McConnell.

"Cigar for forty-five, just as Flint said, and Daisy for sixty, plus fees. A young fellow from Hampshire with a string of ponies bought her, apparently, with an eye toward amateur racing. Criminally cheap. He's in county for the hunt."

"She has the pace for racing," Lenox said.

"Yes, true. Anyhow, Flint's money is going back to him, and Daisy should be here tomorrow morning, with any luck. They're very scared I'm going to write to the *Times*, or the London office, or the police. Chapman was full of apologies and promises by the end. I did let it slip who I was."

"A gray-whiskered man, well dressed," said

Lenox thoughtfully. "They didn't give you any other detail?"

"A local accent," said Edmund. "I was sure to ask about that."

"Well done!" said Lenox, and his brother looked briefly pleased. "And his boots? A walking stick? How did he arrive, how did he leave?"

Edmund's face fell slightly. "I don't know. Chapman said to wire him with any questions, however, at their expense. I'll ask."

"Good," said Lenox.

"And you two?" asked Edmund. "Did you see Stevens? How is he?"

Lenox described what they had done in some detail, then said, "But tell us, Ed, about going back to the gamekeeper's cottage. As I was walking in from the station, I met Adelaide Snow, and she told me that you went over it with a fine-toothed comb. I'm curious what you found."

Just as Edmund was about to tell them, Waller came in and said that dinner awaited—and though their whisky was only half gone, McConnell had an eye on the clock, since he hoped to catch the 8:08 train back to London, so they went into the dining room.

That also gave Edmund the chance to find the notes he had jotted down when he inspected the cottage, which he read over as they sat down to a first course of a rich onion soup, made with ingredients from the house's gardens, topped with thick slices of local cheese. It was hearty enough that a spoon would stand up in it, and eaten along with a cold glass of Tokay, the white Hungarian wine Edmund loved best, it was wonderfully delicious, warming.

As they ate, Lenox's older brother described in detail what he had found at the house, including much that Lenox himself had seen—the remnants of a plucked chicken, the makeshift bed, the small decorative touches that suggested an inhabitation of at least intermediate length. These details were new to McConnell, of course, and for his part, Lenox always liked hearing details twice when he was investigating a crime.

Two new ones struck him. The first was that a small hand-drawn map of Markethouse had been tucked into one of the books. "Was the town hall on it?" asked Lenox.

Edmund nodded. "Not only that, but Potbelly Lane, which is not quite at the very center of town."

"Where is the map now? I should like to see it."

"With Clavering."

"I'll look at it tomorrow, then," said Lenox, frowning to himself.

The other detail was that along with the stolen food there was a slab of butter and several sprigs of herb—mint, marjoram, and rosemary were the ones Edmund had identified—which again suggested both a longer inhabitation, and a certain sophistication, of a piece with the novels and the bed.

As the footmen cleared the soup and brought out plates of steak, smothered with roasted potatoes, McConnell said, "Still, I would prefer dining here," and the brothers laughed.

"There's one thing that puzzles me more than the others," Lenox said. "I understand all the food, our horses, the blankets, even the books. But I don't understand the dog."

"Nor do I," said Edmund.

"Perhaps it was a watchdog," Lenox said. "But then, it never barked at us. And it was surely the thought of the moment to have it act as a decoy, rather than a premeditated idea."

They discussed the dog for some time then, sipping the claret Waller had opened for them to follow the Tokay, the disappearance of the last evening light in the windows making the candle-lit family dining room of Lenox's youth close, intimate, friendly. He asked if Edmund could get hold of a decent scenting dog, and he said he could, down at the Allenby farm, their excellent brindle pointer. Lenox suggested they put his skills to the test the next morning.

When McConnell left at a quarter to eight in the dogcart, both Edmund and Charles stood in the doorway, waving good-bye to him and asking him to pass their love to Toto and Georgianna.

After he was out of sight, they turned back

inside and immediately started discussing the case again, even before they had reached the brandy.

It was good to see Edmund animated; and for that reason, Lenox said, when perhaps he might have kept it to himself, for it was a slender thought, "Gray beard, you know. Well dressed. Does it sound like anyone to you?"

"The Duke of Epping."

Lenox shook his head. "No, I'm being serious."

"Well, who?"

"To me it sounds rather like Arthur Hadley."

CHAPTER TWENTY-EIGHT

L enox had a favorite piece of public wit from his many years of life in London. It had appeared at the north end of Westminster Abbey, which had one of the only walls in the entire city that was not covered in handbills—those familiar bright papers pasted up all over, advertisements for steamships, patent medicines, exhibitions, notices of public auction, whole magazines laid out to read page by page.

The men who posted these handbills were a familiar sight. All of them wore similar fantastically garish fustian jackets, with cavernous pockets to hold their bills, their pots of paste, their long collapsible sticks with rollers at the end.

The abbey was exempt from their energies only because of a large, forbidding placard that read BILL STICKERS WILL BE PROSECUTED in bold lettering. One day, passing nearby, Lenox had noticed an acquaintance—a usually somber fellow, a naval officer named Wilson—standing at the wall, grinning. Lenox had greeted him and asked what was so entertaining, and Wilson had pointed at the wall, where, underneath the placard, some anonymous genius had written *Bill Stickers is innocent!* Lenox had stared at this for a moment and then burst into laughter, and every time he saw Wilson now they smiled before they spoke, remembering the joke.

The next morning, Lenox woke up smiling, with this joke in his mind. He had been trying to remember all of his favorite ones for Edmund—most of which would elicit a groan from his brother, but a smile, too.

This one was good, and Lenox went downstairs thinking about how he would phrase it for maximum effect. But when he came into the breakfast room, he found that his brother was gone.

"Out on a walk again?" he said to Waller, who was carefully laying strips of kippered herring on a tray.

"Yes, sir, out on a walk."

Lenox cursed. He didn't know why this sudden uncontrollable passion for morning walks had arisen in his brother, and they had agreed the night before that they would make an early start to interview Miss Harville, Stevens's secretary, before visiting Clavering to check on his progress. As soon as the morning frost burned off, he also wanted to take the pointer out and look for Sandy, Mickelson's dog.

For twenty minutes he felt modestly irritated, as he ate and read the newspaper, and then in the next twenty minutes he began to grow more seriously vexed. This was a murder investigation, not a boys' adventure. By the time he had waited an hour and ten minutes, he was full of utterly righteous indignation.

Edmund came in with red cheeks. "Hullo," he said.

"Did you leave the dog in the stables?" asked Lenox.

Edmund was reading a letter and looked up from it only after a beat, distracted. "The dog?"

"The Allenby pointer—the one I asked you to borrow."

"Oh, dash it, I forgot. I'll have Rutherford send someone."

"Just a leisurely walk, then?" asked Lenox.

"Why, what's wrong?" said Edmund.

He was pouring himself a cup of tea, as if they had all the time in the world, and Lenox said coldly, "It's nearly half past nine."

Edmund glanced up at the clock on the wall. It was actually about ten past the hour, but he didn't mention it—a piece of discretion that only annoyed Lenox further, in his current mood. "I'm sorry," Edmund said. "Give me a few minutes, and I'll be with you."

"Where in creation do you keep going every morning?"

Edmund frowned and was silent for a moment, as if contemplating how to answer. Then he said, "Do you recall that one of my tenants, Martha Coxe, came to the house on the evening you arrived?"

"Vaguely."

"Apparently Molly was teaching three of the women in the Coxe household to read, the mother and the two daughters. I have undertaken to continue the lessons."

In a different mood, Lenox would have answered differently—but he was put out, and he made a scoffing noise. "Is that right?"

"Yes," said Edmund.

"And you imagine that to be a good use of the time of a person engaged upon a piece of detective work—not to mention a Member of the Parliament of Great Britain."

"I do. Why should it not be?"

"Teaching a parcel of women how to read? Your time is more valuable than that, Edmund, and if yours is not, mine certainly is."

Edmund reddened. "And what was Molly's time, may I ask you, valueless?"

"Of course not, don't twist—"

"Valueless, simply because she did not sit in the greatest assemblage of fools in the history of the British Empire? Am I to consider yet another blue book on coal mining in preference to teaching these women, and leave them halfway through the alphabet? Do you call that honorable? Parliament!"

"Then there's the case."

"The case! It can wait half an hour."

"That is not an assessment you are qualified to

make. But more than that, how can you be so obtuse? You have a dozen duties more pressing than—you have the estate, that on its own, you know, is enough!"

"The estate," said Edmund flatly.

"Your time—"

Suddenly Lenox saw that Edmund was close to vibrating with fury. He realized, a moment too late, that he wasn't even angry at his brother anymore. He tried to go on, but Edmund said, in a very distant voice, "I shall conduct my personal affairs as I see fit, Charles. I do not recall telling you that it was unwise to go into *trade,* though neither of us has to stretch far to imagine how our mother would have felt to learn that you had."

"Edmund—"

"I shall teach the horses to read if it pleases me. I invite you to disengage yourself from any interest in how I choose to spend my time immediately."

"Edmund, I—"

"Please feel free to carry on the investigation without me. Good morning."

He left. When he had gone, Lenox sat back in his chair, thoroughly dissatisfied with his behavior, Edmund's too, and conscious as well of that word, "trade," still alive in the room. For another ten minutes he sat and picked at the toast on his plate, dipping it in jam and eating it absent-mindedly.

When he got up, he thought he might go and apologize. He stood there, indecisively. He noticed the letter Edmund had been reading when he had come in, the one that had distracted him. It was on the piano, atop its torn envelope. Lenox read it.

12 Sept. 76
Midshipman's berth, *The Lucy*
Gibraltar
36.1° N, 5.3° W

Father and Mother,

Writing in absolute haste, as did not expect to put into Gibraltar, but weather muddy and ugly and woke to find leeshore rather closer than comfortable—so cut against the wind and pulled into harbor, and now just time to dash this off before we lie to and tack out of harbor again. The good news is that we ought to be in Plymouth in a month, perhaps even less. That means my birthday at home! Hopes they will give us a week. If I can I mean to bring Cresswell with me—so hide the gin. (Am only joking, do not hide it please.) Mother, if you fancy you could draw Cresswell, he's a great peacock. I do long to be on a horse again. Life aboard ship is splendid however. We passed old McEwan in Gib and he said to say hello to Uncle Charles and would he be so kind as to give him a character, because he is contemplating entering Parliament in Uncle Charles's old spot (which was a joke). Will James come home at Christmas? What odds the four of us can spend it together? Love to all of you and mind you bring the dogs in on cold nights, that stable is fearfully drafty, whatever Rutherford says.

Your loving son,

Teddy

CHAPTER TWENTY-NINE

L enox went to the town hall alone. He could see from the activity in the corridors that business had resumed, albeit uneasily. In the small room opposite Stevens's larger office, where his clerks sat, he found Miss Harville, the mayor's secretary.

She was a quiet young woman with dark hair and narrow dark eyes, aged fifteen or sixteen, very, very young for the job. When Lenox mentioned this, she merely nodded.

He had expected her to be highly emotional, but in fact she was quite poised, and had spent the morning helping Stringfellow, the deputy mayor, catch up on the duties that would fall to him, at least for the time being. Perhaps forever. Lenox asked if there was much to do. A great deal, she said—particularly with the budget meeting approaching. It was the village's most significant public debate of the year.

"Do you know who attacked Mr. Stevens, Miss Harville?" he asked.

Her eyes widened. "No, sir," she said.

"It wasn't you."

"Of course not, sir."

"In that case, it must have been disturbing to find the body."

She nodded solemnly. "Yes. It was."

He asked how she had come to work for Stevens, and she replied that she had been a student at the grammar, where she had shown a flair for mathematics. When she had left school—not intending to work, for her father was an assistant foreman at the factory, and fairly comfortably off—Stevens, searching for an assistant, had found her through the recommendation of her schoolmaster. He had first tested her skill, and then offered her the job.

"Have you enjoyed it?"

"Yes," she said, but dutifully.

Lenox pressed her. "Are you sure?"

"It's a pleasure to have my own money. I do feel quite ready to be married, and in a home of my own. But there are . . . there are not many young men in Markethouse, I suppose, and then, after a fashion, I am married to my work."

Lenox frowned. As with Elizabeth Watson and Claire Adams, there was something reserved in her reaction to the attack upon Stevens.

"Stevens was not married?" he asked.

"Oh, no," she said, as if the idea were outlandish, but added nothing else.

"Tell me about discovering the body."

"I arrived here early yesterday morning, just past seven o'clock, because Mr. Stevens asked me to come in early and run over figures for the budget. We both checked them for safety, though his own calculations were never wrong. I knocked on the door of his office, and there was no answer."

"Were you surprised?"

"Yes. He normally had his office door open."

"What did you do?"

"I knocked again and waited for a response. When there wasn't any, I assumed he had been detained at home. I went and fixed him a glass of sherry with an egg in it, which he always liked to take when he arrived at work and just when he left."

Again that sherry. Lenox remembered Stevens ordering the same concoction at the Horns on Market Day. But could *Stevens,* of all people, have been the one to have broken into Hadley's house? To have stolen the sherry?

It seemed impossible both because of the mayor's character and because he had been the one so eager to put a stop to the thefts. It was Stevens, after all, who had told him that books from the library had gone missing—the titles that matched the books in the gamekeeper's cottage.

"And then?" asked Lenox.

"I went into his office without knocking, thinking I would leave the glass on his desk. It was then that I found him."

"Had you seen anyone in the corridors of the building? Anyone leaving as you came in?"

"No, sir," she said.

"As far as you knew, you were the only person in the building."

"Yes, sir."

Lenox paused. "Did you disturb anything in the room?"

"No, sir."

"What did you do?"

"I called for help straightaway."

Lenox shook his head. "No, you didn't."

The secretary flushed. "Excuse me?"

Lenox nodded toward her shoes. "There were faint footprints in the carpeting that match the size of your shoe—in blood, you understand. They lead to the window. One set is much deeper there. I think you must have stood at the window for a while, more than a few moments. Perhaps you even drank the sherry! I shouldn't blame you. At any rate, I know that nobody was admitted to the room again after you went for help."

"Well, perhaps I did stand at the window. I was very shocked."

Lenox inclined his head. "Did you drink the sherry?"

She was still red. "A sip, to steady my nerves."

Very calmly, Lenox said, "What sort of man was Stevens?"

"A man much like any other."

He noticed the word "sir" had dropped out of her answers. "You liked him?"

"He was not a warm person. But he did . . . he selected me," she said.

"And who do you think attacked him?"

There was a long pause, and then, at last, she said, "I haven't the slightest idea. And I really must pick up my work again."

Lenox's brain was running rapidly through everything this young woman had said. He tried to focus, to remember her face and tone of voice so he could mull them later at his leisure. "Does the name Arthur Hadley mean anything to you?" he asked.

"I believe he's a resident of the village. Why?"

"How do you know him?"

She shook her head. "I cannot recall, but I have seen the name somewhere."

"Where?"

"As I say, I cannot recall."

"In the mayor's papers? Or did the mayor mention him?"

"No, not that. Perhaps in his papers—in fact, yes, I think somewhere in Mr. Stevens's papers."

"You're sure you can't recall anything more exactly?"

"If I do, I'll tell you," said the young secretary. "Please excuse me, Mr. Lenox. I wish you luck in finding out who killed Mayor Stevens, but if you want to speak any further, it will have to be after my work is finished."

"Of course. Thank you, Miss Harville."

Lenox left the building and walked up the square, brooding. It had been a peculiar interview. Why had she been so eager to end it?

He found his feet turning to Potbelly Lane. On an impulse he stopped into Mrs. Appleby's post office first, where he greeted her and then fired off a telegram to Polly and Dallington. In it, he asked if they might spare Pointilleux for a night, and added that if they could, the young Frenchman could pack a suitcase and stay at the hall.

After that he went to Hadley's house. The street was quiet and empty, the morning sun falling softly on the cobblestones, the few clouds slipping soundlessly across the pure blue sky. Lenox paused at the foot of Hadley's steps and took a few breaths of the clean air, thinking.

When he knocked, Mrs. Watson answered the door. "Hello, Mr. Lenox," she said.

To his eye she looked troubled, and after greeting her, he said, "Is everything quite all right?"

"Well—I suppose."

"What's the matter?"

"Nothing, exactly. Only I don't think Mr. Hadley came home last night."

Lenox became very alert. "How do you know?"

"The food I left for him is untouched. As far as I can tell, so is his bed."

"May I come in?"

"Of course, sir."

There was a broom leaning against the front hall table—evidently Mrs. Watson had been sweeping—and Lenox walked past it toward Hadley's sitting room. There he checked the alcohol (all present) and surveyed the room for some time. The charwoman watched him.

Then, abruptly, he turned back into the front hallway, making for Hadley's study. "Today is Wednesday," he said. "When did you last see Mr. Hadley?"

"Monday evening, sir."

Lenox went into the study. There was nothing of very great interest on the desk—but something in the room looked different. What? He forced himself to slow down and look around carefully, as he had in the sitting room.

Then he saw it.

The door of the mahogany cabinet underneath the window hung just slightly open; he strode forward and opened it fully, and found, inside, Hadley's safe, where he kept his collection of gemstones.

Empty.

CHAPTER THIRTY

Back at Lenox House an hour later, Lenox found there were two telegrams waiting for him, both sent by Dallington. The more recent of the two merely reported that Pointilleux was on his way. The first, from that morning, was a disjointed post on their progress in the Muller case:

> When can you return STOP following chandelier per your sugg STOP whole thing damnably confusing STOP suspect Greville myself STOP have just discovered bizarre fct also STOP Margarethe Muller is reported in Paris right this minute by their constblry STOP anyhow come back here curse you STOP Dall

Lenox frowned after he read that. He read it again. *Reported in Paris.* He sat for some time, thinking about all that this information implied.

Thurley had identified the dead woman without hesitation when they found her: Margarethe Muller, Muller's sister and assistant.

It was possible that Thurley had been lying, but Lenox didn't think so. His reaction had been immediate, genuine.

That meant Muller had introduced the woman to the theater manager, and presumably everybody else, as Margarethe Muller. Which, in turn, meant, that the woman calling herself by that name in Paris might well be an impersonator— or that the dead woman had been an impersonator. One or the other.

After pondering this in silence for a long time, Lenox suddenly sprang up out of his chair. Writing rapidly, he drafted a telegram to Dallington.

> Must remain here for now STOP but was Muller married STOP if so possible mistress traveling under sister's name STOP please keep apprised STOP Lenox

No sooner had he given that slip of paper to a footman with instructions to hurry down to the village and send it, however, than he had another thought. This one hit him even harder, with all the force of a revelation.

In his excitement he grabbed another servant and had him stand there and wait as he wrote.

> And if lover then MULLER HIMSELF must be suspect STOP but how did he learn of chandelier STOP and why STOP push hard on Greville and Thurley STOP wine glasses STOP

Lenox sent this missive off—not much more coherent than Dallington's—and after he had watched it go stood stock-still in the front hall, thinking for many minutes on end.

As he stood there, he was wholly in London, wholly bent upon the problem of Muller's disappearance. Had he cracked it? A certain race in his pulse and his thoughts told him he had gotten a step closer to the truth, anyway. A lovers' quarrel. It made sense. If Muller was married—and Lenox strained to recall whether the newspapers had said he was, but couldn't—then his mistress might easily have traveled with him, and been more plausibly explained as a sister than a secretary or friend.

He would have gone on thinking about Muller for a great deal longer, if at that moment Edmund had not come in with a handsome brindle pointer. "Hello, Charles," he said.

"Hello, Edmund. How are you?"

"Oh, well enough. This is Toby, your scenting dog."

Lenox looked at his brother and smiled a smile of forced cheer. "Let's take him out, then. Do you have your walking boots on? Good, because the Lord knows what will happen to our horses this time."

They had to ride very slowly. For a moment Lenox had thought that Edmund would decline to accompany him, but after a beat he had agreed, and now, having given Toby the flannel from the spaniel's neck, they followed him together at a walk, now and then a trot. Occasionally they would exchange a few desultory words. Only when Lenox described Hadley's disappearance did Edmund become engaged.

"My goodness. Did you tell Clavering?" he asked.

"I passed the word by Bunce, and I wired the head office of the Dover Assurance to ask what news they had of Hadley's whereabouts."

Edmund shook his head. "It doesn't look good."

Lenox squinted into the sun. "I know. And yet . . . well, it's simply odd, that's all. Why is his disappearance so different than the attack on Stevens? I mean to say, Stevens is confronted and stabbed, Hadley tormented for weeks and then kidnapped? Isn't it odd?"

"It is. Is it possible that Hadley himself attacked Stevens, though?"

"Yes, and what if Stevens was the tormenter! I thought of that, but then—why would Hadley have come to us, if he knew what was afoot, and that he planned to confront Stevens? His puzzlement seemed completely genuine. And then, even more baffling, why would he draw our attention to him by leaving directly after the attack?"

"Yes, true."

Lenox looked at his pocket watch. It was just

before one o'clock. "At this moment, the Queen is either in my house or not in my house," he said.

"I don't want to puncture your *amour propre*," Edmund replied, "but that's true of my house, too."

Lenox smiled. "I wonder whether she went, that's all."

"Will Jane wire to tell you?"

"Hm. Only in the event of a nonappearance, I would wager. We shall see."

Toby ran along ahead of them, nose importantly to the ground, tail high in the air. They were again walking the perimeter of the village, on the logic that Stevens's attacker, if it was the same person who had been in the gamekeeper's cottage, must have needed a new place to stay until at least Tuesday, the day of the assault.

After a mile or so, they spotted another horse, and as it came closer, Lenox saw that atop it was George Atherton, one of Edmund's closest friends here. Atherton hailed them from a few hundred yards and rode their way, pulling his horse up short from its canter when he reached them, a trim, healthy animal, black all over but for its white socks. Toby smelled its legs and then dismissed it from his mind, coming to take a piece of dried duck from Edmund, then sitting and waiting at his command.

"I call this lucky—I was just riding over to see you, Ed!" said Atherton. He was a large, extremely good-natured fellow, country through and through, bluff, with an easy laugh and his blond hair held back in a clip, in the fashion of the last century. His chief passion in life was farming. He had chaffed Lenox since they were boys, and as a result Lenox had never been as fond of him as Edmund was. "Is that Cigar? What's all this I hear about you selling him to the glue factory for a shilling a pound?"

Edmund shook his head. "He was stolen. You remember Charles, obviously?"

"Of course! How d'you do, Charles? Still scared of roosters?"

"Not for thirty-five years or so. Are you still wet from falling in Sturton Pond?"

Atherton bellowed with laughter at that, and then called Charles a good'un. After that he asked what they were doing, and when he learned they were scenting, offered to come along.

Lenox was irritated when his brother agreed—it would slow them down—but as time passed, and Atherton chatted away without a care, Lenox realized that Edmund was smiling. More than that, it emerged, from one or two stray comments, that Atherton had been a regular visitor at Lenox House whenever Edmund had been here, and learning that, Lenox felt himself warm to the man. He even put in his joke about Bill Stickers being innocent—and was rewarded with another of Atherton's infectious guffaws.

It was when they were three-quarters of the way around the village that Toby picked up a scent. They were near a rutted cart path, and all at once all the muscles in the dog's body came alive. His pace increased, and he quivered and whined, his nose so close to the ground that he bumped it every few inches. Lenox offered him the flannel again to be sure, and Toby barked impatiently and increased his pace.

To Lenox's surprise, the dog led them not out into the countryside but toward the village of Markethouse itself.

Soon there was an air of great suspense among the three men, urgency. They were silent—even Atherton, unless you counted one occasion when he muttered that he'd never seen a dog so full of hell and pepper—and watched Toby intently as they followed him.

Presently they came to the head of Bell Street. "Shall we leave our horses here?" asked Edmund.

"Fool me once," said Lenox.

So they rode in a crowd, almost as wide across as the street.

Toby, on the scent, was possessed—he would break into sprints now and then, and never faltered, turning right onto Markham Lane, left onto Pilling Street, left again onto Abbot Street. The few people about looked at them oddly, including half a dozen women from their windows. This was a quiet, working part of Markethouse, extremely tidy and well kept. In Abbot Street a chicken waddled indignantly beyond Toby's path, though the dog ignored it completely.

"What the devil is he after?" said Atherton.

"He's going to take us clear out of town again," said Edmund.

Indeed, the houses were thinning; they had trailed through some of the densest parts of Markethouse, but now they were in sight of open fields once more.

Then, at the foot of Clifton Street, which actually ran straight from the market to the countryside, Toby became frantic. Lenox had tied a piece of rope to his collar several minutes before, and the dog strained and pulled at it, barking.

And finally it became clear where he was pointed—toward a little cottage at the very end of Clifton Street, set some ways off from the rest of the houses, surrounded by a stone wall. As Lenox could see from the height of his horse, a thick, rich tangle of climbing plants rose up the walls of the dwelling.

Toby leapt and fought at the wall, barking furiously. Lenox saw Atherton and Edmund exchange a grave look.

"What is it?" said Lenox. "Who lives here?"

It was Atherton who answered, in a low voice. "Mad Calloway."

CHAPTER THIRTY-ONE

Edmund and Atherton watched Lenox, awaiting a signal. For his part he was feeling irresolute; he kept glancing from the dog to the door of the little cottage and back.

Then he glanced into the garden. He thought of the mint, the marjoram, and the rosemary in the rudimentary little kitchen inside Snow's gamekeeper's lodge, next to the butter.

"Look," he said to Edmund after a moment, voice quiet, gesturing toward the garden. "Loose-strife growing there on the south wall, just by the second window."

Edmund raised his eyebrows in response, a look that said he understood the implications of that loosestrife. Neither mint nor marjoram nor rose-mary nor loosestrife was *very* uncommon; on the other hand, there likely weren't many gardens in Markethouse or its environs that contained all four.

Lenox recalled watching Mad Calloway walking around the Saturday market with his little stringed-up bundles of herb and flower.

In the twenty or thirty seconds all of this took, Toby remained frenzied, jumping with his front paws against the wall, turning around at them beseechingly every few seconds.

At last, Lenox stepped down from his horse. "Atherton, will you hold the dog? My horse, too, if you don't mind."

"Certainly," said the farmer.

"Thank you," Lenox said distractedly.

He was trying as hard as he could to recall what he could of Mad Calloway. It was very little. Calloway was the next thing to a hermit—disappearing for long stretches at a time into his little cottage, emerging every other market day usually, friendless, unfriendly indeed, and by all accounts truly mad. Lenox had never heard him speak a word.

On the other hand, he hadn't heard of him being violent.

And yet—a full gray beard, that was what the man who had sold their horses to Tattersall's had had, and that was what Calloway had. It was also common to see him ranging across town with a pipe clenched in his teeth, and Lenox hadn't forgotten the tobacco ash that had been piled next to the door of the gamekeeper's cottage, as if someone had been standing there for a long while, refilling a pipe as he waited.

A woman or a child, McConnell had said. But mightn't an old, stooped man strike a similarly weak blow?

He was close enough to Atherton and Edmund that he could say to them, in a low voice, "Do Calloway and Stevens have anything to do with each other?"

Both men shook their heads. "Calloway has nothing to do with anyone," said Atherton.

"What about Calloway and Hadley?" Lenox asked.

Again, both men said that they knew of no relationship between Calloway and any man in the village, and Atherton said that would be doubly true of a relative newcomer there, such as Arthur Hadley. "On the other hand," he added, "Hadley and Stevens know each other well."

"Well?" said Lenox. "What?"

Atherton looked surprised at the vehemence in Lenox's voice. "Yes, Hadley bought Stevens's house when Stevens moved to Cremorne Street," said Atherton. "Ed, you must have known that."

"I had no idea," said Edmund. "In Potbelly Lane?"

"Yes, they've been friendly since."

Toby was making an outright commotion at the gate of the cottage. Though nobody was stirring inside, in the rest of Clifton Street people had noticed. Glancing back, Lenox saw several women in the doorways, peering down toward the group on horseback.

They must do something soon, or risk Calloway running as he had before, if indeed it had been he who'd taken their horses outside the game-keeper's cottage. This new information about Stevens and Hadley—this troubling new infor-mation—would have to wait. He looked back to make sure that Atherton was still restraining Toby. The dog was pulling hard at the end of his leash, forelegs lifting off the ground, but Atherton had him.

Lenox went to the gate. As he pushed it open, it gave a loud creak.

"Mr. Calloway?" he called.

There was no reply. He went in and took one or two steps up the short path to the low front door. Edmund, too, had dismounted. He followed behind his younger brother.

Together they waited at the front door. "Do you hear anything?" Lenox asked in a quiet voice, after he had knocked on it.

"No. You?"

Lenox pushed the door inward. The garden smelled strongly, but as they moved into the house the smell of greenery became all-consuming—neither pleasant nor unpleasant precisely, a jumble of every herb that had ever been, living, dead, growing, dried. In the dim light, Lenox could see dozens of jars on a small table by the door.

"Mr. Calloway?" he called out loudly.

There was no answer, and he began to have a dreadful feeling. What if they found him dead, Mad Calloway? The town's mayor and its hermit in the same week?

What if that chalk drawing was waiting on the wall?

The rooms of the house were tiny. There was a sitting room, a kitchen, and a bedroom, none much wider than the span of Lenox's arms, and none of the ceilings high enough that he felt confident walking entirely upright.

These rooms were also empty.

"What now?" asked Edmund.

"I'm not sure."

"Hm."

"Let's see if there's a back gate," said Lenox. "It's a trick that fooled us once before."

They returned to the front door and walked out the little path. Then, peering around the corner of the house into the garden, Lenox noticed a rickety shed at the end of it, made of what looked like ancient time-blackened driftwood.

Through its slats he saw a movement.

Heart quickening, he gestured to Edmund to follow him, and they waded through the deep herbs growing all around to get to it—trying not to trample them underfoot, which was funny, Lenox thought. After all, Stevens was nearly dead.

"Mr. Calloway?" Lenox called when they had come to the shed.

At the sound of his voice, there was a thin whine for response—a dog's whine.

Without hesitating, Lenox opened the door and saw them both: There was Calloway, still alive, thank God, bent over a small sprig of some herb, pruning it with infinite care and tenderness, and behind his chair, staring up at them with beautiful wet dark eyes, was Mickelson's spaniel.

"Mr. Calloway?" said Charles softly.

There was no reply.

"Mr. Calloway, I'm Edmund Lenox. My brother and I hoped to have a word with you."

Calloway didn't turn away from his project, and Lenox said, "It's about Stevens Stevens, the mayor. Did you know that he's been attacked, Mr. Calloway?"

There was a long pause, and then the old man put down the plant carefully on a bed of wet cotton that he had evidently prepared before beginning this delicate operation—there were similar such beds on the makeshift table, a kind of infirmary for plants—and turned to them.

"Is he dead?" Calloway asked.

Lenox would later learn that these were the first words anyone in Markethouse had heard Mad Calloway speak in eleven years. Not surprisingly, his voice was hoarse. "No, he's not," said Lenox.

"More's the pity. Have you arrested anyone?"

"No, sir."

"And who do you think did it?"

"We don't know, sir."

A look came over Calloway's face then that struck Lenox, a look he would remember, some odd mixture of strain, relief, and exhaustion. "Well," he said calmly. "I did it. Give me a moment to finish this and I'll come away with you."

CHAPTER THIRTY-TWO

It was a few hours later when Mrs. Appleby, highly professional representative that she was of the Royal Mail, came to find Lenox in the jailhouse near the Bell and Horns.

"You have three wires addressed to you at Lenox House," she said, "but I thought you might prefer to have them now."

"Thank you very much, Mrs. Appleby," said Lenox.

"I heard that you were here, you see."

She needn't have added that; the entire village had known within seconds, it seemed to Lenox, that Mad Calloway had been arrested for the violent assault upon the person of Stevens Stevens. This, even though they had tried their hardest to transport him to the jailhouse anonymously. It hadn't mattered. The word had run up Clifton Street faster than their horses, then perhaps north to Pilot Street over a back fence, then probably down Pig Lane with the washing-woman—and now here they were, with half the people of Markethouse again gathered in the square, and half of them convinced that Calloway had killed Arthur Hadley, too.

Clavering had a little desk outside of the single jail cell. Edmund, Lenox, and he were seated in chairs around it, staring at Calloway, who was asleep upon the low straw-filled bed in the cell. Atherton had gone home at last, taking Toby with him along the way as a favor to Edmund—though not before the dog had been treated to a piece of beefsteak from the public house next door by Lenox, who had strong convictions about fairly rewarding anyone who assisted him in finding a murderer, regardless of the number of legs they might possess.

"Damned awkward," Clavering said for the dozenth time, after Mrs. Appleby had left. "He was never a bad sort. Even a very *good* sort, I would have said, before he lost his mind."

They had tried to question Calloway for hours now; they might as fruitfully have tried to question the wall behind him, or the straw in the bed. He was silent.

"What was his motive?" Edmund muttered, yet again.

Lenox had his own thoughts on that score. Until his mind had worked over the facts, however, he was going to stay quiet.

He tore open the first of the telegrams, read it, and sighed heavily. "What is it, sir?" asked Clavering.

"The case began with Arthur Hadley coming to us," he said, "and his problem, at least, I think we have solved."

"We have?" said Edmund doubtfully.

Lenox passed across the telegram, which was from the Dover Limited Fire and Life Assurance Company. "I believe so."

Edmund read it out loud:

Arthur Hadley safe STOP staying night in Chiselhurst STOP plans return home when work concluded STOP sends thanks for concern STOP

Clavering took it from him and read it again, frowning. Edmund, looking at Charles, said, "I still cannot see the thread."

Lenox explained. "As soon as Atherton told us that Hadley lived in Stevens's old house in Potbelly Lane, the pieces fell into place. My first thought was of the sherry."

"The sherry," Edmund said slowly, still in the dark.

"According to Miss Harville, Stevens Stevens drank sherry several times a day without fail."

"Usually with an egg in it," Clavering said.

"Yes, with an egg in it. Now: think of Hadley's house, which someone broke into on consecutive days."

"Presumably Calloway."

They all looked into the cell, where the old man slumbered on. "Why twice?" Lenox said. "Looking back on it, the crucial break-in is the second one. To whoever did it—Calloway, let's assume—it was important enough to break in again that the person sent in a false report of a fire at the corn exchange in Chichester, which guaranteed that Hadley would be drawn away from home.

"But why? The person had already been in the house the day before! They had chalked their strange image on the steps. Why risk being seen to get inside the house again?"

"I confess I still don't know the answer," Edmund said.

"Because they had made a mistake," said Lenox. "What was changed by the second break-in? Only one thing. The sherry."

Clavering frowned. "Hm."

"My belief is that Stevens Stevens was the sole target of this series of crimes. The intruder at Hadley's house actually believed they were entering the house of Stevens. In the course of the break-in, this intruder poisoned the bottle of sherry, counting on the mayor to drink it that very night. A reasonable presumption, given that Stevens always did drink sherry throughout the day. But soon enough—"

"The intruder learned of his mistake," Edmund said, finally comprehending it, "and had to figure out a way to get the sherry out of there before killing an innocent person."

"Precisely right," said Lenox, with a feeling of satisfaction. "Hence the false telegram about the fire in Chichester. And hence the necessity for a second, more direct attack on Stevens—and the second figure drawn upon the wall."

Clavering's eyes were wide. "I'll be blowed," he said. "In Markethouse, no less."

"The difficulty is that it puts us no closer to knowing why Calloway attacked Stevens," said Edmund.

"Mm. Calloway," said Lenox.

"What?"

"Oh, nothing."

Edmund thought for a moment. "Hadley is simply gone on business, then, not vanished. But what about the safe, the gemstones?" he asked.

"He has no family, no close connections," Lenox responded. "Those gemstones are what he cares about most passionately in life. I believe he heeded our advice and removed them from his house. It may also be why he chose to stay away from Markethouse the past two nights."

"Yes."

Edmund sighed then—and Lenox understood the sigh. There was still so much to reconcile in all this. For his part, he kept returning to Harville and the Watson sisters, the two charwomen.

"Tell me, Clavering," he said, "do you know how Stevens is faring?"

"No. I've been intending to run over to the Horns and get Bunce to fetch a report back to us. Shall I do it now?"

They all glanced over at Calloway, who was still asleep. "Yes, why not?" said Lenox. "Who knows—he might have awoken."

When Clavering had gone, Edmund stood up and began to pace the small room, hands in pockets, face pensive. Lenox took the moment to reach for the second telegram.

It was from Jane—and if Dallington was profligate in his style, Jane, in hers, was positively reckless, at least when she got into stride.

Well the Queen did not come STOP I should write 'alas' here but honestly cannot feel so very sad about it STOP she would have made the entire affair very formal and <u>prestigious</u> but instead we had many small conversations and nice food and anyhow we did manage three royals STOP felt badly for them because unless you're queen you're counted just that way like pups in a litter STOP one I liked very much indeed Carlotta STOP she gave Sophia a kiss on the nose and took a ribbon out of her own hair and tied it in Sophia's STOP and of course most important we raised a great deal of money for the hospital STOP Toto ever so pleased STOP people say 'most important' when they mean <u>least</u> important often STOP but you may take it as read that I am altogether more saintly STOP I really do care so does Toto STOP you would be altogether shocked how much Emily Westlake gave too STOP all of us here missed you dearly STOP my love always STOP Jane

Lenox read through this twice, and only when he glanced up did he see that Edmund was looking at him intently.

And in that look, Lenox for a flash of an instant experienced the full force of what Edmund was suffering. The case fell away; Muller, too. He imagined himself without Jane.

The feeling lasted a second—less than a second—but it left him shocked, a buzzing in his ears. He had believed that he was being kind and empathetic to his brother. Only now did he perceive how inadequate his understanding had been.

He said the one thing he could think to say. "Listen, Ed, I'm so terribly sorry that I lectured you about teaching that family."

Edmund shook his head. "No, no, it is I who should be sorry—very high and mighty. And I said that thing to you about trade."

"Oh, that. Anyhow, listen, I think it's a very fine thing to do. Molly would have been happy. She always saw everything through—a very determined person."

"Do you think so?" Edmund glanced at the door.

"Well, perhaps, perhaps not. But I am sorry, Charles, for saying that. Forgive me."

"You're my brother, you oaf. You never hav to ask my forgiveness for anything, in this life or the next. Ah, there's the door—that will be Clavering back. Let's see what he says about Stevens."

CHAPTER THIRTY-THREE

R oughly a century and a half before, in 1714, the King of England had been very, very nervous about the possibility of revolution. He was George the First, a Hanoverian, and therefore persuaded that the Stuarts were going to form mobs and depose him, or perhaps even kill him.

To settle his nerves, the government passed a law. If any twelve or more people were engaged in "tumultuous assembly," a magistrate could stand up and formally demand their dispersal by reading it out loud. If they hadn't separated an hour after the magistrate's proclamation, they could be arrested, and sentenced very harshly indeed, even up to two years of imprisonment with hard labor.

The law the magistrate had to read out loud to bring into effect had a name: the Riot Act.

The act was still on the books, Lenox knew from his time in Parliament, though it hadn't been widely used in a very long time—surviving, instead, in its name, a term for any stern lecture from a schoolmaster or mother or disappointed friend.

And yet when Clavering returned, he looked and sounded as if he would desperately have liked to invoke the old Riot Act. His shirt was torn at the collar—actually torn!—and he was red in the face. He shook his head despairingly at Lenox and Edmund.

"The whole town wants to string him up this evening, the poor devil," he said, nodding toward the cell. "They've worked themselves into a frenzy."

"I know a simple enough way to calm them," Lenox said.

"And which is that, sir, when they've gone through eighteen barrels of ale in the last three hours!"

"Tell them that he's innocent."

Clavering looked confused. "Innocent?"

"Yes."

It was Edmund who glanced at the cell behind them to see, and the other two followed his gaze. Calloway was staring at them. "Is it true?" Edmund asked. "Are you innocent, Mr. Calloway?"

"No," he said.

At least he had spoken. Lenox stood up. "You maintain that you entered the town hall yesterday morning, stabbed Stevens Stevens, left him for dead, and have been in your house since then?"

"Yes."

"Where is the knife?"

Calloway said nothing. Lenox met his gaze, and they stared at each other for some time, Lenox with the feeling that there was perhaps not much madness at all in this old fellow.

Calloway's personal history was murky even to those, like Clavering, who had lived in Market-house their entire lives. Both Atherton and Clavering had said that Calloway had had a wife and a daughter until roughly a decade before, the three of them living happily in the small stone cottage, but that then the wife had died of a sudden fever one winter. The daughter had gone to live with an aunt and uncle in Norfolk, Atherton remembered, her father unable to look after her properly.

Lenox had asked, as they stood huddled away from the cell, whether it was this sudden solitude that had driven Calloway mad.

"Well, he was always an odd bird," Atherton had replied in a quiet voice. Because he was a farmer, and his goods sold at market, he had a much firmer grasp of the local characters than Edmund, so often off in Parliament, did. "Never a very avid gardener until around the time he went silent."

"No?" said Lenox curiously. "Did he have a job?"

Atherton had shaken his head, no. "I believe he inherited some money when his wife died, or perhaps that she brought it with her in the dowry. At any rate he never worked. But it was only after her death that I think he became a—a recluse, you know, for lack of a better word."

Clavering had nodded. "His wife was right

sociable, you know, Mrs. Catherine Calloway."

"And who were his friends? Who are his friends now?"

Neither Clavering nor Atherton had been able to answer that question. A village was peculiar: so deeply intrusive, in a way, and in another way pig-blind. Once Calloway had become Mad Calloway, Lenox guessed, people had stopped acquiring any new ideas about him. They had pegged him to his role as the town's eremite, as surely as the local baker or the local hostler or the local thief.

But somebody in Markethouse would have a sharper recollection than Clavering or Atherton. It was simply a matter of finding the person.

Clavering was just asking Lenox again why he thought Calloway was innocent when Bunce came into the room. He had been down to see Dr. Stallings at Clavering's request.

"Any improvement?" Edmund asked.

Bunce shook his head. "The same," he said. "Weren't no better nor no worse."

"In such a case steadiness may be counted improvement, I hope," said Edmund.

Behind them there was a noise—Calloway had snorted in disgust.

They asked why in every way they could think of, over the next few minutes, but nothing would induce him to speak.

It was late afternoon now; it had already been a

long day. Lenox suggested they leave Bunce with the prisoner, get a bite to eat, and discuss the case, and Edmund and Clavering agreed.

Though the Bell and Horns was the most visible and popular, there were several public houses in Markethouse. Lenox's favorite was the Lantern, in Pilot Street, whose presence was only indicated by a single lantern above a low wooden door. Behind this door was a dark room, full of flickering candle- and firelight, pewter flagons lining the stone wall behind the bar, and long varnished oak tables scored a thousand times with keys and coins. It was a place that served food, but would close shop before calling itself a "restaurant," that London word—in Lenox's youth he had never heard it, and when he first did, at the age of fifteen or so, it referred only to European dining establishments, as opposed to the beef houses, oyster rooms, and coffeehouses that served British food. More and more, though, anywhere could be a restaurant, and the beef houses, oyster houses, they had begun to have an old-fashioned air, a Regency air, which Lenox rather regretted. This kind of simple eatery was being replaced by finer ones, even toward the bottom of the economic scale, with cloth napkins, complex puddings, waiters in aprons. To be at the Lantern was to step back a foot or two from that particular progress of the modern age.

Edmund, Clavering, and Charles were the only patrons there, having slipped the crowds by leaving through a side door. The owner, a quiet but friendly older chap named Lowell, fixed them three pints of mild. Following them soon thereafter was supper: Lady Jane might have dined with three royals, but Lenox was certain that none of them had had as satisfying a meal as he did, which he ate ravenously until it was all gone, and he could sit back with a happy sigh and watch Clavering chase a last dab of applesauce around his plate with a chunk of roasted potato.

"When you said earlier that Calloway was innocent," Edmund said, "were you being provocative?"

"Does nothing strike you as odd about his confession?" Lenox asked them.

"Only that he spoke."

Lenox frowned. "Well, then," he said, "let me tell you what I noticed that struck *me* as odd. First: Why would he take the risk and trouble of inhabiting an abandoned gamekeeper's cottage when he has his own house in Clifton Street? Second: Why would he need a map of Markethouse, after having lived here for sixty years or longer? Third: Why would he need to steal books, or clothes, or food, if, again, he has his own cottage, his own food, his own clothes, and was perfectly entitled to take books out of the library? Fourth: How is it possible that he would believe Stevens still lived in a house he hadn't inhabited in several years?"

Both Edmund's and Clavering's eyes had widened. "Hm," said Clavering, his round face knit with concentration. "When you put it that way."

"Fifth: Why would he have stolen a dog? And sixth, why, for all pity, would he suddenly, after all this time living a few streets away from him, attack the mayor of the town?"

Edmund nodded, tapping his fist lightly against the oak table, his postsupper pipe clasped in it. "On the other hand," he said, "seventh, why would he tell us he had done it?"

Lenox recalled that strange look of relief and exhaustion in Calloway's face when he had asked if they had arrested anybody. "To protect some-one," said Lenox. "The real intruder at Hadley's house, whoever that was."

Edmund frowned. "Who would a friendless loner, a hermit, want to protect?"

"What we need is someone who knows Markethouse backward and forward," Lenox said, "and won't mind filling in all of the missing details of Calloway's history for us."

Clavering and Edmund exchanged a glance, then said, almost simultaneously, "Agatha Browning."

"Who is she?" Lenox asked.

But he would have to wait for his answer. The door of the Lantern swung open, and a handsome young fellow carrying a shining black leather overnight case entered. It was Pointilleux.

"Gentlemen!" he said happily. "The estimable Monsieur Bunce has inform me you are here!"

"Hullo, Pointilleux," said Lenox, "decent of you to come."

The young Frenchman inclined his head gravely. "Of course. Tell me, though, this supper you have all eaten so gluttonous that your plates are clean, in true English fashion, is there another of it? I could not be more hungry, I swear to you, not if I am to ran from here to Marathon and back."

CHAPTER THIRTY-FOUR

The food was ordered, cooked, delivered; Pointilleux fell to it heartily and happily. As he ate, the three men informed him of the situation and discussed their plans.

The clerk said he was refreshed by his trip—he had that incredible constitutional springiness of a twenty-year-old human—and didn't need to sleep. He listened intently as they described their progress in the case thus far. When they had finished, he asked them to put him to work. This was a holiday, and he looked appropriately eager: no clerking for a few days, for once all of his energies put toward detection, ever so much more engaging than copying and filing.

"In that case, I would like to set you loose in Stevens's office," Lenox said. Pointilleux had proven himself adept at parsing documents in the matter of the Slavonian Club. "Look for anything, anything at all, personal, public, particularly anything at all that ties Stevens to Calloway. Don't forget the budget is coming up, either, a contentious local matter."

"I don't think Stevens would like that," Clavering said.

"That's too bad for Stevens," said Lenox firmly. "It would have been very helpful to know before now that Hadley bought Stevens's old house—it would have saved us a measure of time and work. If there's any similar piece of information in his office, we need to have it."

"And what shall the three of us do?" Edmund asked.

Lenox had several ideas on that score, too. He enumerated them now, and the others nodded in agreement. After Pointilleux had thrown off a glass of ruby red wine—"Wretched swill," he said, a phrase he must have learned from Dallington, "but it will do"—they walked him down to the town hall.

Clavering had a key now, and they took him up to Stevens's office.

"Will it not bother you to pass time here alone, with that horrible drawing on the wall?" Edmund asked.

"No," said Pointilleux cheerfully. "Charles, you tell me there are papers here and across the hall, too?"

"Yes," said Lenox.

"And if I slow, how you say, if I desist in feeling awake—how do I arrive to Lenox House, to sleep one hour or two?"

"We'll send a boy back with a horse," Edmund said. "He'll wait outside."

"Thank you."

"And he'll hear it if you scream," Edmund

added in a mutter, as they left the agency's clerk to do his work.

"Chin up," Lenox said as they walked downstairs to leave the hall. "I think the attack was meant for Stevens. Not anybody else."

"It's that blasted drawing which bothers me," said Edmund.

Clavering, who badly needed a rest, nevertheless insisted on stopping by the jail again before he went home, and Lenox felt a flare of admiration—not spectacularly intelligent, this small, round-faced man, but stout, honest, and dogged. They were lucky to have him.

All three of them went and looked at Calloway. He was asleep, as Bunce and his cousin, equally reedy and tall, played a hand of cards by candlelight.

"You're staying overnight?" Lenox asked.

"Oh, yes," said Bunce.

"Fair enough. And Clavering, in the morning you'll take us to see Agatha Browning?"

"Bright and early," said Clavering.

"Good."

They were finished for the day then, finally, and all of them shook hands, before Lenox and Edmund betook themselves slowly back toward Lenox House.

They went by the same route that they had taken so many hundreds and thousands of times in heir vanished youth. Then, of course, their parents had been waiting; more recently, Molly, usually, and often Jane, too; now they were alone together.

As he did at any moment when they weren't actually following the trail of the crimes that had been committed in the village, Charles sensed Edmund's preoccupations returning to him. His silence about them—it did him credit, perhaps, but it was sorrowful to behold.

"Do you know when James will hear the news?" Lenox asked quietly as they walked along.

Though it was dark out, it wasn't too terribly cold. Above them the stars were brilliant as they can be only in the countryside, where the soft whisper of wind in the grass, the motion of the leaves in the trees, seems somehow to make the heavens even more still, more immense, their innumerable scattered lights more mysterious and beautiful.

Edmund waited for a while to respond, eyes on the ground, hands in his trouser pockets. At last, he said, "He may know now." Then he added, "I fear it will be very hard on Teddy."

To an outsider, this would have sounded unkind, but not to Lenox. James had always been more like their Uncle Harold than either of them—sharp-witted, funny, flashy, adventurous, not notably contemplative. He would take his mother's death hard, but on the other hand there was no doubt, either, that he would be able to live past it.

By contrast, Teddy was a vulnerable soul—a thoughtful, worried boy, more inward than his older brother. From what Lenox could tell, this disposition had survived even its immersion in the rough world of the Royal Navy.

"I know," said Lenox.

"They say that you can't protect your children—one of those great saws, you know. It's appalling to find out how true it is."

They approached the gates where Edmund's land began, ahead of them the long, peaceful, tree-lined avenue leading toward the pond and the house. "I'm just so sorry, Edmund, you know. I really am."

"Well, thank you. It's a trial."

"More than that," Lenox said.

Edmund nodded, taking in his words.

Had asking about James and Teddy, Lenox wondered, made things worse? As they came to the door of the house, he feared it had. One thing about Molly was that she had been a person without very many cares—rather like James, now that he came to think of it—and she had always been able to lighten Edmund's mood, whether he was tired from Parliament or cantankerous because they had to be in London.

Who would do that now? For his part, Lenox felt as if he kept making mistakes.

"What's that noise?" Edmund asked, frowning.

Lenox looked toward the house, which was now about a hundred yards off. "Is it music?" he asked.

"I think it is—the piano."

"Waller," said Lenox.

Edmund laughed. "No. Atherton, I imagine, if anyone."

As it happened, they were both wrong. When they came into the front hallway, they heard women's voices from the long drawing room, and when they entered it they found, sitting together at the piano, mauling a sprightly waltz for four hands, Lady Jane and Toto.

"Jane!" said Lenox.

"Toto, too," said Toto.

Lenox laughed. "My goodness, how are you both? Why are you here?"

"We took a train earlier this evening," said Jane, who had risen up and was coming across to them. "London seemed too quiet once the party was over." She embraced Lenox, then Edmund.

"Not quite the thing, living plain old life without a royal in sight," said Toto. "And on top of that, we were desperate to go to Jane's brother's ball in two nights. It's been years since an overweight country gentleman trod on my feet. I intend to make McConnell very jealous."

"I'd forgotten the ball. Is Sophia here?"

"Oh, yes, and George, too, both asleep in the

nursery," said Jane. "The servants looked pretty het up about having to help us, especially because both girls were crying and miserable by the time we arrived, since it was past their bedtimes. But Edmund, can you hold all of us?"

"Of course," he said, and he was smiling. "It will be a pleasure to hear the girls' footsteps."

"Well, until they step in mud and then go into the Palladian room," Toto said. "On the other hand, I bet we can solve all your murders."

"That will be convenient," Lenox said.

"It's not even a murder yet," Edmund put in. "Our mayor is still alive. Touch wood he may be come the morning."

"Anyhow, let's skip all that now. Could we have supper?" Jane asked. "Mr. Waller said it was ready. I'm famished. The royals ate all the food before I could have any, and there wasn't a tea cart on the train."

CHAPTER THIRTY-FIVE

The next morning at eight o'clock, Mr. Chapman, from Tattersall's, knocked on the door at the jail. Clavering let him in, and before they had even introduced themselves, Lenox and Edmund heard him say, "Yes, that's him."

He was looking at Calloway. "Are you sure?" Clavering asked. "This fellow in the jail cell?"

"Yes, not a doubt of it. He sold me the horses. He's welcome to return my sixty pounds any time, too."

"You're welcome not to buy stolen horses," said Clavering.

"Well," said Chapman, stiffly, "that's him. Will that be all?"

"Mr. Calloway, do you recognize this man?" asked Clavering.

Calloway was sitting up in his cell, reading an old newspaper that Bunce, in a moment of kindness, must have passed him. There was a roll and a cup of tea mostly eaten and drunk up next to him.

Unsurprisingly, Calloway didn't respond, and after repeating the question and waiting for a moment, Clavering sighed and thanked the horse auctioneer for coming to Markethouse.

After he was gone, Lenox said, "Mr. Calloway,

you do know we have enough evidence to hang you now. I hope you appreciate how serious your position is."

Calloway looked at them steadily, as if to say they ought to go ahead and hang him, then. He would buy the rope.

They had already been to see Pointilleux that morning. After asking where he could order in coffee and a sandwich from, he had shooed them away. Miss Harville, Stevens's secretary, had been helping him, which was surprising. Then again, Pointilleux was a handsome lad.

Now they went to see Mrs. Agatha Browning. As they had come into the village that morning—by carriage, in case they needed to move quickly—Edmund had told him that Agatha Browning was a widow, nearly eighty, the mother of nine, grandmother of thirty-odd, who was related in one way or another to nearly every other person in Markethouse.

She answered the door of her small thatch-roofed house herself, a wiry, clear-eyed, gray-haired woman, very thin, in a loose shift, not bent even slightly by age. "Hello, Sir Edmund," she said. "Charles Lenox, I doubt you'll remember me, but you once danced with my daughter Eliza, when she was eight, and you were eighteen. She never forgot it. I'm so pleased you've come back to stay."

"Ah, thank you, but in fact—"

"Come in, though, come in. It's brisk this morning, and I'm an old woman."

They went into her immaculate little sitting room, which had a silver spoon over the fireplace, and a knitted sampler next to it: a room of utter respectability. She served them tea in small blue cups, very sweet, too, whether they took it that way or not.

Edmund told her they were there to ask about Calloway. Lenox had expected some resistance— a hard, appraising eye, of the sort a detective grew used to, some stubbornness—but she was only too pleased to talk. Perhaps it was because Edmund, belonging to the village, in a way belonged to her.

"George Calloway was born here about ten years after I was. He's had a hard enough passage, I suppose. His father was a grain merchant."

"Do you ever remember him being violent?" asked Edmund.

"No, I don't, and I wouldn't have picked him for it, either, though I've been surprised too often by people in life to be surprised by them anymore, because they're all so surprising, all of them."

Lenox smiled. "That sounds like a riddle."

She returned his smile and said, "Well, anyhow, you know what I mean."

"When did he become so isolated?"

At that question she shook her head, and her

face grew grimmer. "After Catherine died, his wife. She was a lovely girl. Catherine Adams, as she was. Beautiful dark hair."

"*Adams,* did you say?"

"Yes, why?"

"Any relation to Elizabeth Watson or Claire Adams?"

"Why, their oldest sister."

Lenox and Edmund exchanged a look. Then Lenox said, "But Atherton told us that she had brought money into the marriage."

"Oh, no, quite the opposite. He did. She was poor but very lovely. Calloway was an introspective, quiet young fellow—no interest in continuing in the grain business after his father died, and not very many friends. But he had been left very well off by his parents, and selling the business left him even better off, and he fell head over heels for Catherine. It took time to convince her, but after he did, they had a happy marriage. One daughter, Liza. Then Catherine died very suddenly, and right away George Calloway began to act oddly. Liza went to Norfolk after only a month or two. His family thought it best. She would have been fifteen or sixteen then."

"His family?"

"Yes, he had a lot of cousins in Norfolk, who took her in. She made a very good marriage, actually—a fellow with the East India Company,

I believe his name was . . . oh, my mind . . . oh, yes, Evans. Mr. Evans. They live in Bengal. A bit of a shame for her to be so far, with her father in this state, but she was always much closer to her mother. It was hard on both of them."

"And he became a hermit?"

"He still comes to market. I see him there. He began taking a great interest in his garden. It was, oh, eight or nine years ago that he stopped touching his hat to me—that he became really very mad, you know, twitching, unhappy, shy. So he got his nickname. If I recall correctly it was actually one of the Watson boys who gave it to him, his own relatives, by marriage."

"How on earth can you recall that?"

Mrs. Browning raised her eyebrows philosophically. "It's a small town."

Lenox shook his head, marveling. When he had traveled on the *Lucy*, he had picked up a saying from the sailors: *When an old sailor dies, a library burns to the ground.* Here was an old woman with a thousand histories at her fingertips, not a gossip, really, but rather a storehouse, an institute, a repository of all their memories, here on this little scrap of the world's land. Part of him wanted to stay and talk to her for the whole day.

"Who were his other connections?" Lenox asked. "Besides the Watsons?"

She frowned. "Well—all of us, in a way. My

husband used to invite him for a pint after Catherine Calloway died, but he stopped saying yes to that quickly, very quickly. There are no other Calloways left. His father's brother has probably been dead thirty years. But a great deal of cousinage, as you might imagine."

"Do you know of any connection between him and Stevens Stevens?" Lenox asked.

For the first time, she hesitated—not out of discretion, but because her memory was inexact. They watched her think. "You'll have to let me remember," she said. "I think there must be some connection there, but I can't—I'm running through Stevens's family in my head, and none of them are related to a Calloway or a Watson, not the Edgars, not the Greshams, so it must be . . . no, you'll have to let me try to remember. It will come to me. Some slight connection, though, I'm sure . . . Calloway and Stevens . . ."

"I'm sorry to trouble you."

"It's only that I hate not remembering."

"Is there anyone who might have spoken with Calloway recently?" Edmund asked. "To whom he might have confided?"

Mrs. Browning shook her head. "I know he stopped talking to the Watsons even before he stopped talking to me—his wife's own family. As I say, he was always a peculiar, inward sort of man. Catherine's death was the ruin of him. And now I think he must have gone actually mad—if it's true, that is, if he's attacked the mayor."

"He says he has."

"So it's true? He spoke to you?"

Lenox shifted uneasily in his chair. "I would appreciate it if you kept that to yourself."

"Oh, of course," she responded. "I may seem like a chatterer, Mr. Lenox, but rest assured, I can keep silent. I'm only speaking so openly because I know you need help."

"Thank you," Edmund said.

"Of course. You know, Lady Lenox was a wonderful woman, I always said that."

"She was, that's true," said Edmund.

"Did you know she was teaching the Coxe family to read?" asked Agatha Browning, and looked only a little surprised when first Lenox, and then even Edmund, had to laugh at her improbable breadth of knowledge.

CHAPTER THIRTY-SIX

When they returned to the jailhouse, they found Clavering with Dr. Stallings. "Mr. Stevens is awake," he informed them.

"Awake!" Edmund cried.

"Has he spoken yet?" asked Lenox.

Stallings shook his head. "I fear that speech is still a ways off, but I am heartened by his progress. I give credit to your friend from London, Dr. McDonald."

"McConnell."

"Excuse me—McConnell. He prescribed a very mild dose of phosphorous given in beef soup, and I would swear that the patient's pulse has grown stronger since I gave it to him."

"That is excellent news. The moment he can speak, please ask him who his attacker was."

Stallings looked doubtful. "Calm is probably for the best, at least until he is much stronger."

"Use your judgment, I suppose," said Lenox. "It would be very useful to hear the answer."

A woman or a child. McConnell's description of the attacker: Might it prove as incisively given as his prescription for the wounds of the man who had been attacked? Was Calloway protecting one of the sisters of his late, beloved wife, either Elizabeth Watson, Hadley's charwoman, or Claire Adams, who cleaned the town hall?

Although Claire Adams had an alibi, from the family for which she cleaned. It was Elizabeth Watson who did not. But she could scarcely have mistaken Hadley's house for Stevens's.

A few minutes later, as Clavering was telling them in a low whisper about what Calloway's confession would mean for his trial, there was another knock on the jailhouse door. It was Arthur Hadley who came in.

"Gentlemen," he said, "I came as soon as I returned to the village. I apologize for having left. Word had spread to the pub in Chichester Tuesday evening about the drawing on the wall of Stevens's office, and I admit that the fear I felt kept me away."

"Where are your gemstones, may I ask?" said Lenox.

"In a deposit box in the London branch of the Dover Assurance, under lock and key, and two stories beneath street level."

"An intelligent measure," Lenox said, "though, as it happens, I no longer feel any anxiety on their behalf."

"No?"

Lenox explained his theory of Hadley's case—and as the pieces clicked into place, one by one, a powerful inner emancipation played out across the insurance salesman's features. A mistake, all a mistake. What a relief. At the end of Lenox's explanation Hadley looked five years younger than he had at the start.

"Stevens, though, that's terribly unlucky," he said, barely managing to keep the absolute delight out of his voice. In fairness, he'd just had a stay of execution, for all he knew. His sympathy was at least partly sincere. There were few men on earth who wouldn't rather their neighbor's skin be at risk than their own. "Will he live?"

"We hope so," said Edmund. "He's at least awake."

"I'll go by and see him. He was very decent to me when I first came to Markethouse."

After he left, the three sat and talked for a while. The word "jailhouse" sounded rather severe, but between them Clavering and Bunce had made it a homey little place, with a teakettle in the corner, bits and bobs and old bottles of beer on the scarred desk, newspapers here and there, and a dozen candle stubs, all of it warm enough that the actual cell almost became an afterthought. Edmund, Clavering, and Lenox sat for a comfortable hour, drinking strong tea and discussing the case.

Comfortable, but also not very useful, Lenox knew, and after a while, with a sigh, he stood up. There was still much to do, if he suspected that Calloway was not telling the whole truth.

As he stood up he realized that there was still a

telegram in his pocket. Mrs. Appleby had given him three the day before, one from Jane, one from the Dover Assurance. The third had been sent in at Chancery Lane—Dallington. Lenox had left it for later, and now found that later had come. He opened it.

All here very glum STOP Lacker approached with password STOP by of all people Chadwick STOP good news is was held and admitted only three names STOP still rotten thing dash it STOP no criminal charges Polly and I couldn't bring selves STOP Jukes burst into tears but cannot see how can be kept STOP muller case proceeds promisingly STOP more on it soon STOP best all there STOP

Lenox's face must have fallen as he read this, because Edmund looked at him with concern.

"What is it, Charles? Not bad news, I hope?"

"Oh, of a sort," replied Lenox. He explained: Chadwick and Jukes were the two boys who worked in the office in Chancery Lane. Both had been living on the streets and running farthing errands, including occasionally for Lenox or Dallington and Polly, which was how they had gotten their jobs. They were the two who, upon finding regular work at the agency, had used their first pay to buy the hats of which they were

286

so inordinately proud. "One of them has betrayed us to LeMaire and Monomark."

"How do you know?"

"We left out a false letter, with the name of a lawyer and a password to give him in order to see our full list of clients. In fact it was only Lacker—and Chadwick came to him, I guess."

"And the other boy?"

Lenox passed the telegram. "You can see for yourself."

Edmund read it. "Very hard on him, if he didn't know anything, this Jukes."

"I know it. But Dallington's right, what other option do we have?"

Edmund frowned. "I suppose. I wonder what he means, too, that the Muller case is coming along."

While they had been obsessed with the events of Markethouse, the world, Lady Jane had told them the night before, had redoubled its own obsession with the missing German pianist; there was no other subject in any society now, high or low. The royals themselves had asked Jane if Lenox had any particular information on the matter.

"I wonder myself," said Lenox. "I wish this were solved so I could go up this moment."

"And miss Houghton's ball?" said Edmund.

"I would be willing to forgo even that very great joy."

At that moment, a hoarse voice spoke behind them—Calloway, whom they had all almost forgotten was present.

Clavering looked up from the paperwork he was doing at his desk. "What was that?" he said.

"I asked what's become of the dog," said Calloway.

"How did you come by that dog anyhow?" Clavering replied.

Calloway didn't respond, merely stared at them. At last, Lenox said, "He's been returned to Mr. Mickelson, I believe."

"His owner," Clavering added belligerently.

Calloway nodded once and then looked away from them and toward the one small window of his cell, set high in the wall and barred. They all looked at him expectantly, waiting for him to speak again, but he didn't—not even after Clavering tried to prod him into speech with a few harmless questions about his garden.

Why did he care about that dog? Lenox wondered. Why had he taken it in the first place?

Just then the door of the jailhouse opened again. This time it was Pointilleux, bleary-eyed, with his black hair pushed up in a stiff wave. "How are you, gentlemen?" he said.

Clavering stood up. "Let's go next door, just to be safe."

They went into a small cloakroom through the door, out of Calloway's earshot, where they stood, huddled among their own jackets, and the boots and whistles of all the volunteer night watchmen.

Lenox noticed that Pointilleux was holding a notebook. "I believe I have now consume every paper in this office," said the young Frenchman.

"You must be very full," Lenox said.

"Excuse me?"

"Nothing, nothing."

"Did you sleep?" asked Edmund wonderingly.

"Not yet I have not."

"Never mind that," said Lenox, who was less solicitous than his brother of Pointilleux's health. "What did you find?"

"I find something, I believe. A connection between Mr. Calloway and Mr. Stevens."

CHAPTER THIRTY-SEVEN

The sheet of paper Pointilleux passed Lenox was a list in three columns. Clavering and Edmund crowded around to look over his shoulder as he read it.

Harville	44 p.a./quarterly	3/9/75
Barth	46 p.a./quarterly	30/1/73
Snow	41 p.a./quarterly	22/12/72
Tuttle	36 p.a./quarterly	4/5/69
Ainsworth	35 p.a./quarterly	27/4/69
Moore	36 p.a./quarterly	14/2/66
Calloway	34 p.a./quarterly	21/7/65
Sather	30 p.a./quarterly	11/11/61
Claxton	55 p.a./semi-annually	9/1/57
French	55 p.a./semi-annually	6/12/54

Lenox read the list twice and felt his mind prodding the case at its edges, looking for where this information might fit into it.

"This is a simplify copy I have construct," Pointilleux said. "In the book, the ledger, each name takes one page, and the salary payment are recorded by quarter, by date."

"These must be his secretaries," Edmund said. "Miss Harville top of the list and most recent."

"I think so, too," Pointilleux said.

"Does this mean Calloway was his secretary?" asked Edmund.

"Not Calloway. Calloway's daughter, perhaps, or another relative?" said Lenox. "Stevens only hires women."

Clavering corrected him. "Now he does, but French and Claxton are both men. French still lives in town here—seen his way to a fair-sized trading company, furniture, makes a very handsome set of chairs, too."

"Well, that explains that," said Lenox. "Stevens hired women because he could pay them less. Look, Miss Harville still isn't making what Mr. French did in 1854, twenty-three years ago."

Edmund shook his head. "It may be Calloway's daughter was Stevens's secretary eleven years ago, then, for about eight months. She left his employment, it looks like, around the time that her mother died, and her father went mad—and she went to live in Norfolk. I don't see what it has to do with this attack."

Neither did Lenox. He kept thinking of Elizabeth Watson. Was it possible his theory of the break-in at Hadley's was wrong? That it wasn't a mistake?

"Clavering," he said, "who is this—Ainsworth? She only worked for Stevens for a few weeks."

The constable's face fell. "That was sad, that, Sarah Ainsworth. She was a troubled girl from the start, though. Clever, which was why Stevens took her on. But she disappeared one night, run away to London, we always heard. Her mother was proper heartbroken over it. The daughter hasn't been back since."

"Are any of these people related to Watson?" asked Lenox.

Clavering took the list and scrutinized it, then shook his head. "No. All of these young girls are from the more educated classes than Claire and Elizabeth—respectfully meant, you know."

"Another excuse to pay them less, perhaps, if they came from comfortable families," said Edmund.

Lenox nodded. "There's another name I know here, too. Snow. If that's Adelaide Snow, I met her outside of the village."

"It must be her, I believe," said Edmund.

"We might call on her. I've been meaning to quiz that family about their gamekeeper's cottage." He looked over at Pointilleux, who was following the conversation. "Very well done. Was there anything else?"

"No. I still peruse the papers, however."

"Good—stick at it. Thank you."

With a flourish of his hand, Pointilleux said, "It is my job."

They bundled into the carriage then, and went to visit Snow.

He lived in a handsome two-story limestone house, albeit one with various barns and outbuildings visible from its front steps—a working farm. An elderly housekeeper answered the door. Snow himself was not in, she told Lenox and Edmund, but Miss Snow was, yes.

In the drawing room where she received them, Lenox found that she was the same pretty fifteen-year-old girl he had met on the lane just outside of Markethouse, with a naturally happy expression on her face—a person young, confident, eager to be pleased by life.

She welcomed them with very ladylike grace (he remembered Edmund calling her father "rough," but apparently none of his manner had descended to his progeny) and introduced them to her darker-haired cousin, Helena Snow, who was staying at the house for two weeks. They had been in the midst of a game of backgammon, the older about to gammon the younger.

"She has come at a very thrilling time," said Adelaide, "to what I had assured her was the least interesting village in England. You have arrested Mr. Calloway?"

"Yes, how is he?" asked Helena Snow, the cousin. "I hope he is not confined to a dungeon somewhere."

"Quite the contrary," said Edmund. "He is very comfortable—altogether comfortable."

"Is he provendered?" she asked anxiously.

"Certainly—food brought in from the public house next door."

She looked relieved. "Good," she said.

Adelaide Snow said, "And are you quite sure he's the one who did it?"

Lenox inclined his head politely but ambiguously and said, redirecting the conversation, "I understand that you worked as a secretary to Mr. Stevens?"

"That! Yes, I did. I have some talent for numbers. But I couldn't stick it out. I didn't like the job."

"No?"

"I suppose I'm an airy, head-in-the-clouds sort of person, and it wasn't for me. I hope Miss Harville does enjoy it. I gave her fair warning that she might not. I'm happier back in school. It's quite a good school—and I only go two days a week, so I can be here with Papa most of the time."

"Did Mr. Calloway and Mr. Stevens have any contact in the short time you worked for the mayor?"

She shook her head. "I would recall seeing Mad—seeing Mr. Calloway. It was a very brief time, as you noticed, Mr. Lenox."

"Miss Snow," said Edmund, "this is your land. Have you noticed anyone odd on it, in the time that your gamekeeper's cottage had its stowaway?"

Adelaide Snow looked at her cousin, uneasy for the first time. "Go on," said the older cousin, encouragingly.

The girl shook her head. "It will sound peculiar, but I did, once, see a man walking across just that part of my father's land, near the game-keeper's cottage. At the time, I didn't think anything of it. All walkers have the right of way, of course. It was only after the attack on Mr. Stevens that I thought anything of it."

"Did you recognize the person?"

"Well, that's just it. I didn't *think* I had recognized him. But the more I thought about it, the more I thought that perhaps it might just have been—well, Mr. Stevens himself."

Lenox looked at her, surprised. "Near the gamekeeper's cottage! How confident do you feel in that guess?"

"Only a bit. And yet I would have said it was him—I would say it was him. But he couldn't have been staying in the cottage himself, could he? It seems impossible."

"He might have been meeting someone there," said Edmund. "Calloway, for instance."

Lenox asked several more questions, Edmund occasionally interjecting. They stayed for another twenty minutes, teasing out the details of Adelaide Snow's memory. After a while Snow himself came in—a stringy, singularly ugly man, whose face softened out of recognition when he spied his daughter.

Soon after he had entered, Lenox rose, saying that they ought to go. He badly wanted to speak to Elizabeth Watson. He could sense that he was close to the solution now. Perhaps very close.

He thanked Adelaide Snow and then added, "Incidentally, if you have time, I'm sure you would both be very welcome at my brother-in-law's house tomorrow night. He's having a ball. With your father's consent, obviously."

"The Earl of Houghton?" said Adelaide incredulously. Her cousin's eyes widened, too. "Are you quite sure?"

"By all means," said Lenox.

After some further cavil, made solely out of propriety, both cousins agreed, happily—the father, less happily. When they had left, Edmund asked him if he ought to have done that. Lenox replied that it would do Houghton's wife good to have something to complain about, and they were very nice girls, a demographic often in short supply at Houghton's balls as he recalled, and anyhow everything was much looser in the country, wasn't it?

CHAPTER THIRTY-EIGHT

Hadley himself opened the door to the little house in Potbelly Lane. "Hello, gentlemen!" he said welcomingly. "Please come in, please. I cannot tell you how happy you have made me with your conclusions, Mr. Lenox. Even now I am restoring some of the collection I had to leave here to their superb little display cases. Would you like to see them, I wonder?"

They then passed the most stultifying forty seconds of Lenox's life, pretending to be fascinated by what looked like a piece of common granite, but which Hadley assured them was a rare and invaluable example of something-or-other-in-Latin.

"Mr. Hadley," said Lenox as soon as he decently could, "I wonder whether we could have a word with Mrs. Watson?"

"Mrs. Watson? Of course! She's in the kitchen. You know the way, if you would like to speak to her privately."

"That would be ideal—thank you so much." Seeing from Hadley's face that he had been abrupt, he added, "I hope we may hear more about your collection at a moment when our time is more our own. You understand, of course."

Mollified, the insurance salesman nodded. "I do, gentlemen, indeed I do."

The charwoman was polishing a silver teapot. Lenox and Edmund greeted her and asked whether they might have a moment of conversation, to which she assented.

Not altogether happily, Lenox noted. The first question he asked was whether she had had any contact with Mr. Stevens in her life.

"Only to see at the market, sir," she answered, "or I suppose I must have seen him about the hustings, election time."

"Has your sister told you anything about him? About interacting with him at the town hall?"

She shook her head. "She goes in after everyone's gone for the evening, you know."

"And yet Stevens worked long hours sometimes." Without a direct question to answer, she looked unsure of how to reply, and Lenox forged on. "Are you close with Mr. Calloway?"

Her face took on a look of pity. "We tried to be family to him, after my sister died, poor Cat. She was a ray of light, that one."

"He rejected your friendship?"

"For a year or two he would sit down to a glass of wine with us, right enough. But in the end he lost his mind, did Calloway. Never had a *very* firm grip on it to start with, mind."

"Do you know of any reason he would attack Stevens?"

"I've been puzzling over that all morning myself," she said.

"Could it have been for you, or for your sister?"

She laughed with disbelief. "For us? He wouldn't open the door of his 'ouse for us."

After this response, Lenox asked her to look over the list of Stevens's secretaries. It became clear very quickly that she couldn't read, however—and equally clear that she would stand there till the final battle between good and evil on the day of judgment rather than admit it—so Lenox took the list back and read her the names.

She knew all of them; her face screwed up in anger and pity at the name Ainsworth. But she didn't have anything particularly useful to say. She wasn't related to any of them.

Lenox paused. "This is a small town, Mrs. Watson," he said, "so I will come out with it plain. You are connected to Mr. Stevens and Mr. Calloway in a dozen different ways. Both you and your sister, in our conversations, seem to me not to have a great affection for the mayor. The mayor—who has been attacked. I'd feel more comfortable if I knew why."

This gambit of openness, Lenox saw almost as soon as he started speaking, was destined to fail utterly. A pitiless blankness descended on the maid's features. "Don't have any feeling about him one way nor the other, sir," she said. "I'm sure I wish him quite recovered."

The repudiation in her voice was absolute. By asking about her sons, Edmund managed to bring her around to a better humor before they left, but a last casual question about Stevens from Charles elicited no further information.

Peculiar, peculiar.

They were standing out on Potbelly Lane in the brisk air a few moments later, looking up and down the cobblestoned street. The sky was white, wan, a net of birds rising from a field and turning across it as they looked toward the countryside. Lenox sighed.

"What now?" asked Edmund.

Lenox stood still for a moment, thinking. Then he said, "Let's walk back to the house. I would like to sit alone with a pot of tea and think for a few hours."

"Why? Do you have an idea of who did it?"

Lenox shook his head. "No. And yet I'm sure that I also know exactly who did it, if I can merely piece all of the clues together and realize that I know it! Something . . . something about the whole business . . . something about Miss Snow and Mrs. Watson . . . and Miss Harville . . ."

Edmund waited patiently after he trailed off, and remained mostly silent as they walked across the town and out across the field toward Lenox House, blessedly. Lenox was deep in thought. Back at the house he gave quick, distracted kisses to Sophia and Lady Jane, said hello to Toto and

George, and then, mumbling his excuses, made immediately for his father's old chess room.

Charles and Edmund's father had been a devoted chess player; his fiercest lifelong opponent had been an illiterate farmer named Paxton, who had come up to this room every few evenings for thirty years. It was an odd, very small chamber on the second story, barely more than a closet, with just space enough for two chairs and a tiny table, inlaid with a chessboard—but it had a vast window and, sitting near the corner of the house, gave a long and beautiful view of the dipping and rising green countryside.

Lenox sat down in the chair closer to the door, with the view. Edmund had left the room exactly as their father had had it, though he wasn't a chess player himself. After a few minutes Waller came up with the pot of strong tea that Lenox had asked for and set it down. Lenox stood up and cracked the window, which let in a bracing coolness. Then he poured himself a cup of tea, added sugar and milk to it—and set about considering the case.

There were many aspects of it that he pondered. A few kept returning to him.

Adelaide Snow, for instance, saying *I would recall seeing Mad—seeing Mr. Calloway.*

Calloway's behavior; and the behavior, too, of both his sisters-in-law.

Those library books.

That terrible drawing on the steps to Hadley's house; on the wall of Stevens's office.

Paxton had been a superior player—Lenox's father would have been lucky to get three out of ten games from him—and as Lenox fiddled with the chess pieces, thinking, he felt a burst of love and fondness for his father, who would come downstairs with his rueful smile and see Paxton off, promising his revenge next time. They'd been friends, though they'd spent most of their lives in such different ways, Lenox's father with the great men of the land, Paxton amid turnips and pigs.

Now they were both gone. How was it possible? It was amazing how real the dead could seem, as if they might walk in from the next room. Where had they gone? When would they come back? Why shouldn't they sit at this table again, each smoking, Charles's father in his red evening jacket, Paxton in his heavy brown cardigan, pondering their respective strategies? It was so strange. When his father had died, a great comfort had gone out of life, and being back here made him see that, and made him pity James and Teddy for losing their mother. To have Jane was an enormous consolation, but a parent—while one's parents were alive, if they were decent parents, one was always at least in some small part of one's self protected from life, from fear, from reality.

Lenox thought of Molly, and then of the line, the greatest line written by an Englishman between Chaucer and Shakespeare: *O death, thou comest when I least expected thee.*

He made his way through cup after cup of tea, sitting there in silence, staring into the countryside. It grew dimmer and then dark. The hours passed.

When at last he stood up, it wasn't with a snap of recognition, or a revelation—but he had it. He was suddenly extremely tired.

He went downstairs, where his brother, Toto, and Jane were in the long drawing room, chatting amiably. "Charles!" said Jane. "How are you?"

"Oh, fine, thank you," he said, smiling. "Edmund, do you think you might send word asking Mickelson if we could borrow his dog for the day?"

"Sandy? She's not a scenting dog."

"Yes, Sandy, if you wouldn't mind. Unless Stevens steps to it, I suspect it's that dog who will tell us the truth at last."

CHAPTER THIRTY-NINE

Lenox spent the whole next morning with Sophia. It was still just warm enough that they could comfortably clomp around the dewy fields in their boots, kicking up puddles. They visited the horses in the stables and had a walk around the pond—terrifying several hapless ducks as they went—before settling in to a long spell of picking themselves apples from the trees on the west side of the house. They threw the bad ones at a stump nearby, which was satisfying.

He had refused at breakfast to tell Edmund his suspicions, just as he had refused the night before. "I'm probably wrong," he said.

"Is it Calloway?" asked Edmund. "Just tell me if it's Calloway. I'm the one who told you about the mint and marjoram, after all."

"That's very true," said Lenox, "but I don't want to say anything. Just be patient a little while longer."

"You're a bore," said Lady Jane. "And if you know who did it, oughtn't you be out putting them in jail? The public's safety is in danger."

"The public will survive another day," said Lenox.

After lunch, when Sophia went up to the nursery to have her afternoon nap, he did go into town.

Edmund was busy catching up on a great deal of the estate's business—what he had returned to Markethouse to do in the first place—so Lenox went alone. He took possession of Sandy, Mickelson's spaniel, from his owner, and went to see Clavering in the jail.

The constable continued to look besieged. "Mad Calloway still won't say a word more," he told Lenox, "and I would swear that he's laughing at us—daring us to hang him."

They were standing on the porch of the Bell and Horns, which blazed with the welcoming light of several fireplaces from its small windows. "I think I may be able to settle his hash," Lenox said, "with the help of the dog."

"Are you sporting with me, Mr. Lenox?"

"You have my solemn word that I am not. But listen—will you get Claire Adams and Elizabeth Watson for me, a little bit later on, and Miss Harville, too?"

"Arrest them? Claire Adams has an alibi, for one."

"No—not arrest them. But I would like to speak with all of them this evening."

They fleshed out the details of the plan, and then Lenox walked with the spaniel down to Dr. Stallings's house. There he learned that Stevens had relapsed into something that looked like a coma.

"Will he die soon?"

"I would have said he would be likely to die yesterday," said Stallings, "and then he woke up briefly—and now—well, I cannot say. Nobody could say. It is all contingent."

"I wish he might wake up," said Lenox, shaking his head. "It would be enormously helpful."

Stallings frowned. "No doubt of some personal consequence to Mr. Stevens himself, too."

"Yes. Of course—of course."

He made his way home with Sandy, tipping his cap at the window of the barbershop, where old Mr. Widaman was apparently still shaving people—though his hand couldn't have gotten steadier since Lenox had been a boy, when he had already seemed of a very advanced age. In the window of the shop there was a card that said, in bold letters:

PURE GREASE OF A LARGE FINE BEAR!

Which meant that old canard had migrated from London out at least to the Home Counties. Ten to one it was plain old cooking grease. It was considered an extremely sophisticated thing to have in your hair, bear grease, but bears were not so very common, whereas grease was. From time to time one saw an actual bear in the window of a barbershop in the West End, with the promise that this was the bear to be killed for its grease later that week. Lenox was convinced that there was only one bear, who moved from shop to shop and would live to a fine old age—not unlike Lady Jane's theory that there were fifty fruit-cakes in the whole of England, and everyone kept passing them around to each other, year after year, at Christmastime.

At home, he found his wife writing letters in the quiet, light-filled front drawing room. Toto had retired; she always rested after her midday meal.

"Tell me about the party, then," he said, as she sealed an envelope.

He was in an armchair next to the delicate walnut desk where she was sitting, and she smiled. "I wish you had been there—it was very fun. Though I'm afraid the sherbet was not all I could have wished. Toto agreed, she called it lackluster."

"Shakespeare invented that word, you know."

Lady Jane nodded. "He was pretty bright. Any-how, it wasn't very cheerful to serve lackluster sherbet to three royals—but on the other hand the soup was the most delicious soup I ever had, and everyone did get along famously. And then, of course, sherbet is not very important when you consider the children of the hospital. So I say, forget about the sherbet, life is too short."

Lenox laughed, and asked another question about the party, and soon they were rattling along in conversation, trading names, their acquain-tances—and more importantly their opinions of their acquaintances—so familiar to them that the conversation would barely have been comprehensible to an outsider. After a few minutes they turned to Sophia, and whether her nose was a little runny, whether she had outgrown a certain wooden toy, all the minor subjects that make having a child together so fascinating. Having already loved each other, Charles and Jane, he had nevertheless found, to his surprise, that by becoming parents, they had reached a different level of affinity he hadn't expected, a whole unexplored variety of friendship and attachment.

After some time had passed, Jane said that she thought she had better prepare herself for the ball now. A woman would be coming from the village shortly to sew her and Toto into their dresses, and there was her hair to be done, too.

"The seamstress was Molly's particular friend, I believe," said Lady Jane. "Edmund recommended her very strongly."

"How does he seem to you?"

She hesitated. "I think, very close to giving up," she said. "He is still friendly and lovely. But I don't . . . I don't know. I wonder when James and Teddy will return."

"So do I. Soon, I think."

"That will be very hard." She was silent for a moment and then said, "I wish there were something else we could do for him."

"At least we're here," said Lenox.

"And yet I wonder if he wouldn't be better off in London," Jane replied. "For its being less associated with Molly in his mind."

"Do you think so?"

She sighed, then smiled sadly. "I just don't know."

The next few hours were very busy for Toto and Jane, and very idle for Lenox and Edmund, who went out and looked at the horses—Daisy was back, and Lenox had hopes of riding her in the morning—and then, at six o'clock or so, quickly changed into their dinner jackets. So dressed, they spent a profitable fifteen minutes entertaining Sophia and George (Lenox saw some fleeting joy in Edmund's face when he made his niece laugh) and then went downstairs to have a glass of hot wine and wait to leave.

"Go on, Charles, do tell me," said Edmund. "Haven't we been in it from the start?"

Lenox realized he had a point. "All right, then," he said.

He told Edmund what he thought—and his brother, brow darkening, listened attentively and then asked a few pointed questions. When these were answered he shook his head. "A black business."

"Yes, I think so."

"We ought to go soon. I'll just check that the dog is in the carriage."

Lenox nodded. "Good."

CHAPTER FORTY

The house in which Lady Jane had grown up was very grand and beautiful. It was situated on a rising hillside, giving views of its crenellations from a long way off, as well as the Capability Brown gardens that descended the hillside in front of it.

"Wellington turned down the first house they offered him after the war because it was on a hill," Edmund observed as they came within sight of it. "He thought it would be bad for his horses."

"Wellington was a fool," she said. "What kind of sledding could he have had for his children without a hill?"

"He also said in public that he wasn't the least in love with his first wife," Toto put in. "I remember reading that. 'I married her because they asked me to do it.' Can you imagine saying such a thing! I'm against him forever, just for that."

"He did win the Battle of Waterloo," Lenox pointed out.

"That was *ages* ago," replied Toto.

"Still, it was pretty well managed."

"Well, perhaps," she conceded.

As they approached Houghton Manor, ablaze

with light and ringing with faint music, they continued to talk. In the back of Lenox's mind, however, the case was always present. He suspected the same was true of Edmund. Sandy was riding up on the box with the driver, barking at every bird and beast they passed.

It was those drawings, in chalk and then blood, that had finally settled it for him, he thought.

They were a bit early, as suited the house's daughter, and Jane led them from the carriage into the sumptuous front hallway. It was lined with servants; she helloed them, smiling, and they nodded or curtsied their greetings to her.

"Where is my brother?" she asked.

The earl was in his library, they learned, and they found him sitting there and sipping a brandy, poring over the newspaper.

"Hello, Houghton, you layabout," said Jane affectionately, embracing him and then leaning back with a hand on his cheek to look at him more closely. "I do hope you've been well. I missed you."

"Is that a dog?"

"Yes, it is. Are you a natural historian now too? We need somewhere to put him during the party."

The earl, who had stood up, considered this for a moment. He had a look of happiness on his face, a younger brother from whose clever older sister attention has not always been automatic.

"The kitchen is boiling hot," he said. "We can put him there. But I say, welcome home, Jane. I want to show you the ripping new wallpaper we have in your room now. I chose it myself—very carefully, too, very carefully, and wouldn't let the paper-hanger go till it was smooth."

"I hope it's not ripping already, then," she said.

He laughed. "No, I meant—"

"I know, I know," she said, putting her arm through his and leaning her head against his shoulder. "Let's put this dog in the kitchen—he's a very important dog—and then I want to look."

Half an hour later the ball began, very slowly and then very quickly. First there were one or two people who arrived, removing their fur stoles and coats, calling cheerful country hellos to Houghton, then moving to the ballroom and making it somehow feel emptier and larger by their presence, the half a dozen of them—and then suddenly there were fifty people there, and then a hundred, and then almost an infinite number, in that way parties grow. The line of carriages outside became very long, and their drivers stood in small groups near them, smoking and talking. Lenox saw faces he hadn't seen in years: Matthew Quill, who had lost an incredible fortune at the track and then made it back in shipping; Samantha and Serena Boyer, two witty, aged sisters who had known his mother well; Ellis Fermor, a drunk and a cad, but the most beautiful hand with a cricket bat. New faces, too, pretty young girls, handsome young men. The atmosphere was electric with hope; weeks of anticipation before this evening now culminated in sheer happiness that it had come, and with it the magic of being drawn out of one's routine, the sudden magic of other people. The older men and women lined up near the punch, and the younger ones were already dancing. Through the black windows, rain fell softly on the ground.

Edmund had an official role to play at functions like this—and an official smile, too—but he broke into something like real warmth when Atherton arrived.

"Hullo, Houghton," said Atherton, clapping their host on the shoulder. "How are you off for soap?"

When Adelaide Snow and her cousin Helena arrived, Lenox was sure to be on hand, and he was glad he had thought of it. They both looked tentative, and perhaps just slightly overdressed, but after a moment's conversation their uneasiness melted, and soon Adelaide especially, young, pink-cheeked, and with shining eyes, looked very pleased to be there. Lenox accompanied them into the ballroom and then lost track of them; both were in demand as dance partners.

At a little before eight o'clock he took a glass of champagne from a tray and went into the cloakroom by the front door alone, where he sipped it and watched the drive. Soon he saw what he had expected—Clavering's arrival, in a humble dogcart, with the reedy Bunce near him. Clavering was dressed in his uniform, and had lantern, whistle, and truncheon dangling heavily from his belt.

Lenox greeted them with a smile and ushered them into the small sitting room near the front door that Houghton kept for guests he did not know—a chamber prettily decorated, with oak chairs and a bronze bulldog over the fireplace, but without a single personal memento in it— where he left them with a bottle of wine. A few moments later he returned with the dog, Sandy, and put his lead in Clavering's hand, promising he would come back again soon.

His mind and body were taut as a cello string— from the blended excitements of the champagne, very little food, the warmth of the house, and above all the knowledge that they were close, very close. He felt a tremendous lucidity of thought; there was no doubt of his hypothesis, none at all, he felt.

Back in the enormous ballroom the noise had reached a crescendo. It was nearly impossible to hear the band, in fact, and the dancing had attained a kind of loose, improvisational quality, only faintly connected to the music, perhaps just to its most essential rhythms. Atherton was dancing with Toto, and Edmund with Jane—the formal step, turn, and return of Jane Austen's days, fashionable then, still just clinging to life out in the country. You would never see it in London now.

When the dance was done, Lenox asked Edmund if he wanted to come away for a bit, and his brother, comprehending, said of course, immediately. Together they found Adelaide Snow and her cousin Helena and asked them, cheerfully, if they might be willing to spare a moment of their time.

As they walked through the hallway toward the small sitting room where Clavering, Bunce, and Sandy were waiting, Lenox felt something about this deception—guilt, perhaps, or self-regret, especially with Adelaide Snow talking brightly just at his side about how great the fun of the evening had been so far.

They came to Houghton's little sitting room, and there were four people in it now, arrayed along two dark blue couches: Clavering and Bunce on one, and on the other, faces irritable, as if they quite rightly wondered why they had been compelled to be here, two sisters, Elizabeth Watson and Claire Adams.

Clavering and Bunce rose as Edmund, Charles, and Adelaide and Helena Snow entered. Claire Adams and Elizabeth Watson remained seated—and their faces remained impassive. Lenox glanced at Helena and Adelaide. Their faces, too, were blank. There was perhaps a red color in Adelaide's cheeks.

He drew the door closed behind him softly, waited a beat to see if anybody would say anything, and then, reluctantly, asked Clavering, "In the closet?"

The constable nodded. "Yes."

Adelaide, looking flummoxed, said, "Why have you brought us here, may I ask?"

Lenox went to the closet in the back corner of the room. There was a happy whine behind it, and a scratch of paws on the other side of the door—and when he opened it, Sandy, the springer spaniel, burst out of it.

The dog bolted directly for Helena Snow, Adelaide's quiet older cousin. He was hysterical with happiness—yelping, jumping for her with his front paws up, trying desperately to kiss her hands and her face. And despite what she must have known her position to be, she smiled, half-smiled, and murmured, "Good boy. Good boy."

"Miss Snow," said Lenox, "or Mrs. Watson—Miss Adams—would you like to come clean with us now?"

Elizabeth Watson shook her head, a look of total stupidity on her face. "About what?" she said.

"Yes, about what?" asked Adelaide Snow.

"I'm curious, too," said Edmund.

Lenox inclined his head toward Helena. "This is the person who attacked the mayor of Markethouse, I fear," he said.

"My cousin?" asked Adelaide, her demeanor stubborn but, to Lenox at least, transparent.

"Not your cousin, no. Your father was an orphan, was he not? My brother told me so, anyhow. If that's true you shouldn't have made her a Snow, when you invented her—you should have made her one of your mother's relations."

Clavering, his small round eyes squinched up in confusion, said, "Who is she, then?"

Lenox inclined his head toward the young woman, whom the dog was still happily circling and pawing. "Unless I am mistaken, this young person is Mr. Calloway's daughter, Liza."

CHAPTER FORTY-ONE

There was a moment's pause, and then the young woman burst out, "Well! I am! What of it!"

"Liza, no!" cried Claire Adams.

The young woman tried to hold herself steady, but after a moment she began to weep and fell back into the sofa behind her, hiding her face in the arm. Adelaide—her own face full of sympathy and grief, as if they really were cousins—sat down, too, and put her arm around Liza Calloway's shoulder.

Adelaide glanced up at Lenox with a look of reproach in her eyes, and he felt it fully. He had needed some proof. The dog's reaction had given it to him. Nevertheless, it was cruel to send any person into such collapse.

"At such a lovely ball, too, shame," murmured Elizabeth Watson, as if privy to his thoughts.

It was absurd on its face, if Liza Calloway was guilty of violent assault upon the mayor, and yet there was a kind of county justice in it, too. The feeling of the room—even Clavering and Bunce, even his brother—was against him, not wrongly.

In his boyhood, one of the least reputable streets in Mayfair had been a few blocks down from the family house in London. It was a shabby, paint-chipped little lane, with a cheesemonger, an unsavory pub, and a number of scroungy fourth-rate lodging houses—oh, and at number 10, for it was the street called Downing, the residence of the Prime Minister of Great Britain.

To Lenox, raised in the rigid divisions of country society, by which two neighboring land-owners might not enter each other's houses for forty years because of slightly uneven ancestries, it was enthralling to see how London pushed every kind of person together into cheek-by-jowl life. Gladstone and the boot boy at the pub next door had the same right to the pavement. Downing Street had become more refined since the 1840s—in fact, partly at Gladstone's insistence—but you could still find anyone out upon it at any hour, a merchant, a duke, a vagrant, drunks, priests, bricklayers, paviers, basket-men, a greengrocer, the Prime Minister, a cabman or chimneysweep. A detective. The Queen.

Here, however—well, he had played a London trick on Liza Calloway. The fact was that he bore one of the well-known surnames of Sussex, and now he stood in the sitting room of his brother-in-law, who bore another of those great last names. All of the advantage in the room was his, therefore, and in Markethouse that meant that he had a greater duty to the others than they did to him. Elizabeth Watson was a charwoman, Claire Adams a housemaid, Adelaide Snow the daughter of an orphan, and Liza Calloway was a thready pulse away from being a murderess. He had forgotten—something, *noblesse oblige*, perhaps, you could call it.

"I am sorry to have tricked you, Miss Calloway. I needed to see if the dog would identify you."

Calloway's daughter ignored these words and went on weeping. Edmund handed her his handkerchief. "Would you like a glass of champagne?" he asked. "Or something to eat?"

"Yes, sort her something to eat," said Elizabeth Watson commandingly. Now she, too, had risen and come to the sofa. "She'll feel better."

It took a minute or two for a footman to return with a glass of champagne and a wooden board of cheese, apple, ham, and bread. By this time, Liza Calloway had wiped her tears. She drank a sip of the champagne and nibbled at a small hunk of bread, holding what remained in the fingertips of her two hands and staring at it, as if willing herself not to cry again. And then she did start crying again. Her aunt and Adelaide Snow embraced her.

"Can you explain to us what's happened, Charles?" asked Edmund.

"Miss Calloway, would you like to explain?"

"Mrs. Evans," she said. "My husband's name was Evans—may he rest in peace. He contracted cholera and died last year."

"Mrs. Evans," said Lenox gently. "Would you

care to explain how you've come to return to Markethouse?"

She was silent, though at least she was no longer crying. After a moment, Lenox nodded and began to explain.

"Mr. Calloway may not be a murderer," he said, "but his confession was the most important clue we had about the case. Why? Well, from all we've heard, he has no strong personal ties remaining in Markethouse. He may live here, but his allegiances are dissolved. His wife's family—the wife whom by all accounts he loved passionately—"

"He did," said the daughter of that marriage.

Claire Adams nodded her agreement with this assertion.

"That family, including the two sisters present in this room, had become strangers to him, and though both Elizabeth Watson and Claire Adams seemed to me to bear some personal animus toward Stevens, it was impossible to imagine that Calloway would care enough about their prejudices to act upon them, or to sacrifice himself for either of them.

"Add that, of course, to the other facts that didn't square with the idea of Calloway as the murderer—the use of the gamekeeper's cottage, when he had his own house, the theft of the library books, the map of Markethouse, the mistake of thinking that Stevens still lived in Potbelly Lane, in what is now Mr. Hadley's house. It was clear to me that an outsider to the village was involved."

Calloway's daughter looked up. Though he was old and bearded and mad, it was possible now to see the resemblance between them; both had strong cheekbones and penetrating eyes. Hers were trained on Lenox. "How do you know that I went to Hadley's house?" she asked.

"Hush, Helena," said Adelaide.

"How did Miss Snow come to be involved?" asked Clavering.

"Give me a moment and I'll explain," Lenox said.

The mood of the room had changed. Now they were upon the terrain of firm fact. Sandy was curled up happily at Mrs. Evans's feet, eyes already settling closed in the warmth of the fire. Edmund, standing near the fireplace, was gazing at the scene with a calm, steadying sympathy.

"I asked myself," said Lenox, "whom Calloway might then have cared enough about to protect. He more or less invited us to hang him, after all. And I thought: Who could inspire such a cheerful suicide but a child? I myself am a father—and it is no sacrifice, the idea of sacrificing yourself for a child. Your self doesn't even come into it.

"So it was that I came to the answer: this woman, before you. Mad Calloway's daughter."

"Please don't call him that," she said.

"I apologize. In fact, I remember Miss Snow, Miss Adelaide Snow here, stopping herself just short, yesterday, of saying Mad Calloway, and saying, much more politely, *Mr.* Calloway. It struck me as an odd hitch in her speech at the time, until I realized she was sparing your feelings, Mrs. Evans. I also wondered why you took such a pressing interest in the condition of Calloway's imprisonment, about which you asked us several questions. As a cousin visiting from out of town, you could scarcely have known anything about him. Now, of course, I understand."

"But what was it for?" asked Edmund suddenly. "If Mrs. Evans did indeed attack Stevens, *why?*"

"Ah." Lenox looked at the two young women on the sofa. "There I enter into the realm of speculation. Mrs. Evans?"

She remained silent. Lenox glanced at Adelaide Snow's usually kindly face and was startled to see in it something stony and strange. It took him a moment, but then he realized what it was: rage, sheer rage.

He looked at the two Watson sisters, and upon their faces, too, was deep emotion.

"I suspect that Stevens Stevens is not a—not a good man," he said lamely, and then went on. "Mrs. Evans, Miss Snow, you have both been in his employ. Can you tell us the truth of his character? Of what happened?"

"Never," said Adelaide Snow fiercely. She gripped Liza Calloway's shoulder again. "Just leave us alone. You can't prove a thing."

Lenox glanced at Edmund and raised his eyebrows slightly. He was about to speak again when there was a knock on the door, and then, without waiting for a reply, the knocker pushed it open a few inches. It was Lady Jane.

"Charles, there you are, and Edmund, too," she said. "What have you been doing?"

Despite the circumstances, Adelaide Snow rose to her feet, and Lenox realized that of course his wife was famous in this part of the world. He watched her take in the entire scene with her quick, intelligent gray eyes.

"This is Miss Liza Calloway," he said, "or more properly, Mrs. Evans."

"Ah," said Jane. She still had a hand on the doorway. There was a long pause, and then it was clear that she had apprehended the situation, the tenor of the room, and she said, "Well, perhaps I might sit with you."

It was Edmund who saw the merit of the idea most quickly. He strode forward. "Listen, perhaps all of us had better clear out," he said. "You and I, Charles, and us, Clavering and Bunce. Jane—these young women have had some trial. Ladies, you may speak to my sister-in-law with utter confidence that she will keep your secrets—or not, if you prefer, but at any rate you ought to have a few minutes to yourselves. It's been a difficult night, I'm sure. We'll return in a little while."

CHAPTER FORTY-TWO

They left. Lady Jane was closeted with Adelaide Snow, Liza Calloway, and Elizabeth Watson and Claire Adams for the better part of an hour. Halfway through she came out and told Lenox to go and find Toto for her, which he did. Clavering and Bunce were in the kitchen, eating and drinking; the two brothers sat in the hall outside the room, on a wooden bench beneath a comically bad portrait of the seventh King Henry, waiting. Off to their left was the ceaseless roar of the ball, and behind them the close little room, from which a raised voice would occasionally emerge.

They passed the time first by playing five-across noughts and crosses (Edmund won five games out of fourteen; they drew six; Lenox won three) and then by attempting to throw playing cards into an empty wastebasket across the hallway. Lenox had a blue deck, Edmund a red one, and after each had thrown all of his cards they would go and count up how many of each color was in the basket. They were more or less even, Edmund perhaps edging his younger brother more often than not. His sideways flick of the wrist achieved less glamorous results than Lenox's tomahawk motion—but was more reliable.

He didn't ask about the case until they had been sitting there for forty-five minutes or so. And then all he said was, "Stevens, then—from the sound of it he was a kind of—of vicious exploiter of young women, you believe."

Lenox nodded. "That's my guess."

"How do you know?"

Lenox sighed. "A feeling, I suppose. He hired this long series of young girls as his secretaries, and the list Pointilleux found showed that almost half of them left immediately. Including Miss Adelaide Snow, for example. Do you remember her saying that she hoped Miss Harville enjoyed the job—and then adding, 'I gave her fair warning that she might not'? And don't forget Miss Ainsworth, the young girl Clavering told us disappeared to London after only a few weeks of working for Stevens."

Edmund shook his head, disgust on his face. "It wasn't because it was less expensive to hire women, then, or because he believed them to be more intelligent than men."

"I doubt saving the village fifteen pounds a year was his first priority, in a budget of so many thousands. Though perhaps it added to his pleasure."

"And Miss Calloway—or Mrs. Evans, I suppose we should call her—"

It was then that Lady Jane opened the door. er face was sad, full of concern. "You may come in again, if you like," she said. "I think we can have a reasonable conversation. I've assured them that you're not trying to hound them onto the gallows. I hope I'm right."

"Don't be absurd," said Edmund.

They followed her into the little room, where the four women were sitting as they had been. Toto, perched on a small armchair next to the fire, her arm resting on a card table, had tears on her face, and the spaniel, which was still lying between Liza Calloway's feet, looked up as they entered, thumped his tail once, sniffed the air, and then laid his head between his paws again, his eyes quickly closing.

"Charles," said Lady Jane, "tell us exactly what you know, please, and then we can have a conversation."

Lenox and Edmund were still standing. "What I know?" said Charles. "Very little, really. The timing is suggestive."

"Timing?" said Miss Calloway—Mrs. Evans—looking up at him. Her own face was now dry.

"Your father began to withdraw from society approximately ten years ago, a little while after your mother's death, and more exactly after your departure. To Norfolk, from all we learned—but I wonder if that's true. It seems to me that perhaps his grief was at losing you without an explanation. Did you think that he knew about Stevens's treatment of you, and leave without telling him why?"

He saw that his supposition had gone home. "Well. Go on," she said.

"Perhaps it was your own grief at the death of your husband that drove you back here, seeking revenge on Stevens. You had nothing else to lose, after all. I take it that you don't have children?"

"We were not so blessed."

Lenox didn't need to look at Lady Jane to know that he was correct—that she knew the whole truth. "The drawing on the wall, of a schoolgirl," he said. "Was it some kind of message to Stevens?"

Suddenly Toto stood up. "This is all very well," she said angrily, "but what are we going to *do?* This young woman cannot go to prison—not after what she has endured. I'll put her on a train myself, and you can try to stop me, Charles Lenox."

Lenox shrugged. "I have no legal standing here," he said. "Clavering is downstairs. I think you could do worse than to place your trust in me."

Calloway's daughter looked him in the eye for a long moment and then nodded, inhaled to brace herself, and began to talk.

The mayor had come into her life on the day she first made that drawing. Or a version, anyhow—that particular schoolgirl had been smiling. She had been nine years old. Stevens had seen her drawing as her father socialized on the steps of the Bell and Horns and praised her for it, asked, even, if he might have it.

After that, he had always been very friendly to her and to her father, and when he had seen her he had nearly always mentioned the drawing. ("Still drawing, my dear?" "Well enough supplied with charcoal, I hope?" That kind of thing.) Finally, five years later, he had offered her a position as a secretary. She had been unusually young for the position, just fourteen, but as he had told Calloway, he'd had his eye on her for a long time.

Lenox had known Stevens as an acquaintance for many years, and even the euphemistic description of what he had done to his young secretary seemed . . . well, impossible. Dull, number-bound, impersonal old Stevens, his name the only interesting thing about him, a market mayor in a market town.

And yet there was Adelaide Snow's face: confirming every detail. Lenox hoped that her short term as Stevens's secretary meant that she had been strong-willed enough to resist his assaults.

I gave her fair warning that she might not.

"I was in a savage grief after William died," Mrs. Evans said. "You were correct about that. I had a little money, and no connections at all in the world. His family were mostly dead, my own was a father I believed had betrayed me. I

decided that I could at least—at least right one
of the wrongs of my life, I suppose."

"You poisoned the sherry," Lenox said.

She nodded. "I did. The sherry, well, he
enjoyed it, of course. And he always offered me
a glass—after. As if I were an adult then."

"The scoundrel," said Toto.

"I chalked that drawing on his steps, first,
though," said Calloway's daughter. "I wanted
Stevens to know that I was back—to go in, pour
a drink to calm himself, and then know, as he
was choking on the floor, dying, who had done it
to him."

"How did you find out that it was the wrong
house?"

"I went straight to my father after it was done,
to spite him. I was exhilarated. I was planning
to leave that night, return to London."

"Did you never live in Bombay, then?" asked
Edmund suddenly.

"We did, yes, for several happy years."

"I'm sorry—go on."

"When I saw my father, my heart broke," she
said. Next to her, Adelaide Snow gave her arm a
little extra squeeze. "He looked a thousand
years old to me. And then, his garden. He had
always liked plants, but now, I could tell right
away, it was all he had. His garden—all these
years taking care of *something,* if you see what I
mean, after my mother and I had both left him. I

think I would have forgiven him then and there, regardless of the past. But it emerged that he hadn't even known about Stevens. Foolish child that I was, and missing my mother, too, I had assumed he was as evil as the world. I'd been wrong. And to think—he never met William!"

She burst into tears, and it was some while before she could resume. "Take your time," Lenox said.

"No, it's better to get it out," she replied, collecting herself. "Well, it wasn't until a long time had passed that I even told him about the sherry I poisoned. He put the pieces together and realized that I had gone to the wrong house.

"In a panic I went back. I stared at the house for a long time. For all I knew the wrong man was on the floor inside, dead—but then, the lights were off, which made me hopeful that this poor Hadley person was still alive. He might not have been a sherry drinker. Fortunately for me, he wasn't.

"The next morning, with my father's help, I lured Mr. Hadley out of town and then took the sherry and destroyed the bottle. After that, it was a matter of planning anew how to kill Stevens."

"Your father didn't attempt to dissuade you?" asked Lenox.

"If anything, he was readier than I to do it." She gazed toward the low blue fire. "I suppose if two people are mad together, they can talk each other into thinking anything makes sense."

Lenox looked at Claire Adams. "You gave her the key to the town hall?" he asked.

"I did, yes," said the maid stoutly. "I would do it again."

"My father suggested that I visit Aunt Claire and explain—ask for her help. He was quite right."

"We've known what Stevens was for a while," said Claire Adams.

"Sarah Ainsworth," muttered Elizabeth Watson.

"It's simply a coincidence that your aunt was working in Hadley's house, then?" asked Edmund.

"It's a small village," Lady Jane said.

Lenox turned to Adelaide Snow. "Miss Snow," he said, "tell me, how did you come to be involved in all of this?"

"I found Liza in our gamekeeper's cottage."

"And then?"

"I asked her instantly whether she was the person who had tried to kill Stevens. She said she wasn't. I said that was too bad, because if she had been I would have shaken her hand—that I had worked for him briefly, and thought he was the devil. I only wish I'd had the courage to tell my father about him. After that we became friends. I vowed I would help her."

The Watsons, Calloway, Adelaide Snow—a

village was like that, Lenox supposed, with justice elusive for a long time, and then everyone agreeing on it all at once, and converging to help bring it about.

He was about to speak again when there was a knock on the door. It was Houghton's butler, Lane. Behind him was Pointilleux. Lenox had sent word that he would be here and told him to come to the ball if he'd finished his work.

The young Frenchman bowed to all of the ladies in the room and then said to Lenox, with some urgency, "Two things."

"Yes?"

"First, this. I find it in his ledger."

He passed Lenox the folded paper he had been carrying. It was the drawing—the schoolgirl, preserved all these years, its crease so deep that a gentle tug would have ripped it in two. In the bottom corner, in childish scrawl, a signature: *Liza Calloway.*

"Well found," said Lenox. "What was the second thing?"

"The victim, Stevens—he is dead."

CHAPTER FORTY-THREE

The reaction in the room was confused, as well it might have been. A bad man was gone, there was no doubt of that; anyone who might have been inclined to question Calloway's daughter's story had Adelaide Snow there to confirm that it was true.

On the other hand, it made this young woman, her eyes red, the dog still resting between her feet, a murderer.

"Why the dog?" asked Lenox suddenly. "I understand why you stayed in the gamekeeper's cottage—at first to avoid your father, and then to avoid being seen with him, to protect him, for of course you would have been noticed. I understand as well why you took the blankets and the books, and the herbs from your father. You wanted to stay out of the shops. The chickens I understand. It must have been easy to take the carrots when they presented themselves. But why the dog?"

Liza put a hand down and scratched the dog's ear. He growled happily. "I saw his owner kick him, the poor creature, before going into the pub. I couldn't let him stay there. He came away quite happily."

Human beings never ceased to surprise Lenox—

a person who could plot the brutal stabbing of a man in cold blood, but couldn't abide a dog being kicked. It was true that Mickelson was a very rough fellow.

"We must decide what to do," he said.

Toto made an indignant noise. *"Do."*

"Think, Toto. Calloway is in prison now, a confessed murderer," Lenox said, "and he'll hang for this crime unless we stop it. On the other hand, Mrs. Evans, I understand—well, no. That would be false. I cannot accept your actions, honestly I cannot. You might have gone to the police about Stevens."

"What, to Clavering? Ten years after the fact?"

"Yes," said Lenox. "I feel certain Clavering would have done his best by you had you gone to speak to him."

All of the women in the room seemed to roll their eyes simultaneously. "What have I miss?" asked Pointilleux.

"Too much. I'll tell you in a moment," said Lenox, and then, looking back at Liza Calloway, Evans, he realized he had no idea what to do. Just as he had when they were little and in the same position, he glanced at his brother. "Edmund?" he said.

The Member of Parliament for Markethouse stepped forward, and though his face was mild, his hands in his pockets, he had a certain authority in his bearing—greater than it might have been in London, though he was an important political figure there, because here his position had been sown into the soil many centuries before, and he only a season of its long existence.

"We cannot conceal the truth from Clavering, nor should we," he said. "Mrs. Evans, your father cannot die on your behalf, whether or not he believes it to be just."

"Edmund!" cried Toto.

"On the other hand, you are at the moment a free agent, at any rate for a little while longer. Have you any money?"

"A small legacy from my husband, and a little more from selling our house."

"Friends?"

"Me," said Adelaide Snow.

"No, Adelaide," said Calloway's daughter gently. "You have already been kind enough." She looked up at Edmund. "How long will it be until I am arrested?"

Edmund looked at his watch. "Clavering and Bunce are enjoying themselves in the kitchen. Call it—morning."

"Morning."

Lenox thought that Edmund was right to offer her a way out, but he also understood the feeling of hesitation in the room. Where was she to go? What was she to do?

It was Lady Jane who took charge. "Right, then," she said firmly, "that's six or seven hours, which is an eternity. Charles, Edmund—perhaps you would go back to the ball, to make up the numbers for poor Houghton, who must be working like a dog. Take Pointilleux with you— he looks as if he could use an hour of entertainment. There are six women in this room. It would take fewer than that to run England. I'm certain we can solve this problem. The three of you will only slow us down."

Lenox glanced at Liza Calloway. He was hesitant to leave. He knew this was his last chance to do what was proper and place her under arrest. The question he had to ask himself was whether she was capable of murdering again.

No, he thought. Or rather—yes, but not wantonly, not randomly. Stevens had ruined her life, and chance, a disease contracted by her husband, had ruined it again. He could understand how this second unhappiness might reverberate back toward the first.

"Very well," he said, and bowed slightly toward Calloway's daughter. "Good evening."

In the hallway again, the three of them stopped and looked at each other. Lenox picked up one of the decks of cards they'd been playing with and began to cut it into itself, feeling restless.

"Can you explain me the situation?" asked Pointilleux.

"Do you remember Lord Murdoch?" asked Lenox. Murdoch had been a Member of the House of Lords who had been brought down by similar charges two years before. "The same. But it was death, not prison, for Stevens."

Pointilleux's eyes widened. "*Mon dieu.*"

"What is it about politics?" Lenox asked, his voice speculative. "A fellow like Stevens, dry as a stick."

The young clerk sighed. "Perhaps we should pass the evening in the ballroom, if there is nothing else to be done, then."

"You ought to," said Edmund, "but not us." He took a sheet of paper, folded several times, from the ticket pocket of his waistcoat, and read from it. "Harville, Barth, Snow, Tuttle, Ainsworth, Moore, Calloway, Sather. Those are the eight young women who worked as secretaries for Stevens. Snow and Calloway are in the room behind us, Ainsworth who knows where. Still, that leaves five women. Markethouse has let them down badly. We ought to go and apologize."

"It's too late to visit them tonight," said Lenox.

Edmund shook his head. "I'm going now."

Lenox paused, then nodded. "Very well."

"Shall I come?" asked Pointilleux.

"No," said Edmund. "It's our village, not yours—our responsibility, too, not yours."

Pointilleux shrugged, and they walked down toward the noise of the party, where they left him in the care of Houghton. When that was done, Charles and Edmund went to the kitchens.

Clavering and Bunce were having a fair time there—but Clavering, conscientious soul that he was, had stayed sober.

"How is Mrs. Evans?" he asked.

"She is returning to Adelaide Snow's house to fetch her things," Lenox said. It was what they had agreed to tell the constable.

Clavering stood up. "If you believe she attacked Stevens, I ought to be going with her."

"Killed Stevens," said Edmund. "We just learned that he's died."

"Cor," said Bunce, and removed his cap.

"Where is she now? Already gone?"

"I believe so. But she doesn't want her father to hang. She's going to return here when she's finished."

"Fine," said Clavering. He shook his head. "I'd like the whole story. An ugly business, and now Stevens dead, too. The mayor!"

"Yes, the mayor," said Edmund, his voice less impressed than Clavering's by the title. "Charles, you and I had better go."

Together, the two brothers made five visits that evening, Edmund's carriage moving briskly through the narrow cobblestoned streets of the village, five slumbering houses roused to wakefulness again. It was the baronet who led their way in each time—apologetic, greeted in each case with puzzlement, but his well-known face enough to earn them admission.

Lenox was mostly quiet. Edmund spoke, stating to each woman at the outset of the conversation that they now had some evidence that Stevens Stevens had been guilty in his lifetime of very serious trespasses upon his secretaries; they were here to gather information, anonymous information, and also to offer the apology of the town.

The reception they received was different each time—and in truth, Lenox wasn't entirely sure at the end of their trip, at nearly midnight, that they had been right to make the visits. One woman, formerly Miss Sather, now Mrs. Berry, a bony middle-aged person, wanted no part of their apology: "Out," she had hissed. "I only thank God my husband is away. If he knew I had entered our marriage in a state of sin he'd thrash me within an inch of my life. And I would deserve it."

On the other hand, Miss Barth, who had worked for Stevens relatively recently, and still lived with her father on a street adjacent to Potbelly Lane, burst into tears, offered them tea, and said, in a roundabout, halting way, how inexpressibly relieved she was that it hadn't been her alone upon whom Stevens had preyed.

"I wondered what I had done to make him— to make him that way," she said.

"Nothing at all, I am quite sure," Edmund said softly.

There was another blank reaction from the woman who had been Miss Moore, now Mrs.

Clarendon, but there was a restrained look of grief on Miss Tuttle's face, after she heard them out—and then asked them to go without responding, though she spoke politely.

The last person they visited, Miss Harville, lived alone in a set of rooms on the High Street; she stood up after Edmund had spoken, poured herself a glass of sherry, drank three-quarters of it, and then stood by the window, looking out at the town hall, whose spire was visible from her window.

As they left her house a few minutes later—promising as they had to all the women that she would have the protection of their silence, offering her whatever help they could—Edmund said, "There. Now that's done."

"Mm."

"What an unforgivable thing to happen in Markethouse." He stopped and shook his head, his face illuminated by the silvery light of the moon. He pulled his pipe out of his pocket and jammed it moodily with tobacco. Then he turned to his brother. "I know it's late, but I propose we walk home. So much has happened tonight. A walk might clear our minds."

"With pleasure," said Charles.

"Stevens, damn him. I wish I had known years ago. I would have been tempted to kill him myself."

CHAPTER FORTY-FOUR

At the breakfast table the next morning, Lenox, Jane, Toto, and Edmund gathered, a little later than usual perhaps—only Lenox among them at all fresh or lively, because he had risen early to go out on a horseback ride, and returned just in time for a bath and a bite to eat. He would fall to earth again later in the day, but for now he was full of energy.

The other three were not, and the responses Jane and Toto made to the brothers' inquiries about Liza Calloway were first sluggish, then obstinate. This came to a head when Edmund asked if they knew, at least, what Clavering's night had been like, and Toto stood up from the breakfast table, stormed across the breakfast room, and speared a few kippers angrily onto her plate.

"Stop asking so many questions!" she said.

Lenox adopted a conciliatory tone. "Please," he said, "you must understand how hard we've worked—and how intimately it's of interest to Edmund, particularly, who lives here."

Jane and Toto exchanged a glance, and he saw both of them relent. "Our worry is that she's still not safe," said Lady Jane.

"Why not?" said Edmund.

"She's going to London first, to collect her husband's legacy in a lump sum."

"Jane!" said Toto. "We promised!"

"We gave our word that nobody would follow her if we could prevent it. Will you set the law after her?" Both Lenox and Edmund hesitated, and Jane shook her head gravely. "Only two men could equivocate after the story we heard. I suppose there's a limit to what you can understand of how it is to be a woman."

"I won't set the law after her," said Lenox.

"Oh, how decent of you," said Toto.

"On the other hand, I am more experienced than you are when it comes to things of this kind, and I can assure you that setting a killer free—even with the best intentions—does not always have a happy sequel. I lost the arrogance of thinking I knew when to do it a very long time ago."

"Well—that's fair," said Jane. "But you won't tell?"

"I won't."

And so Jane and Toto explained. After Lenox, Edmund, and Pointilleux had left the night before, they said, the people remaining in the room had hurried into action. Elizabeth Watson and Claire Adams—largely silent while the two men were present—became the leaders, more or less, of the initiative: Where would she go? What would she eat? What would she do?

As Jane and Toto described it together, the plan

emerged fairly easily. The two of them could provide her with enough money to survive for a while, long enough to claim her husband's legacy in a lump sum, hopefully a bit longer. Adelaide Snow's father had a small house in Shepherd's Bush, in London, and when they returned to gather her things, Adelaide would give Liza Calloway the key and an address.

She had also offered to go along with Liza, in fact, Jane recounted with admiration. ("I think she's a very warmhearted and bright girl. I'm going to ask her to tea. When we asked her about Stevens, she said he was only a bully, and hadn't had his way with her—and then added that all she'd had from him were a few bruises, which only lasted a week, and which she refused to let settle in.")

Elizabeth Watson, however, had said that she wanted to be the one to go to London with her niece. It had been ten years: ten years since her sister's death, too, two lights gone out of her life simultaneously. Her husband, her sons, and Mr. Hadley could survive a week without her.

"Is it clever to stay in Shepherd's Bush and leave a link to Adelaide Snow?" asked Lenox. "Mr. Clavering may not be very savvy, but I fear the case will attract wider attention than the local police force."

"We thought of that," said Toto. "She'll only be there a day. Then she hopes to move on."

"To where?"

Somewhere, was the answer. She didn't quite know herself. Her only question had been whether she could be allowed to write to her father and Adelaide (it was safe enough, they had all decided together), and her only request that she be allowed to take the dog with her to London.

"Wonderful, a dog thief, too," said Lenox.

"The farmer kicked the dog!" said Toto.

"Farmers do kick dogs," Lenox replied.

With Liza's plans settled, Claire Adams had gone down to the kitchens to cajole a packet of sandwiches out of them for the journey, Elizabeth Watson home to pack her things into a carryall, and Adelaide and Liza to Adelaide's father's house, where they would act as if they were simply returning from the ball. (Her father had known only that his daughter had a friend she wished to claim as a cousin—and was too besotted by his child to question her judgment, said Lady Jane.) Jane and Toto had given them ready money and devised a plan by which they could all credibly contend that she had slipped away unnoticed; both had also offered help farther down the road, should she need it.

The whole thing filled Lenox with trepidation, as he sat there sipping his coffee, the sun rising to cast its pale morning light over the hills—but with respect, too. Here were two maids, two aristocrats, and two women somewhere of the middle, for Liza Calloway's father had some distinction of birth, while Adelaide Snow's had none, but did have a great deal of property.

So perhaps it was the case that the country, too, could push people together, force them to know each other. In extremity, anyhow.

"She gave you no hint of what she might do after she leaves London?" asked Lenox.

"I doubt she knows. I think she's had the worst year of her life," said Jane.

"Do you know what she told me as I put her into the carriage?" said Toto. "She said she'd always wanted to be an actress. I told her to go to Edinburgh and look up Madame Reveille at her theater—to use my name, if she liked, as a reference."

"Did you really?" said Edmund.

"That's where I intend to picture her," said Toto, a piece of toast held meditatively in her hand. "At least until we hear from her again. The wretched thing. Fourteen!"

At that moment Pointilleux came in. He had been up very, very late—and from the looks of it had made an excellent time of the ball—and after greeting them all he asked, eagerly, what had happened.

"Oh, we've just been over it," said Lenox. "I'll tell you later."

Pointilleux scowled. "I am miss everything," he said.

"Get married, then you can be Mrs. Everything," said Toto.

That afternoon, Edmund and Charles made the rounds of Markethouse, tidying all the stray details of the case.

First they went to see Hadley and told him that they had confirmed their suspicions about the odd incidents at his house: He was not their target, but an accidental victim of the circumstances that had eventually led to the death of the village's mayor. He nodded gravely and thanked them again; they gently declined his offer of a tour through his gemstones, explaining that their time was still not their own. He saw them out himself—Mrs. Watson, he said, had been called away unexpectedly, a damned nuisance, but she was generally very reliable . . . and if they needed their lives insured, the Dover Assurance, gentlemen, first-rate service, honest and reliable service, he was happy to wait on their needs at any time . . .

Their next stop was to see Mickelson and tell him that his dog had been stolen. He was sitting in the Bell and Horns—being a practitioner of that certain variation of professional farming that involves mostly sitting at the bar, telling loud stories—and he took the news philosophically, though he added that it was a shame, because he had drowned a litter of puppies not a week before, and he would have held one back had he known.

Then it was Stallings. Lenox wanted to hear

about the details of Stevens's death, though to his disappointment, the mayor had never spoken.

"He revived a little before evening, but then fell comatose again," the doctor reported, "and by nightfall he was scarcely breathing. Indeed, my assistant called me in three times, certain that he was dead. At last he stopped fogging the mirror at just after eight o'clock."

"His wounds killed him?"

"If his clothing or the knife was unclean, his internal organs may well have become infected— a case of sepsis, as the medical journals have begun to call it now, from the Greek. I plan to be present at the autopsy."

Their final visit was to Clavering. This was the one they had both been anticipating unhappily, given that they would have to deceive him.

As it happened, however, he was ahead of their news. "She's gone," he said, greeting them. Calloway was still in the cell behind him, and Clavering gestured toward the old man. "His daughter. Fled. Adelaide Snow's already been in to tell how it happened."

"We heard," said Edmund, and indeed several people had stopped them to tell them the news.

"And I can't blame her," said Clavering grimly. "Not with what's passin' about—the word about Stevens."

"The word?"

It was the day of the market, and there were stalls

and sellers in the square, chattering; a small village could never half-keep a secret, Lenox supposed, it was either buried, or everyone knew. Who had spoken about it to whom, igniting the chain of gossip? One of the women they had visited last night? Another one of Stevens's victims?

Clavering's face was black with anger. "At least he's dead."

"Amen," said a voice from the cell—Mad Calloway.

They looked at him. "Would you like to speak to us now?" asked Clavering. "Take back your confession?"

Calloway shook his head firmly and decisively. "On the contrary, I stand by it. I killed him. I hope I have a chance to say as much to a court under oath."

Lenox, a father, understood—and glancing over at Edmund, he saw that his brother also did.

Apparently Clavering understood, too. He took the key to the cell from its peg and said, "I suppose you might as well stay at your cottage until it's all sorted out, Mr. Calloway. We can't spare the staff to stay overnight any longer. You won't leave Markethouse?"

"I will not."

"Very well, then. On with you. There's market today, if you haven't kept track of the days. I'm sure your garden is a right mess, too, before you can sell anything. I'll have my eye on you."

CHAPTER FORTY-FIVE

They all spent the morning at the market together, where there was every kind of gossip running up and down the little lanes of the village. A little bit after noon they returned to Lenox House with a whole variety of parcels: oranges in brown paper for Sophia, a small silver mirror that Toto had bought for herself, a basketful of vegetables Lady Jane had acquired.

When they came into the front hall, Lenox saw straightaway that waiting on the silver tray was a letter, its return address visible, from James Lenox, Edmund's older son.

Edmund spotted it a beat later. He turned pale, took it, and without a word went to his study. He was there for nearly an hour before Lenox decided to knock on his door.

"Come in," Edmund called.

Lenox entered and saw his brother staring out of the window, a hand at his chin. The letter lay across a small card table next to him.

"How are you?" asked Lenox.

"I think James is the kindest soul that ever lived. He expresses a great deal of concern for me, which of course is unnecessary. Anyhow, better still—the best news I've had in a long time—he's returning here for a visit, as soon as he's handled a few small matters in Kenya."

"That's wonderful."

"I think he may be home in time for Christmas, with any luck from the wind," said Edmund, smiling.

He looked younger—and Lenox realized, knowing Edmund as he did, that it wasn't simply the news that James would return home. It was the letter itself. What did it mean to be left alone to take care of the children, when it was two of you who had brought them into the world together? It was a part of Edmund's burden that Charles hadn't quite considered; he had thought of the companionship that was gone, the love and care, but less of how solitary and grave Edmund's responsibilities as a father had become.

James would be all right. That was why he looked so relieved.

"That will be a treat," said Lenox.

Edmund sighed and smiled wanly. "Yes. Only Teddy to tell, now. And who knows, James may be able to tell him with me. Teddy's always looked up to his brother."

"I know it. So have I!"

"Oh, shut up."

Lenox hadn't been joking, but he let it pass.

The supper that evening was the nicest one they'd had yet. Atherton came, and afterward the five of them played cards in the convivial blaze of fire and candlelight, drinks and small biscuits on the table with the cards, the dogs sleeping on the thick rug, and Toto losing so steadily and spectacularly that she owed them a theoretical fortune by the end of the night.

She declared that she hated Sussex.

"You might as reasonably say that you hate this deck of cards," said Edmund.

"I *do* hate this deck of cards, that's what you don't know about me, Edmund Lenox."

"Shall I deal out one more hand?"

"Oh, go on."

Lenox asked Atherton, who had been in Markethouse until just before supper, what he had heard about Calloway and Stevens.

"Pickler told me confidentially that he'd heard Stevens had cloven feet—Dr. Stallings had found them upon examination. Part devil."

"Pickler the milkman?"

"That seems implausible," said Lady Jane.

"Oh, the rumors are out of control. Nobody ever trusted him an inch, if you believe what they say now—but I swear I am astonished at it all, astonished. I freely admit that I saw Stevens every market day for the last twenty years, and I never had him down as anything except a human abacus. And I consider myself a pretty good judge of character, let me assure you."

Every farmer Lenox knew considered himself a uniquely penetrating judge of character, and most of them couldn't tell a parson from a murderer. Atherton shook his head, and Lenox merely nodded sagely. "Yes, of course."

"Tell me, what did he do—exactly? There is every kind of gossip abroad."

Lenox glanced at Edmund. "I think we must keep it to ourselves. He's gone now."

"But tell me this—he was bad? We aren't ruining the name of a good fellow, are we now, for local sport?"

"No," said Edmund. "He was a second devil. His name ought to go straight through your thresher."

Atherton accepted this, sipping his whisky. "And Mad Calloway has been freed. People were lining up Clifton Street, hoping to catch a glimpse of him. There was smoke from his chimney. Then he came out at five and posted a letter. Mrs. Appleby was cordial to him when he did it, from what I hear."

Lenox and Edmund exchanged glances. If Calloway had written to his daughter, he had done foolishly. On the other hand, it might have been hard to resist. There was no doubt a great deal for him to say. Ten years!

Toto put down a card. "The knave of diamonds. Can you beat that, Charles?"

At a little past noon the next day, Toto and her daughter, along with Pointilleux, who had spent the last thirty hours dead asleep, took the train headed back for London, waving at them all on the platform from the window.

After the train had gone out of sight, Edmund said, "How much longer do you plan to be here?"

"We have nothing urgent to take us back to London," said Lady Jane, taking Sophia by the hand and leading her down the few small steps. The carriage was waiting for them. Lenox knew that she had canceled, oh, twenty or thirty appointments to be here with Edmund. "How long will you be in the country?"

"Another week. But you must go, really. I shall be fine."

"No, no," said Lenox.

"What about the missing pianist, though?"

In truth, Lenox had thought about little else in the past day. That morning after breakfast he had lain out all of the papers from the previous week and read through them avidly, using Lady Jane's nail scissors to cut out a dozen intriguing scraps of information he hadn't seen.

"Perhaps I might stop and wire Dallington on the way home, if you wouldn't mind taking Jane and Sophia," he said. "I can walk the rest of the way."

"It's a cold day," said Edmund.

Indeed, the sky was a severe gray, the trees bending in the wind and scattering more and more of their leaves, which fluttered down to rest in their soft layers for the winter.

"I have my cloak," Lenox said. "Tell Waller to keep lunch warm, and I'll be back in time to eat with you."

He walked into town with his collar turned up. Despite the cold, six or seven people were gathered near the little ledge at Mrs. Appleby's house where the mail arrived and left; Markethouse had been in a breathless conversation for several days, and it didn't look likely to stop anytime soon. Lenox went forward to the postmistress and asked if he could send a wire.

"Certainly," she said, "and you can take one. I was just about to send it to Lenox House, but it's easier to give it to you now. In from London this morning."

"Thanks," said Lenox, accepting the slip of paper.

It was from Dallington.

Polly and I closing in STOP haven't slept days STOP hopeful of success STOP will send word to Queen's Arms of whereabouts every few hours in case you are free to return STOP Dallington STOP

Lenox felt his nerves tighten and hum. A solution. What could it be? He remembered his last communication with Dallington, when he had suggested that Muller might not be the victim of this crime—indeed, that he might have been the murderer of the woman they had found, either Margarethe Muller or, if the real Margarethe was indeed in Paris, per the reports they had received, her impostor.

He thanked Mrs. Appleby distractedly—"Didn't you need to send a wire?" she asked his retreating back—and tried to calculate how quickly he could be at the Queen's Arms.

Could he leave, though? There was Edmund.

His brother quickly disposed of that question upon Charles's return to Lenox House. He had Sophia dandled upon his knee, where she was studying with intense concentration his pocket watch, but he was able to muster his authoritative squire's voice. "You must all three go. I've gotten far too little done since you came down."

"There was a murder," Lady Jane pointed out.

"Never mind. I'll follow you to London in only five or six days. We'll see each other then."

"Are you quite sure?"

"Absolutely sure."

Lenox looked at Lady Jane. "Darling?" he said.

"You take the soonest train. Sophia and I will follow you."

Lenox nodded. He wouldn't have gone if his brother hadn't received that letter from James, but he seemed just enough improved to desert. "Lend me a horse, Ed, and then I can get a train direct from Chichester at 2:12."

Edmund stood up, putting Sophia gently on the

ground. "I'll ride with you so I can bring the horse back."

"You'll pack my things, Jane?"

"Go!"

Lenox nodded and bent down to kiss his daughter on the top of her head. "Thanks. On our way, Edmund. Hopefully we don't lose the horses this time."

Lenox and his brother had spent their whole youth riding together, except for two appalling autumns when Edmund had been allowed to ride with the hunt and Charles had still been forced to ride with the children, hanging back as the adults thundered over the heather.

Now, galloping across the countryside, he felt the years fall away—the cold sharp air stinging his skin, the tears forming involuntarily in his eyes and then streaming away in the wind, the happy blur of the fields they crossed toward the low spires of Chichester. Occasionally a slight turn of his head or a roll in the landscape would give him a glimpse of his brother's serious face, and he would feel his heart fill with affection.

They arrived at the train station with nine minutes to spare. Getting down from his horse, Edmund said, "Thank you for coming to visit, Charles. It was a nice time for it. Useful, too, as turned out."

"My pleasure."

"Do you have anything to read on the train?"

"Blast it, no."

Edmund nodded toward the stationmaster's small hut. "He sells newspapers and scones, though I warn you they're both about equally edible."

Lenox smiled. "See that Jane gets on the train safely, would you?"

"Yes, of course."

"And don't stay down here too long."

Edmund sighed. "No—I need to be back in Parliament soon, at any rate. Good-bye, Charles, safe travels."

They shook hands, and Lenox turned toward the platform.

A little over eighty minutes later, he was flying through the door at the Queen's Arms. All he had noticed on his dash from Paddington was the smell—the rich, middlingly unpleasant, river-and-waste-and-horse scent of London, which one forgot after any time away, and also after any time back, which meant that it existed only on in-between days like this one.

It was pungent.

The Queen's Arms was the pub across from their office on Chancery Lane. Behind the bar was the reliable taverner named Cross. "Had word not ten minutes ago," he said before Lenox could speak. "Said to tell you, at the theater."

"At the theater," Lenox repeated.

"That's all he said, sir."

"Thank you, Cross." He put a coin on the bar. "Have your next on me."

"Thankee, Mr. Lenox."

The cab he had taken was waiting outside for him still. He stepped into it and gave his directions to the Cadogan, desperately curious what he would find.

CHAPTER FORTY-SIX

W hen they finally picked up Muller's trail, it was nearly midnight.

They were deep in the recesses of the famous Jermyn Street Baths: Dallington, Lenox, Pointilleux, their lanky friend Nicholson from Scotland Yard, Thurley, the manager from the theater, and a friendly waddling constable named Cartwright who had never made an arrest before. (Out of his hearing, Dallington had made some rather cruel guesses as to why that might be, mostly to do with Cartwright's weight and almost supernatural stupidity—but he had been the closest constable to the entrance of the baths.) Poor Polly, though she had worked herself three-quarters to death on the case, had been barred admission from the inner rooms of the house, as a woman. Instead of going with them, she had taken up a post in the front hall and started writing out a list of journalists for her assistant, the hulking ex-seaman Anixter, to go and collect.

When Lenox had arrived at the theater earlier that day, he had spotted Dallington, and the young lord—looking fresh, as he always did, whatever exertions he subjected himself to—came straight over.

"There you are."

"You're close?" said Lenox.

"Yes, old Greville broke."

"The theater owner."

"He's in a state. Did you know that was a wig, that tearing fine head of hair he had? Underneath it he's only got a grizzled bare pate, I can tell you, and right now he's weeping in the box at the Yard."

Lenox, whose own close-cropped brown hair was still blessedly full, but nevertheless thinner than it had been when he was on Dallington's side of thirty, said only, "What did he tell you?"

"You were right on two counts. First of all, that woman was Muller's lover, not his sister. His sister really was in Paris, is in Paris, I suppose. Second, it all came down to the chandelier. Muller couldn't have known about it—nor about the passage above his room."

"And?"

"We told Greville he would hang for the murder if he didn't come clean. That flustered him. I'm no admirer of Broadbridge, but he can certainly put the fear of Jehovah into a chap.

"According to Greville, it all happened at intermission. Muller came offstage and told him, immediately, that he had a problem. Well— the problem was a dead woman."

"Poisoned, though?" Lenox asked.

"Eh?" said Dallington.

"Nothing, nothing. Go on."

"Greville has never sold more tickets at a higher price, and he made a quick calculation. It didn't count on Muller running. He's greedy. He told Muller about the chandelier and the passage. I suppose he thought that nobody would miss a German woman without a single friend in London, and that they might go on selling tickets together for another week at least, and deal with the problem then. Only Muller did a runner."

"And now you're on Muller's track?"

"Actually we've come back here because we lost it," said Dallington. "At this moment Polly is asking Greville where Muller could possibly be—what he knows in London. We already asked him, and we've chased down every place, without finding any fresh sign of him. We want to see if Greville can think of anywhere else Muller might be."

"Which places did Greville already give you?"

"Muller's hotel, the York, though of course that's been torn into a billion pieces. Two restaurants, Thompson's and Wilson's. A pub called the Earl of Thomas, where he liked to have a glass of port alone before his concerts; Green Park, where he took his morning walks; and the music shops on Lillard Street."

"No sign of him at any of them."

"None. We asked pretty forcefully at the music shops in particular."

Lenox frowned. "No, he wouldn't go there if

he had any intelligence, which I think we can assume he has. It's funny, though—Thompson's and Wilson's are in very different directions, and neither is close to the theater."

"So?"

"Is there a bookshop nearby?"

"Hatchards."

"Yes, of course, that's right. Give me fifteen minutes to get there and back—don't leave."

Hatchards, with its sober hunter green exterior and comfortable interior, was the best bookstore in the West End. A bookseller nodded at Lenox and asked if he could help.

"Where is your travel section?"

"At the rear of the store, sir. Let me show you."

The shop carried a shelf's worth of guides to London in foreign languages, including three in German.

The first of these was useless, but in the second, Lenox saw with a little thrill, two of the restaurants recommended with the highest number of stars, three, were Thompson's and Wilson's.

He confirmed that the third guide didn't have the same offerings, then bought the second one, which was by Karl Baedeker, and ran back to the theater with it, heart beating quickly.

He found Polly and Dallington speaking to Nicholson and interrupted them. "Look here," he said.

"Oh, hello, Lenox, welcome back," said Polly,

tiredly but sunnily. "We've just heard that LeMaire is still at the York. Out of ideas."

"Oh, good. But look—Thompson's and Wilson's." He stabbed at the page with his finger. "Every German I've ever met has traveled out of a guidebook."

Dallington's eyes widened. "Yes!"

Polly nodded slowly. "So what do we do?"

"Muller knows a very small section of London. I think we can cover it all today."

And indeed, in the course of the afternoon and evening they had several tantalizing glimpses of him. No, he had never eaten at the Florence, as far as the manager of that restaurant could remember—but the highly touted tobacconist the next street over had had a German fellow answering to Muller's description in the shop twice. Moreover, he had bought the same kind of cigars that Thurley (enlisted as an aide) remembered Muller smoking.

What had he been wearing? Where had he come from? The tobacconist couldn't answer, but a little ways off, at Thompson's again, Lenox pressed the manager there for every detail of Muller's visits. Had he ordered dessert? Cheese? Coffee? The manager admitted that he hadn't ordered coffee, which led him to recall for the first time that perhaps Mr. Muller *had* mentioned that he liked a refreshing walk before he took his post-prandial coffee, when declining it at the restaurant.

It was this that led them to Frank's, the most heartily recommended coffeehouse in Baedeker's book. It was owned by a German and carried the latest editions of the German newspapers, apparently.

It was the proprietor here who inadvertently gave them the clue that sent them to the baths.

"He would have been in later in the evening, probably," Polly was saying, pressing him. "Around ten o'clock."

"Ah, there I lose you. I am generally at the Couch Street Baths after six o'clock."

"Couch Street? Is that where the Germans go?" Lenox asked.

Mr. Frank, who spoke excellent English, said, "The working Germans, sir."

The working Germans. Muller, by contrast, was well-off. Lenox looked in Baedeker: There were two pages, there, dedicated to the wonders of the Jermyn Street Baths . . .

And indeed, these were the most luxurious baths in London by a wide margin—not a place to Lenox's taste, but many people swore by it, and after they had raced there and located the manager, he told them that yes, a small German man with a mustache and a receding hairline did come in. When? Generally very late—eleven, or twelve. Was that uncommonly late? Not at all. They didn't close until four in the morning, of course, and only for an hour or two then.

It would have taken a very dim person not to perceive that they were after the missing German pianist, and, having put two and two together, this manager grew extremely agitated and excited.

"Is he here? Is he here?" he asked, a brilliantined forelock of hair falling down upon his forehead and quivering there as he repeated the question, and then offered vehemently his utmost assistance, whatever he could do at all, the reputation of the baths, gentlemen ("and Mrs.—ma'am," he added, to Polly).

The small company, impatience mounting, retreated to a nearby chophouse, before finally returning to the baths at half past eleven.

"I wonder where LeMaire is now," said Dallington as they went in. "Probably China."

"Hopefully far from here, if we're correct," said Polly. "I want the glory for ourselves."

It had started to drizzle, and Dallington said maliciously, "I hope he's stuck out in the rain somewhere."

The baths were spectacular, Lenox had to admit as they walked through. They were set up in a series of connected rooms, each tiled in a different brilliant pattern, all with divans and sofas and chairs at their edges, turbaned servants standing close by at every turn. Their little crew made for an odd intrusion upon the leisure of the prosperous gentlemen who were using the baths, but they only received glances of curiosity, no challenge to their progress.

Following the manager, Smythson, they passed through the hot room, then the "very hot" room, which wasn't pleasant, then the sluice room, where they didn't pause at the waterfalls of cool water, though Thurley, in his three-piece wool suit, red as a beet, looked as if he wouldn't have minded.

After that it was the massage room, the cool room, the plunge pool—room after room after room, the steps in a sequence that aspired toward what must have been a nirvana-like relaxation.

"You haven't seen him, Mr. Thurley?" Nicholson whispered after each room.

"No," said Thurley. "And it is exceedingly unpleasant to examine these fellows so closely when they're—when they're disrobed. I don't like it a bit, and I don't blame them for disliking it either, I can tell you."

"Stick it out a bit longer," said Dallington encouragingly. "If we find him, I'll treat you to a bath myself."

Thurley, who liked a lord, colored and said, oh, it was an honor to help, no remuneration necessary, though of course anyone might find it refreshing to enjoy a bath, after suchlike exertions.

And then, in the middle of this speech, the theater's manager spotted him: the man that all of London had been looking for.

CHAPTER FORTY-SEVEN

He was even smaller than Lenox remembered. They found him in the sitting room just beyond the last of the baths, a large chamber that had been decorated marvelously, such that it could easily have been the inner sanctum of a Turkish palace, he thought. All of the men in it, as they entered, were dressed "à la Turque," having been wrapped in robes and turbans by attendants against the cool air, then seated on comfortable sofas to be served flavored tobacco, sweet coffee, and honeyed pastries.

"There he is," Thurley said.

Even as he said it, the little man, sitting in an armchair and reading a book, saw them.

He stood up right away, with an uncertain expression on his face. He looked absurd in his turban, his sparse graying chest hair emerging from his robe.

"Hello, gentlemen," he said, when they approached him.

"Take word back to Polly to get going," Lenox murmured to Pointilleux.

"Mr. Muller?" said Nicholson.

The little German nodded. He was standing up very straight. "Yes, it is I. I let her die. There is no point to deny it."

He spoke in a squeaky German accent, which took some of the gravity away from this admission. Everyone in the room was staring at them, and Nicholson asked Smythson if they could speak somewhere more private. The manager led them to a little side room nearby, which was overly bright. Muller was extremely docile; he sat with them readily, asking only if he might have a glass of brandy. Smythson dispatched someone to bring it.

"I am Inspector Nicholson, Mr. Muller," said the man from the Yard.

Muller sitting, nodded. "Very well."

"You say you killed this woman? Tell us, please, who was she?" asked Nicholson.

Muller smiled. "Who was she! It is a strange thing to love a madwoman, gentlemen. Love her I did, however. *She*—she was Katharina Schiller, the beautiful Katharina Schiller, famous throughout Berlin society, the companion of my heart. Nobody has ever understood me as she did. Nobody ever will again, either, alas."

"Why did you kill her?" asked Nicholson.

Muller hesitated. Lenox thought he knew why.

Poisoning—it had been on his mind all day, ever since his return to London.

It bothered him. Men who killed their lovers almost always did it out of passion, and by passionate means, a gun, a blow.

They were supposed to believe that Muller, on

the other hand, had murdered this woman by the most premeditated of methods, and at the theater no less, the place and time when having to dispose of a body would be least convenient to him.

He stepped forward. "Mr. Muller didn't say that he killed Miss Schiller. He said that he let her die."

Nicholson looked at the pianist quizzically. "Mr. Muller? You've given us all a great deal of trouble—I do think you might favor us with an explanation of what you did and where you've been."

At that moment the glass of brandy arrived, and Muller drank most of it in a single draft. Then he studied the glass for a moment, before taking a deep breath and responding.

"I could never have broken it off with her in Berlin," he said. "Her father . . . her personality . . . well, I could never have broken it off with her in Berlin, gentlemen. Yet if I was to survive another day with my sanity intact, I had to leave her.

"And here, with the success that has met me in London, far from home, I felt—finally, I could tell her that it was finished, our affair. The day she died, I informed her that I would be traveling on to Paris alone, to meet my real sister, which meant that it would not be convenient to me to have her travel with me any longer. I was very tender, you know! I told her that we would always be friends.

"She left my dressing room without a word. Just before I was to go on that night, however, I found her there again. She had her own key to the theater and to the room. She had insisted on that when we arrived. In my dressing room she had poured two glasses of wine from a bottle she had brought with her.

"Little did she know how transparent her offer of a final glass of wine in friendship was! She had told me many times that she would rather kill me than lose me. When her back was turned for an instant at a knock at the door, I switched our glasses. Yes, it was thus that I killed her. I expected her to take a sip and taste the bitterness, and see that I had found her out. Instead, when I took a sip, she laughed like the madwoman she was and drank the entire glass before I could stop her.

"I cannot describe anything more horrible than seeing her face as she realized what had happened. She died very quickly. I cannot describe . . ." A funny distance came over the German's undis-tinguished little face. "And yet, gentlemen, I do not know that I have ever played better. I felt I was playing for her."

The story they eventually teased out of Muller was much longer than this, and went back to the history of his initial meeting with Katharina

Schiller in Berlin. There were a hundred details that Nicholson pursued, while Muller was in a cooperative mood: how Greville had helped, how the pianist had hidden Miss Schiller's body.

The essentials of the tale never deviated from the original version, first to last, and finally, Nicholson, sighing, said, "Regardless of intent, I must inform you that you are under arrest."

Muller stood up immediately and drank the rest of the brandy. "Of course. Let us go now. The hour is late."

They left. In order to depart from the baths, they passed back through the rooms of the bathhouse in reverse order.

Muller joined uncomplainingly in this unusual procession. Only when they were in the ante-chamber to the baths did he pause. "Mr. Muller?" said Lenox.

They all followed his gaze, which was trained on a pianoforte in the corner, with a broken wooden back. "Gentlemen," he said, "might I have a moment to play? It may be some time before I am seated at my instrument again."

They looked at each other uncertainly. He was a diminished figure, and had come along so quietly.

Still, it seemed wrong. But Muller took advantage of their silence to go sit at the piano, and nobody stopped him. Testingly, he played a note. It sounded very uncertain—an instrument meant for drinking songs, jangly, probably warped by the steam in the baths, certainly not what he was used to. Muller ran his fingertips along the keys noiselessly, feeling them. It was only now that Lenox noticed the single remarkable thing about the fellow: his hands, which were extraordinarily delicate, long, slender, and muscular.

Muller began to play. He started with a few notes that sounded unrelated, but which resolved into a tentative chord. Another followed it, three simple notes. Then the initial chord again, held, sustained.

He played a short run from the first chord back to the second, then paused, then played a few more stray notes, seemingly unrelated.

And then suddenly they were in the midst of it.

Lenox had only an intermittent relationship with music, but he was enthralled. As Muller played, the room, the world, were transformed. The unassuming little German seemed to melt into the piano, his body wholly connected to it. The music was fluid, major, then minor, irreducibly magical.

"Bach," murmured Dallington, who knew more about the subject than Lenox did. "For organ, usually. A variation."

Muller played on and on, and even Cartwright, who had taken the heat of the baths worse than the rest of them, couldn't pull his eyes away. Thurley's mouth hung open. As for Lenox—well, as the music went on he felt as if he were in a room with everyone he had ever loved, his brother, his parents, Lady Jane, Sophia. It was the strangest thing. When Muller began to play more softly, in a minor key, it was almost intolerably moving. When he moved back into the major key, all of them felt the strength and suppleness of the emotion behind it, neither triumphant nor defeated. Loss—the loss of Katharina Schiller—was present in all of the notes, but so was life, the force of life.

At last he began to soften his playing back toward those first chords, the notes quieter and quieter, fewer and fewer.

When he had finished there were tears in Dallington's eyes. "My goodness," he said.

Muller let his hands rest silently on the piano for a moment, and then he stood up. Lenox would never forget the look on his face. He looked renewed, not exhausted. He bowed. "Thank you," he said, and then, after only a few seconds, he was again the absurd little German man he had been before he played.

Genius! Who could explain it?

In the front room they met Polly and Pointilleux, who had been listening to the piano music, too. They watched Nicholson and Cartwright put Muller into a police dray, promising they would call in the morning to inquire after his status.

"He did it, then?" said Polly.

"Yes, he admitted it straightaway," said Dallington.

She shook her head. "How beautiful that music was, though."

"Was it Pascal who said that all of man's miseries come from not being able to sit alone quietly in a room?" said Lenox.

"Very odd. Still, the good news is that we shall be famous throughout Britain tomorrow, fellows. We found him."

"And thoroughly routed LeMaire," said Dallington.

Yet none of them could feel quite as enthusiastic as they ought to, watching the dray—and after they parted, agreeing to meet early the next morning, Lenox, for his part, carried that melancholy all the way home, hoping that Lady Jane, who could always cheer him up again, would still be awake.

CHAPTER FORTY-EIGHT

T wo weeks later it was truly winter at last, and Lenox, more fool he, was sitting outside on a public bench near Wallace Street very early in the morning, as slow, heavy snowflakes drifted down in the windless air, whitening the awnings, dotting the streets. He was warmly bundled, though, and the company was fair: Graham sat next to him, just as deeply buried in warm cloaks and wrappers and gloves, only their eyes and mouths exposed to the cold. Between them on the bench was a large stone bottle of hot tea that Lenox had brought, from which they frequently replenished their small tin cups.

"There he goes, meeting that gentleman in the carriage," said Graham.

"Damn him," said Lenox.

"The third time."

They watched as Obadiah Smith stood at the door of the carriage for a few moments, then, after receiving a piece of paper, ducked back into the begrimed public house that served as his headquarters—the sort of backstreet establishment, not uncongenial, that would put your cut of beef on the gridiron if you bought a drink, and bring it to you with mustard and walnut ketchup.

"What is he doing, I wonder?" Lenox asked for the tenth time.

"All three carriages have been well appointed."

"I noticed."

Smith was a long-term quarry of Lenox's, a score he intended to settle on his own time, and this sort of casual ongoing observation of him wasn't unpleasant, a piece of the puzzle, not a moment of urgent action. The afternoon before, Graham had asked him to breakfast, and Lenox had invited him instead on this escapade—a dirty trick, to be sure, except that Graham had always enjoyed this extracurricular aspect of his work, when he'd been Lenox's butler, and they'd had the better part of an hour to talk.

"Back to the subject we were discussing— spring, you are fairly sure?" asked Lenox.

"I think so," said Graham.

"In that case we will have the supper outdoors."

"Supper?" Graham said, raising his eyebrows.

"Myself, Jane, you, Miss Winston of course, McConnell, Dallington, Lord Cabot—" Cabot was an old political ally of Lenox's, in failing health but still stubbornly sociable, who had become extremely intimate with Graham in the past year—"and anyone else you care to invite."

"Neither Miss Winston nor I wants any bother. I say that quite sincerely."

"I'll see you to hell myself before I let you get married without a supper, Graham."

Graham shook his head. "My calendar is full this spring."

"Every night!"

"Every night."

Lenox laughed, and was about to reply when Smith came out again. The detective scowled and leaned forward slightly, peering through the narrow slit between his scarf and his hat. "What could he be doing?"

Graham studied Smith, who was a hardened criminal, a diabolical and clever person. "I wonder if he's working in his old line again."

"Prostitution?"

Graham nodded. "He's only receiving papers. Addresses, perhaps?"

Lenox narrowed his eyes. "Perhaps. But why would the carriages come to him? And why would they leave behind a trail of paper? I wonder if it's something more complex. Stockjobbing, for instance."

"You could find out by following him at night. If it's prostitution, that's when he'll be busiest. If it's stockjobbing, he'll be off the clock then."

Graham had always been an invaluable second set of eyes. "You're right. If only it were warmer out."

"Mr. Pointilleux is enthusiastic, is he not?"

"I wouldn't want to put him in the way of danger. It's my case."

"Then you and I might do it one night this week."

"I can't risk the neck of a Member of Parliament, Graham. Not to mention what Miss Winston would think of it."

"I think my neck will be all right," said Graham drily.

Lenox continued to peer at the public house, wishing Smith, who'd disappeared inside once more, would come out again. They had a cab waiting and intended to follow the next carriage that came for him. "Well," he said, still staring, "if you're busy all spring it will be a luncheon. And if you're not careful, I'm going to ask Jane to speak to Miss Winston directly."

"Heaven help us," Graham said.

Lenox laughed.

Several hours later, still pink-cheeked but dried and warmed, and having dropped Graham near Parliament, Lenox was sitting with Polly and Dallington at the weekly meeting of the agency's three partners.

"Our finances are not spectacular," Polly was saying, tapping the end of her pencil against the balance sheet she was studying. "Not disastrous, but not spectacular."

"Not disastrous has always been my ambition in life," said Dallington, and smiled at the look of exasperated affection that Polly shot him. "Anyhow, why be so gloomy? We've wiped LeMaire's eye, we're the heroes of Fleet Street, and we have half a dozen meetings with new clients today alone."

"All six of them put together won't add up to what we lost by Chadwick. I'm not joking. If it weren't for the reserve fund, we would be in debt right now. I still think we might be wise to let one of the new detectives go. Mayhew probably."

Lenox grimaced. It was true—Chadwick had cost them a few of their steadiest clients. "This is why it's quite right that Polly is in charge," he pointed out to Dallington. "Best to have a pessimist making the decisions."

"I'm not a pessimist!" cried Polly. "A realist, perhaps."

"Are you not pleased that the *Daily Mirror* called you 'fetching,' then?" asked Dallington.

"I'll quit if you mention that again."

Muller was in dock; the newspapers agreed that he wasn't likely to serve a long sentence, since murder would be near impossible to prove, and a half-emptied sachet of arsenic had been found among Miss Schiller's effects at the Hotel York. More than that, the palace had a strong interest in a pleasant relationship with Germany, as several of the John Bull–ish rags took pleasure in pointing out.

Lenox and Dallington had been to speak to him twice more, and also been to the Yard to receive Broadbridge's brusque praise. (Most of that credit they pushed toward Nicholson, who looked likely, all fingers crossed, to be promoted on the strength of running Muller to ground. It would be valuable to have a chief inspector among the agency's friends.) It was true that the three detectives had become briefly famous recently—to such an extent that even the Monomark papers had given them a few terse mentions, because it would have looked odd had they not.

But would it translate into income? That was the devilish thing about business, Lenox had discovered—never knowing quite whether the blend of publicity and word of mouth and good work would come together to create something that might be sustainable. If they sacked Mayhew he would probably be outraged, given how the business had hummed since Muller's capture. What he couldn't know was the difficulty of living by the books.

Let nobody say that Lenox, as he approached fifty, couldn't learn new ways.

"Not spectacular," said Polly again, glaring at the paper. "I really would like spectacular."

She was their best chance of spectacular. He glanced over at Dallington, who was staring at her with unconcealed fondness, and thought that perhaps the notion wasn't unique to him. "Let's give it two weeks," said Lenox. "We have quarterly payments coming in from Deere and Steele. Then we can decide about the staff."

Polly nodded. "Fine. Next order of business, then. Dallington, have you spoken to your friend at Bonhams about looking at my client's porcelain collection? She is adamant she has been defrauded."

Lenox only half listened to Dallington's reply to the question, sitting back in his chair, turning his head to look through the window at the snow that was still falling outside. He'd accept Graham's offer to come out with him that night and follow Smith, he thought. Not far from Parliament there was a prison called Tothill. In another country, where criminals were held far away from the footpaths of respectable daily life, that would have seemed odd—but in London, the prisons were as integrated into the streets as surely as the banks and the baths. With any luck, Smith would be behind the bars of a cell there before the calendar turned over to 1877.

CHAPTER FORTY-NINE

T ake my word for it, the great thing with a Smoking Bishop is to use *oranges,* not lemons," said James Lenox, who was twenty-two, and consequently knew everything. "It's much finer that way. And first you put cloves in the oranges and roast them over a fire."

The debate was on the verge of growing heated. "You must be mad," Edmund said. "Lemons are the most important ingredient of a Smoking Bishop."

"Surely wine is the most important ingredient," said Lady Jane.

Just to cause trouble, Lenox said that he had heard of making it with Rhine wine—and then it was called a Smoking Archbishop. James nodded and said you could also make it with raisins and burgundy and that was called a Smoking Pope. He was about to continue when Edmund, running his hands through his hair and looking ready to move into Calloway's cottage and dedicate his life to silent study, said that it was his house and the wassail would be made with lemons—that was all.

This was Christmas at Lenox House, and though all of them missed Molly, they were making a fair fist of it. There was going to be a little party that evening. Everything was planned for it except the punch, which was what they were debating in the most beautiful room of Lenox House, which stood at the corner of its L-shape, with enormous windows looking over the pond and the front avenue. There were life-sized portraits along one wall, and above them a small minstrels' gallery where musicians might sit. The floor of this particular was always beeswaxed and shining, and Edmund and Lenox had often passed the time playing badminton here in their formative years, until they broke a window and had been whipped for it, after which they had played in the stable.

Lady Jane, Lenox, and Sophia had been here two days. That afternoon, after the punch debate was finally settled, they had gone into town and walked around the market—a notable one, because people saved their fattest gooses and gleamingest trinkets for this time of year, an especially cheerful day—and only thirty or forty people had congratulated him on moving back to the country, which he considered progress.

On the way home he took Jane and Sophia to the turnoff where he and Edmund had waited every morning for the mail coach—known as the mails—to pass, usually just after nine o'clock, driven by Fat Sam, a jovial figure in a crimson traveling shawl. Lenox could vividly remember the cart's four strong dray horses, so familiar that when one was replaced he had spotted it half a mile down the road.

"What a thrilling boyhood you had," said Lady Jane. "How did you stand the excitement?"

"It *was* exciting, too, I'll have you know," said Lenox. "For one thing it meant news from London. It was painted on white pasteboards they hung alongside the coach. I can still remember when they announced that King William died. I was ten, I think, or thereabouts. It was Edmund and I who broke the news to the chaps at the Bell and Horns. Everyone gathered in the square. I remember all the men removed their hats, and the women were crying."

"Funny, I remember my father coming into the nursery to tell us the King had died," said Lady Jane. "And he never came to the nursery."

Lenox had followed after Fat Sam that day—his usual smile nowhere to be seen—and seen him accept a "pint of wet," the dark local ale, from Lenox's father's butler, then hand across the mail and the London newspapers, which had been full of Victoria's somber reaction to the death of her uncle: grief, respect, reluctant readiness to take the throne.

"It's true, then?" one of the men at the Bell and Horns had asked.

Fat Sam had nodded. "Which we a'had the news at the Swan just afore we left. Erased the boards and wrote um again meself."

The Swan had been, to the Lenox brothers, a place of legend—the Swan with Two Necks, the famous coaching inn of Lad Lane, where the mails departed from before dawn each day. In Lenox's mind, back then, London had been little more than a street containing the Swan, Buckingham Palace, a few street urchins (these had always been held out to him as an example of his great good fortune, and therefore the especial awfulness of his disobedience), and perhaps a large stone bridge, London Bridge. Though of course, that had been replaced, just a year or two before—after six hundred years as the city's symbol of itself.

Long-ago days! Now he had lived in London for twenty-five years himself, and probably passed the Swan a hundred times, going to and from the scene of a crime or a witness's house. As they walked away from the turnoff, he looked down at Sophia, splashing in the puddles (after weeks of snow, it was unseasonably warm now) and wondered what her memories of childhood would be like. That was an unexpected joy of fatherhood: It was living a second time, in a way.

It was just after four when they returned to Lenox House from the market. It was draped with pine garlands and wreaths, festooned with red ribbons, had candles in every window—a credible imitation of Molly's old decorations, whose exact placement James and Edmund had spent many hours squabbling over in the last few days.

Lenox thought that his brother did seem better. Except—there were still moments when he didn't think anyone was looking, and Charles caught a glimpse of his face and saw that it was desolate, haggard, old. If he could just make it through the winter, Lenox thought, he would be all right. It was a shame Teddy wasn't back, but at least James had made it home in time for Christmas.

In the front hallway they stamped their boots, and Edmund, who was just around the corner in the long drawing room, a newspaper under his arm, came out to say hello. "Edmund, do you remember where we were when King William died?"

"I'm sure I have an alibi."

Lenox smiled. "No, I mean—do you remember Fat Sam breaking the news to Milton, and taking a pint? He never took a pint, either."

"Vaguely. I remember Fat Sam proposing to Mrs. Appleby."

"What!" said Lady Jane.

"She declined. I don't think he was much bothered, though, because he was married within a month. Wanted any old wife, I suppose. He'd just turned forty."

"I would have guessed he was six thousand years old," said Lenox. "Is he still alive?"

"Oh, yes. His son drives the mails now. In fact, I was going to go down and pick Atherton up from it in half an hour."

"Atherton takes the mails?" said Lady Jane, who was removing her final wrapper. "I thought he was so prosperous."

"He is, too," said Edmund. "The train makes him ill. It's very bad luck, because it takes three times as long and sometimes you have no choice but to sit outside. Still."

"I'll ride down with you," said Lenox. "I want to meet Fat Sam's son. We could have a chat with him."

"Well, I would moderate your expectations of his conversation. I've never gotten him to say more than 'good morning' to me, and if I ask after his father he looks as if I might be trying to dun the old fellow for a debt."

Charles and Edmund left the house just when it was in a whirl of preparation, the servants crossing every room ten times a minute, polishing, cooking, carting. They rode down to the turnoff in the carriage. It was less than a mile, but Edmund thought Atherton might be tired, especially as he was coming directly to the party. They drove themselves, trading off the reins, and when they arrived they tied the horses to a hitching post and stepped down, and Edmund lit his pipe, Charles his small cigar, and they stood and waited.

Lenox asked about Stevens, Clavering, Hadley, Adelaide Snow. He had already heard the former mayor's name several times at the market—always in a tone that made him sound like the murderer, not the murdered, and in every instance it was accompanied by a broad wink that implied that the speaker knew Calloway had done it, but that he couldn't possibly be blamed, either. Indeed, Lenox had asked several people if Calloway was at the market, but he hadn't been—not for a month. On the other hand, he had seen Clavering and Bunce, who were giving a stern word of reprimand to Elizabeth Watson's younger son for playing with a rasp, a small rolling ball on a stick that sounded exactly like the sound of tearing cloth. The boy had nodded very contritely, and then Lenox had watched him rasp Bunce about fifteen minutes later. So Markethouse was much the same.

According to Lenox, Calloway's low profile—among men who knew—was reckoned a good thing, saving the village the embarrassment of arresting him.

"Do you think he's with his daughter?" said Lenox.

Edmund shrugged. "I hope he is."

As for Adelaide Snow, she had taken charge of the local library now; her father had just put in a new well; Hadley had offered Edmund life insurance more and more aggressively each time he had seen him; the Adams sisters nodded to him very civilly when he saw them, though, he admitted, without smiling, exactly.

"There's the coach," Lenox said.

"Thank goodness it's on time. It's getting colder."

It trotted up, and Lenox called out his hello to the driver, who ignored him completely. Atherton stepped down heavily, but smiling, a small leather bag in hand. "Edmund, you're a prince to meet me. And Charles! Pleasant surprise—I don't know how you stand London, either. I couldn't wait to be gone."

Atherton's tone was pleasant and his words customarily lighthearted, but there was something peculiar in his face.

It took a moment, but then Lenox saw why.

Stepping down behind Atherton from the coach was a young man, much taller, much slenderer than he had been when he first went aboard the *Lucy*. Instinctively Charles looked over at his brother, and saw in his expression first a graveness, and then behind it a barely contained delight, a full burst of love. It was his son, Teddy, thank God, and that meant that Edmund's family, what family he had left, would all be home for Christmas.

Center Point Large Print
600 Brooks Road / PO Box 1
Thorndike, ME 04986-0001 USA

(207) 568-3717

US & Canada:
1 800 929-9108
www.centerpointlargeprint.com

mm — 11-16

ML

6-16